Walker's Pub

Jaclyn E. Robinson

For Daddy, my veteran,
and for the First Responders of 9/11.
Your valor will never be forgotten.

Table of Contents

Prologue 1
Chapter One 9
Chapter Two 22
Chapter Three 32
Chapter Four 44
Chapter Five 55
Chapter Six 70
Chapter Seven 83
Chapter Eight 93
Chapter Nine 103
Chapter Ten 115
Chapter Eleven 125
Chapter Twelve 137
Chapter Thirteen 148
Chapter Fourteen 161
Chapter Fifteen 171
Chapter Sixteen 181
Chapter Seventeen 193
Chapter Eighteen 106
Chapter Nineteen 218
Chapter Twenty 229
Chapter Twenty One 240
Chapter Twenty Two 251
Chapter Twenty Three 261
Chapter Twenty Four 273
Chapter Twenty Five 281
Chapter Twenty Six 296
Chapter Twenty Seven 305
Chapter Twenty Eight 316
Author's Note 325
Acknowledgments 327
Appendix 329
Author's Play List
Nick and Laura's Mix Tapes
About the Author 331

"Valor is a gift. Those having it never know for sure whether they have it till the test comes."

-Carl Sandburg

Prologue

September 11, 2001

Laura Howard stepped inside the large, open kitchen of her parents' house using the side door opposite the barn. The sun had yet to make an appearance in the sky, and the only sign of morning on the horizon was her father sitting at the table with a cup of coffee, newspaper in his hands, and reading glasses perched on the end of his aquiline nose.

"Morning, moon pie. Happy birthday," Cal said, peeking over the metal rims.

"Thank you, Daddy," she said, leaning in to kiss his weathered cheek. "Momma is in the stable rubbing Willow down but said to tell you she'd be in soon." Her mother woke with the birds every morning and thought everyone else should join her. Laura rubbed the sleep from the corner of her eyes once more.

"I figured. She's a creature of habit like your sister."

Laura smiled. She and her siblings all had a little of their mother's stubborn streak, but Kate resembled her the most, both in looks and demeanor. Whereas Laura was more like her father, beginning with a shared love of coffee. It didn't need to be fancy, only caffeinated, and roasted to perfection.

She inhaled deeply through her nose. "Please tell me that heavenly smell is French roast, already made."

"Would I make anything else for the birthday girl?" he asked dryly.

She walked toward the center island in expectation and immediately noticed the envelope with her name, propped in front of the coffee pot. Next to it sat a ceramic mug with a ginormous lizard in a wedding dress plastered on the front and the word BRIDEZILLA covering the other side.

"Oh, and your fiancé asked me to make sure you got those first thing this morning."

Laura let out an obnoxious snort, but Drew's loopy handwriting had her tearing into the envelope with giddy excitement. She laughed loudly as she read the words on the card within. He was good at making her laugh. It was the reason she had said yes to their first date, and one of a million reasons she'd said yes three years later when he proposed the summer after high school graduation.

"Counting down the days?"

"Of course; October is just around the corner. Are you sure we can fit all of Midwell inside the barn? I think we should set up a couple of tents with heaters in the meadow," she said, nervous about the details.

"Your momma has everything well in hand," her father assured her.

In three weeks, she and Drew would speak their vows in front of family and friends in the barn she had come from moments before. Laura would continue working on her family's horse farm for the time being while Drew commuted back and forth from school on weekends and holidays.

Once he graduated, it would be her turn to attend the University of Virginia. Since her heart was set on becoming a large animal vet, the money Laura made working on the farm in the meantime would help pay for her school expenses when she transferred from community college to finish her biology degree. Drew was adamant about them paying their own way, despite her trust fund status.

Folks struggled to understand why they were in such a hurry to get married in the first place. The simple truth was, they were in love, and Laura had no intention of letting the love of her life slip away because the timing didn't fit everyone else's ideal. Drew was her first love, and she wanted him to be her last. Finding real love was a miracle, whether a person was nineteen or ninety-nine.

Nick Kelly looked down at his watch once more as he trotted up the stairs from the F-train into a beautiful September day, a U2 song playing in his ears. Yesterday had been cold and wet on the eastern seaboard, but the predicted storm had moved out to sea overnight, leaving clear skies and balmy temperatures in its wake. Unfortunately, he didn't have time to admire its perfection for long. He was late for his eight o'clock law and society class at NYU. Though he had considered getting a place closer to campus, living at home meant free rent, which also meant he could afford the extra class he took each semester in order to graduate on time.

He thought about the acceptance letters tucked into the drawer of his nightstand. The last detail left was actually deciding whether to attend Stanford or UC Berkely. Both were solid options.

Sunday dinner with his family was going to be an interesting affair this week. Nick's head hurt even thinking about the numerous opinions sitting around his parents' oversized dining table. He knew the first argument would be about why he didn't want to go to NYU or Columbia for law school.

He could hear his mother now. "Nicky," she would start in her most disappointed tone. "Why do you need to go all the way to California? New York has good schools."

The hardest part would be convincing them how important it was for him to experience life away from Brooklyn while he made something of himself. Nick knew he'd move back home one day, but the only thing his family was going to hear was that he wanted to leave them.

Forty minutes into class, sirens began blaring outside at the same time someone shoved open the classroom door and shouted, "One of the towers is on fire!" before running back into the hallway again. With the five boroughs' combined population being more than eight million people, emergencies were nothing new. If it wasn't the NYPD, it was the FDNY responding, and usually both. Nick lived his life steeped in it every day, thanks to his family's devotion as "New York's Bravest and Best."

The entire class, including Dr. Keating, had dispersed by the time Nick stepped into the hallway, which was filled with students and faculty who were visibly upset or holding onto each other in mutual comfort. Some had sprinted outside to see the emergency for themselves. Nick headed for the nearest exit at a jog. Once outside, he could see smoke billow above the World Trade Center, a mere twenty-five minutes away on foot at a quick pace. The cacophony of sirens blaring from every direction clearly signaled impending chaos. This was definitely a five-alarm response.

Nick put on his headphones, hit play on the mp3 player tucked into the side pocket of his backpack, and headed in the opposite direction, the first chords blocking out the panic of those on the streets around him. He could catch the next train back to Brooklyn if he hurried. Pop and his brothers would know what was going on anyway. The last thing he wanted to do was get in the way of crews trying to do their job.

A half hour later, he could hear the news pouring from the television in his grandfather's former bedroom as he came through the backdoor of his childhood home, setting his ball cap on the kitchen counter per house rules. His mother had the patience of a saint but the temper of an Italian mob boss when crossed.

It was only by the grace of God that he and his five siblings survived to adulthood with the number of stunts they had pulled growing up. But absolutely no one made Luna Romano Kelly cry, which is why the tears falling down her cheeks garnered Nick's complete attention. She rubbed the beads of her favorite rosary, stumbling through Hail Marys and adding to his concern.

"Ma, what's going on?"

"It's the towers, Nicky," she said, her voice breaking on a sob.

He automatically reached for her, tucking her small stature in close to his broad chest as she soaked his t-shirt with her tears.

"I know, I was at school. One of the towers is on fire, but they had at least a dozen crews on it with more on the way."

"No, it's both towers. They're saying planes crashed into them. Nicky, all those people…" she cut off as another sob wracked her body.

Nick waited, speechless, because he already knew what she was going to say next.

"Your father and Donnie were at the station when the call came in. They're on their way to the Center. Vinny called to say Leo is enroute with his crew, and Aria left a message. Nate and Miles are on the scene, and Gina decided to stay at the hospital to help with those coming in."

Nick grabbed a set of car keys from the hook by the backdoor. "If I hurry, I can meet up with Pop and the guys—see how I can help."

"They already closed the bridges to everyone but emergency vehicles."

"I'll take the train then…" Nick could hear the desperation in his own voice, the pity on his mother's face evident as more tears slipped over her cheeks.

"They closed the tunnels a half hour ago. All we can do is wait and watch."

Like always, he thought angrily, but conceded defeat with a shake of his head. As Nick's mother began her rosary once again, his voice joined hers. He hoped it would be enough for those they loved.

"Holy Mary, Mother of God, pray for us sinners, now and at the hour of our death. Amen."

Chapter 1

Laura

Cal Howard watched the black sedan come closer and closer as it drove the long, dirt road shaded by tall sugar maples lining either side. His great grandfather had planted the saplings during his own youth, thinking to frame what he considered a humble dwelling with nature's grandeur. In a month's time every leaf would proudly display his forebearer's vision as they turned a glorious autumn red to challenge every other shade, be it apple, tomato, or cherry. Only Mother Nature could claim such a brilliant color.

His wife leaned further into his side, drawing his attention once more, and he soaked in her scent of linen mixed with warm sunshine as she sighed with concern.

"She'll be okay," Cal promised comfortingly and kissed her temple, watching as his youngest child emerged from the barn off to the side of the house.

"I know," she replied out of habit. "I wish she would finally settle down somewhere…anywhere. It's hard to find what you're looking for when all you do is wander."

"Give her time, Beth."

"It's been ten years. How long are we supposed to let this go on? We stayed silent when she asked for her trust fund to travel instead of going to school." Beth tried to pull away, but Cal held fast.

"And I'd do it again if it meant keeping her whole enough," he said firmly.

"I know," she conceded. "But it's like she's running, hoping to find the part of herself she lost along the way. What if she never does?"

"Darlin', she's not the same girl she was before Drew came along, and she can't be the same with him gone."

"Gee, that's comforting," his wife replied tartly, trying unsuccessfully to pinch his waist.

Cal wrapped his hand around the ample curve of her hip and squeezed, enjoying the way she filled his palm. "She's headed Joe's way. I have no doubt your brother will take care of our baby. In fact, I'm willing to bet the farm he's the one to help her figure things out."

"Yeah, yeah. A fork in the road is always on the menu at Walker's Pub," she mimicked, the omission of the "r" in fork reminding Cal of where she'd come from.

"Kate seems to think Laura will find whatever she's looking for there."

"Don't get me started on our middle child. Let's hope Kate finds as much success in London as she has in Brooklyn. Putting an ocean between her and that ex-husband will certainly help me sleep better. Please tell me he still hasn't gone looking for her?"

"Not as far as I know, but he won't go near her unless he wants to get up close and personal with my rifle." Cal hadn't shot at anything aside from a tin can since he'd left the army as a young man and didn't consider himself prone to violence. But he'd make an exception for any man who dared to lay a hand on one of his daughters.

"Our oldest would be more than happy to take his anger out on someone else right now, not that it would solve his problems," stated Beth, the lines on her forehead crowding together in worry.

"I'll have a talk with Lon again when he's home next week," he promised, noting the disgruntle underlying her words. Apparently, their son had something to answer for.

Everyone always talked about how fast the time would go—how children grew up in the blink of an eye. *No one ever said how difficult it was to live with the pieces of your heart running amuck in the world once they left home,* thought Cal. He glanced up at the kitchen ceiling, thinking God might know exactly how he felt and hummed in agreement as though he'd received a reply.

Beth released another weighted sigh and slipped out of Cal's hold. He let her go this time without another word, knowing she needed time on a horse to sort out her worries and the ache in her heart. The screened door slammed shut behind her as she marched toward the stables behind the house with a purposeful stride he recognized well.

Cal turned back to the window again and waited. If anything, he'd learned life was too short and unpredictable to miss the opportunity to say goodbye, even when it took a third of your heart with it.

The bell chimed on the barn door at the bottom of the stairs, rousing Laura from her stupor in the loft above. "Right on time," she muttered and made her way toward the waiting car. Mentally shaking herself, she tucked the ring and chain she had a habit of fidgeting with back into her shirt, close to her heart.

"Thanks," she said, handing the shuttle driver her carry-on luggage. Laura tended to travel light and had little in the way of stuff, by most people's standards. She had no interest in acquiring more roots than the ones she had with her immediate family. Besides, it was difficult to collect anything when someone moved around as much as she did. Traveling light had become her motto, both materially and relationally. She ran through her departure checklist once more as the driver lifted the last of her two medium-sized backpacks into the trunk of a black sedan.

Oven turned off—check.

Thermostat set—check.

Door locked—check.

Her life in a holding pattern—triple check. Laura's mother had made that one blatantly clear while she'd been home for foaling season.

Laura waved one last time to her father, framed in the kitchen window of the white farmhouse she'd grown up in. Renovated by previous Howard ancestors over the years, her dad often joked about tearing down the house to start from nothing, but her mother wouldn't hear of it. Unlike the new, multi-million dollar homes built in the hills surrounding the Howard acreage, this house contained the long history of her family in a town that had started out as nothing more than a varied group of people from diverse backgrounds intent on building a new life.

Laura looked back once more as the car left the drive, another goodbye amongst too many to count in the last ten years and thought about the previous day's interaction with her father.

He'd been waiting with coffee as usual, but instead of a birthday card propped against the pot, she'd found the newspaper.

"I thought perhaps you could use a little perspective this morning," he said and left the kitchen.

Laura had wrinkled her nose as she eyed the headline of the Midwell Chronicle: *9/11 Memorialized Forever.* She didn't want perspective; she wanted to forget. Forget her birthday. Forget how

Drew had disappeared from her life on the same day ten years prior. Forget that she wasn't the only one to understand grief as intimately as a lover.

No one ever wanted to talk about how lonely it was, or that each experience was personal; not a one-size-fits-all. Laura had tossed the paper into the trash bin, refusing to indulge her father's request, and stomped back to the barn, kicking the gravel with her work boots to vent.

Twenty minutes later, her sister picked up where her father had left off. Laura would've bet money they'd planned it, except it went against Kate's nature to be outright mean.

"Hi Kate," Laura had said expectantly when the phone rang.

"Happy birthday, sweetie!"

"Thanks," she replied flatly.

Her sister deliberately ignored her tone, and the reason behind it, when she asked, "Any fun plans to celebrate?"

"Nope, I'm packing the last of my things before I leave tomorrow morning."

Kate finally took the hint and relented. "How was foaling season this year?"

"The same as always," said Laura while putting toiletries into one of her bags. "You know, exhausting, messy, and completely miraculous all at the same time. I don't think I'll ever get tired of watching new life come into this world."

"I wish I could've been there."

"We missed you, but at least you didn't have to witness the group of men Momma paraded in front of me."

"You know, she has your best interest at heart." Kate continued softly, "It's been ten years since Drew."

When Laura grumbled in response, her sister switched topics.

"Anyway, you're going to love Brooklyn in the fall. I'm so glad you're willing to stay with Micky. He's going to adore his Auntie Laura. Uncle Joe has the key to the apartment and, who knows, you might even decide to finally settle down."

Laura laughed in disbelief. "I haven't stayed anywhere longer than a few months at a time in a decade; why would I start now?" she asked rhetorically. "So, are you all set for London?"

"I am. My manager has the shop covered, and if all goes well, I'll be back home for a Christmas visit. I thought we could make the drive to the farm with Uncle Joe together this year."

Laura laughed under her breath. "Why Uncle Joe won't get on a plane is beyond me, but it'll be easier to transport gifts in any case." Laura paused before asking, "Speaking of Christmas, did you know Lon is planning to be gone? He said something about traveling for work."

"Now that you mention it, he did say he'd be gone for the holidays, but I'm not sure it has anything to do with work," she said hesitantly, as if she knew something Laura didn't. "Don't get me wrong; I'd love to see him, but he spirals into a pit every time he sees Abby."

"I know," said Laura with a scrunch of her nose. "I gave her the stink eye the last time I saw her in town. Of course, Momma caught me and gave me a good scolding," Laura complained.

"Don't worry; Momma hasn't forgiven her either. She's trying to kill her with kindness. Besides, Lon's moved on, even if it's only with any woman who looks at him twice."

"I'm not sure hooking up with someone in every bar he walks into qualifies as moving on. It's more of a cry for help," said Laura under her breath, knowing it sounded judgy, especially coming from her. It wasn't as if her coping skills were a stellar example of how to deal with heartache. In the background, she could faintly hear the boarding announcement for her sister's flight.

"I've got to go, but I'll call you once things settle down across the pond. Oh, and you'll need to pick Micky up from the vet. I'll text you the address. Love you, moon pie!"

"Love you more, cow eyes," she recited right before the click of the line sounded.

Everyone in her family thought Laura was floundering, and if she was being honest, she wasn't entirely sure they were wrong. When life had thrown her a curveball, she had used her trust fund to travel the world instead of getting an education and pursuing her dream of veterinary medicine.

Laying her head back against the headrest, Laura scrolled through her email, looking for any flight updates. A song floated through her earbuds, the perfect accompaniment to the moment, while she tried to convince herself the more things changed, the more they actually stayed the same. Going to Brooklyn was a truce, not a surrender. She would eventually find herself somewhere, and though she was tired of disappointing her parents, she couldn't quite bring herself to conform to their expectations either. Drew would've been so proud; except he wasn't there to see it.

The official report had said the truck flipped multiple times on its way down a ravine three miles from her parents' property. The F-150, more rust than baby blue, had belonged in a pasture with the other junk rural communities seem to collect, instead of on the road. Drew had worked three summers at Hanson's Feed Store to be able to buy it the day he turned sixteen. It was where they'd made out, made up, and made plans for a future which would never happen.

Drew was supposed to be in his dorm, not on a winding road in the predawn hours of a Tuesday morning. The day was dry, and visibility good. Highway patrol couldn't find any evidence for why he'd lost control other than common wear of tire tread on top of washout from the rain earlier in the week. He never regained consciousness, and while the rest of the country mourned the lives of those lost in the terrorist attacks of 9/11, her hometown said goodbye to the boy she'd loved all because he wanted to wish her happy birthday in person.

Not long afterwards, she had said her own farewell. Everyone kept insisting it was okay to grieve and to give herself time, as though enough time would eventually make everything better or normal somehow. But what could they know about the way she felt? It was her pain to bear, not theirs.

Everyone else could move on when they were ready, but there had been no reason to give herself more time. Because no matter how long she grieved for the boy she'd loved and the loss of their future, no matter how much time she gave herself, it would never be enough. Drew would still be gone. How could anything in her world be the same without him?

Nick

Standing up, Luna Kelly brushed the dirt from her knees and arched her sore back in a stretch, hearing the chorus of creaks and pops from what her body had become with age. She glanced around, the hazy sunlight causing her eyes to water without her oversized gardening hat to shade them. The headstones in this section of the cemetery were newer, but only by a decade. She ran her hand over the top of the cool white marble in front of her and tried to picture what her husband would look like if he were standing there, but she could barely remember what he'd looked like ten years ago. All except for his eyes.

In her mind, he would always be the first boy she'd kissed, the only man she'd ever made love to, and the father of her children. But he would never age beyond the crow's feet at the corners of his eyes. Patrick Kelly was forever frozen in time, and he would never grow old beside her. What would he think if he could see her now, she wondered. Would he mind the added wrinkles and gray hairs, or the extra pounds she carried courtesy of menopause?

She kissed her fingers and laid them gently on the cold marble once more before putting her small shovel and spade into a bucket beside the excess daffodil bulbs. Next spring her husband would still lie beneath the ground, but like his smiling Irish eyes, the world above him would bloom with a promise of better things to come.

Nick grinned at her from where he leaned against a brick pillar at the entrance gate, dressed in his uniform and a leather jacket.

"Where's the bike?" Luna asked, looking around for the 1947 Harley-Davidson Knucklehead he normally rode these days. He'd spent the last eight years overhauling the motorcycle according to the plans his oldest brother had drawn up but had never been able to use.

"Leo told me you were here, so I hailed a taxi," he said, taking her bucket as they walked toward the parking lot. "I see the diocese finally gave you permission to spruce things up."

"I didn't bother to ask. He's not their husband or father."

Nick chuckled low at her audacious behavior. "Fair enough. I would've come with you if you'd waited."

"I know, but I wanted time alone with your father. Besides, I like to garden in the morning when the ground is moist, and sun is kind."

"How is the old man?" Nick asked as he opened the driver's side door of the decrepit wood paneled station wagon she still insisted on driving, closing her inside. He jogged around to the other side and placed the bucket behind the passenger seat before sliding onto the torn leather seat no longer worth trying to patch.

"The same. How was your shift?" she asked, more out of habit than curiosity. Nothing he could tell her would be a shock. She'd heard it all before during the thirty years her husband had been in the department.

"The same," he said, deliberately using the phrase she had. "Five-car pileup on the bridge. No major injuries. And a fire in one of the old buildings downtown."

"Those derelict buildings should've been torn down years ago."

"They aren't safe, let alone sanitary, but they provide shelter for the homeless these days," he said with a shrug of his broad shoulders.

"Anyone hurt?

"Sent three to the hospital. A toddler and her mother who got stuck in the stairway on the third floor, and a guy, strung out and lying in his own vomit."

"Anyone in the Squad?"

"Nah, we're a well-oiled machine," he said lightly. "No one gets hurt on my watch."

Luna glanced sideways at her son as they rolled to a stop at the red light. He sounded so much like his father, but she knew there wasn't any real arrogance behind the words. If anything, Nick merely meant to reassure her.

Pride and fear warred to fill the places of her duct-taped heart, but she smiled and said, "I have no doubt." When the light changed color, she tapped the gas pedal and moved forward. There was today and, if she was lucky, tomorrow. As the saying went, nothing in life was certain except death and taxes.

Chapter 2

Laura

Fall was claiming New York, and for the first time in ten years she didn't miss being away from home for the season. Taking a key from her pocket, Laura turned the corner of Walker's Pub, and bounced up the stairway that led to the apartment two floors above. It was crazy to think about living in the same place her mother had called home once upon a time. No one would ever guess Beth Howard had been a city girl. Her mother lived and breathed the Howard horse farm as if it were all she had ever known.

When Laura's grandmother passed away shortly after her grandfather, Uncle Joe had offered the apartment to Kate, who needed a fresh start where she could hide from her past. Fortunately, her sister had spent the last two years renovating the dated space, which was closer to a moderately sized home than an apartment.

While the charm of built-ins, trim, and molding remained, it was nice to have new paint on the walls and refinished hardwood beneath plush rugs. The kitchen was a cook's dream, fortunately for Laura, because one of the benefits of traveling the world had been experiencing how other cultures ate and used food to nourish and celebrate.

Laura loved to spend her free time searching local farmers' markets and docks for spices, produce, and seafood. Brooklyn also boasted an assortment of butcher shops and kosher delis from which to choose a variety of meats. She believed any meal had the potential to be more than simply food for the body. It could bring together communities living continents apart, which was part of why she had accepted the offer from Uncle Joe. She may not have fulfilled her veterinary dream, but a new dream had begun to take root in her heart.

She dropped her keys in the ceramic dish colored in shades of lilac and gray on the entry table opposite the door. Removing her shoes and coat, she put them in their respective places and walked through the French doors her sister had recovered from a refurbish store in the warehouse district. Kate claimed the doors were a formal demarcation line between the entrance and the rest of the apartment. Laura rolled her eyes, thinking about how prissy it sounded.

She'd slept in so many hostels and occasionally the friend of a friend's floor over the years, her appreciation for interior design was admittedly a little lacking. In her experience, it was a luxury for the wealthy, and while beauty certainly added joy to life, she'd known the poorest of the poor to appreciate a humble meal and a full belly more than a wealthy man took note of his possessions.

She walked past the couch and an overstuffed reading chair with matching ottoman, nearly catching her toe on the corner of it for a second time. Her sad little appendage had yet to recover from the first time she'd tried to locate a light switch in the dark.

"It won't be long before you know this place like the back of your hand," she consoled herself in the otherwise quiet room.

Though the entire apartment reflected Kate's impeccable taste, Laura's favorite spot was the set of grass-woven, wingback chairs sitting in front of a picture window in the kitchen. It was from there she drank her morning coffee, and where she retreated to at the end of each day to watch the sunset over Brooklyn Bridge. The view was the antithesis of the one from her parents' back porch in Midwell, which overlooked rolling hills and vast swaths of trees. When the sun streaked across the water to torch the buildings on the other side, setting the Manhattan skyline afire, she reveled in the polished beauty the city held. Comparing the two would be like comparing apples to oranges and utterly impossible.

Her sister's Australian Shepard trotted in from the guest room, where he'd no doubt been lying on her bed instead of in his, and sat directly in front of her with his soulful eyes as if to ask, *What's the problem, lady? You sleep on the bed; why shouldn't I?*

Unfortunately, she couldn't make up a reasonable answer for him. "I don't care, but your mom is not going to be happy if she finds out, so let's keep this between us, buddy." She leaned down to ruffle his coat around the neck as he leaned further into her hands for her to scratch his ears, the plastic cone he was supposed to wear for an ear infection nowhere in sight. Standing back up, she led the way toward the kitchen and said, "Come on, let's make an early dinner. How does Risotto Alla Milanese and Caprese Salad sound?" When Micky bumped his head into her hand, she agreed, "I think it's a *favolosa* idea too."

Laura tapped the music app on her phone and the strains of her favorite Macy Gray song filled the quiet room. She perused the kitchen's amenities: a professional-grade oven range, a subzero fridge, and a dishwasher with more settings than Laura deemed necessary—all of which she thought a tad ironic since Kate didn't actually cook. She was more of a takeaway kind of gal.

Kitchen scissors in hand, Laura reached for the basil growing in a clay pot on the wide windowsill above the kitchen sink. Next, she grabbed the heirloom tomatoes resting in a small bunch next to the other potted herbs she had picked up from the farmers' market last weekend. Fresh was always better, in her opinion. Placing her sliced tomatoes on a plate, she layered them with fat slabs of mozzarella and basil leaves, a sprinkling of salt, a dash of olive oil, and a drizzle of balsamic reduction.

Laura sang along to the song in the background, a memory

of senior prom and the last time she'd danced with Drew keeping her close company. He had worn the one thing his father had left him five years prior: a black suit meant for funerals. The coat hung loose around broad shoulders that had barely begun to fill out with impending manhood, and when she laid her head on his shoulder as they swayed back and forth, she felt certain. Certain of who she was and where she was going in life, so long as he went with her.

She swallowed hard, and tried to ignore the emotion choking off the words she sang. After a quick wipe of her hands on the towel tied at her waist as a makeshift apron, Laura added the cooked chopped onions and shallots, followed by a generous pour of Sauvignon Blanc to the Arborio rice simmering in beef stock and saffron. Lastly, she grated parmesan over the top while Micky caught the slivers that fell to the floor and padded after her in hopes there would be more to come. Laura looked toward the canvas outside the double-pained glass framed in white, neoclassical trim, and then to her companion sitting in the other grass chair. "Perfect timing."

<hr>

"Mick, stop coning me." He looked up at Laura briefly before going back to pawing at the ants on the sidewalk, ramming the plastic cone around his neck into her shin again. It was totally Kate's style to leave a note telling her about Micky's recent ear infection, instead of giving her a heads up on the phone before she arrived. At least he swallowed his medication, which proved what she already knew: peanut butter solved life's most serious problems. Need a dog to take his antibiotics without a wrestling match? Jif's got you. Gum in your hair? Skippy to the rescue. PMS? Butterfinger is your best friend. Broken heart? Ben & Jerry's Chubby Hubby knows how you feel.

"Come on, buddy; your cone is killing me." When that didn't garner the desired result, she resorted to threats. "Mick, stop it or I won't give you what you want, and we both know how much you want it."

Micky looked up at her, his light eyes watching her with an uncanny intelligence while he cocked his head as if to ask, *Well then, where's the treat you keep promising, lady?*

She didn't know if she believed in reincarnation, but occasionally thought Micky's soul was more human than canine, one she adored with equal parts love and annoyance. The sentiment came close to how she felt about her sister at the moment. Kate was her best friend and the bane of her existence, all wrapped up in a pretty package. As far as Laura was concerned, it was her sister's fault she was in Brooklyn working for Uncle Joe to begin with—well, sort of. The actual reason was more complicated, and she had no intention of looking at her life under a magnifying glass any time soon. At least being here gave her space from the parental units, especially her mother.

Nick

His back to the person in front of him, Nick passed the time with a new playlist in his ears as he waited for the Squad's order at Ruth's Deli, two blocks from the engine house. The first time he heard his name he assumed it was a coincidence and continued to mind his own business. Hearing his name again, this time in an agitated tone, he turned toward the woman standing directly in front of him and removed an earbud from his left ear. She didn't look familiar, and the words coming from her mouth were odd, but she must have a problem with him.

"Yes, can I help you with something?" Nick asked, his lips turning up at the corners good naturedly. She might be upset with him, but that didn't mean he had to get worked up in return.

Her eyes opened wide in surprise until her forehead crinkled.

"Uh, nope. We're doing fine, thanks."

The woman was petite with a blonde pixie cut, a stunning pair of light green eyes behind tortoiseshell frames, and a diamond stud in her dainty, slightly upturned nose. She reminded him of Tinkerbelle, his niece's favorite cartoon character. Well, before Sofi had become a teenager preoccupied with the opposite sex, much to his chagrin.

He typically dated women who were on the taller side, mostly so he didn't feel like such a giant when he stood next to them, but Tink was cute, even with their height difference. When she snared his eyes again with something akin to a challenge in hers, he did a double take. Changing his original assessment, Nick crossed his arms over his wide chest and shifted his legs slightly to plant his feet firmly on the ground.

Never mind. Tink is completely worth this odd conversation, wherever it leads.

"Well, so far, you've asked me to stop coning you, and now you're threatening to take away what I want, when we both know how much I want it," he said with a smirk.

Heat filled the woman's face, turning her cheeks a bright shade of fuchsia at the implication. She finally found her voice and managed to squeak out, "I was talking to the dog."

"The dog's name is Nick?" he asked, confusion creating a furrow between his brows.

"No, the dog's name is Mick. Well, technically, it's Micky Mouse," she replied with a roll of her eyes. "Don't ask. Micky belongs to my sister. I'm only dog sitting as a favor."

"Ahh, funny." Sticking his hand out between them he said, "I'm Nick Kelly. Nice to meet you..."

She kept her fingertips tucked into the pockets of her jeans but said, "Laura."

Micky looked back and forth between the two, lifting his paw in response to Nick's outstretched hand. Not deterred, he shook the dog's proffered paw instead. It wasn't the greeting he'd been hoping for, but at least the dog liked him.

"Nice trick, pal. Sorry about the cone of shame." Looking back at Laura, he suggested, "You know, you could call him Eminem instead."

"Like the candy?" she asked skeptically.

"Nah, like the rapper. You know, the white guy," he said confidently, as if it made perfect sense.

When Laura continued to stare at Nick as though he'd grown two heads, he sang the words to one of the more popular songs on the radio, losing himself to the beat in the moment. His sisters would no doubt tell him now was a suitable time to shut his mouth, but figured he may as well engage an attractive woman's attention while he waited for the Squad's order.

She shook her head from side to side and said, "Nah, I don't think so."

Smiling despite her reluctance to give him any room to continue in the conversation, Nick asked, "So, do you live around here? Fairly sure I would've remembered seeing you in the neighborhood before."

"That's a really personal question."

"And one you're not going to answer. I don't blame you. I wouldn't want my sisters to tell a random stranger they met in a line anything personal either. Especially, if that someone was talking about coning."

With a half laugh and a snort, Laura looked over her shoulder as the line finally moved forward. When she turned back around again and swept a glance over him, from steel-toed boots to hair, she

muttered something about a sasquatch before saying, "This was...
interesting. I'll see you around the neighborhood, *Nick*," she said
and gestured for her furry companion to stay by the door to the deli.

Nick watched her disappear inside, grinned, and tucked his
earbuds back in with one hand while reaching with the other to take
the paper bags Ruth Abrams held out the shop's sliding window.

"Tell Squad 2 hello for us, Nick."

"Will do. Your sandwiches are the best in Brooklyn," he said
with a wink.

"I know," she agreed, dismissing him in the next breath with,
"Next!"

Chapter 3

Nick

Nick killed the engine on the bike, removing his helmet as he paused to glance up at the sign on the old brick building in one of Brooklyn's recently gentrified neighborhoods. The traffic on the street behind him moved like ants in a line, a fury of honking horns and yelling from open car windows. Pedestrians filled sidewalk corners, counting down the moments until they could cross the street, only to join a new crush of bodies. His brother Donnie had been right; a motorcycle was the equivalent of freedom in the city.

Walker's Public House had opened in 1946 when a young Charles Walker brought his new bride home from London. It was far from being the lone drinking establishment in Boerum Hill at the time, but Charlie had a mind to join in the economic boom flooding New York post World War II, and his wife knew how to run a business like the one her parents had operated prior to the war.

It was from the pub's polished walnut bar that Nick's grandfather had listened to Jackie Robinson play his first major league game with the Brooklyn Dodgers in 1947, and again, when they'd won their first World Series in 1955.

"Son," said Patrick Kelly, looking Nick in the eye as if he were a grown man instead of a twelve-year-old boy. "You should always stop and pay your respects when entering an icon like Walker's."

Nick smiled over the memory. The pub had been there long before he was born, and he imagined it would still be there long after he was gone. A morbid thought, but no less true. He entered the muted space he knew as well as his childhood home and headed for his usual spot. His date sat waiting in a pleather upholstered corner booth, squinting at the dappled light coming from the windows behind Nick.

"Bill, my main man, how are you?" Nick asked, setting his helmet on the table in front of him.

"Still better looking than you, but what else is new?"

Nick laughed under his breath and ran a hand through his thick hair as he sat down in the booth across from his grandfather's best friend. They had buried Gramps in Holy Cross Cemetery thirteen years ago, but Nick still made the weekly visit with Bill Davis, both to honor his grandfather and because the man had been like a second father when his own died.

The pub was usually mellow in the early afternoons on a

weekday which made conversation easier. Bill couldn't remember his hearing aids to save his life, or to make Nick's any easier. The man swore he didn't need them anyway, but after being in the fire department for almost forty-two years, Nick was willing to bet good money he did. More than that, he was glad hearing protection had improved in the years since he had joined.

As the two continued their usual banter, a couple of coasters followed by waters with lemon were set down in front of them. The weather was warm for a mid-September day, making the glasses sweat beads of moisture onto the walnut stain. Nick looked up to thank their usual server, Teresa, but as the words slipped off his tongue, he realized he was looking into a set of familiar green eyes, minus the tortoise shell frames this time.

Startled to see the woman from the deli, Nick racked his brain and tried to remember her name but all he could think of was the dog's. Not surprising since it rhymed with his own. Stalling, he asked, "Where's Teresa?"

Or it's nice to see you again, he admonished himself. *Smooth, Kelly, real smooth.*

"I think she's in the back helping Joe with inventory. What can I get you fellas started with?" she asked.

The woman…why couldn't he remember her name all of a sudden? Regardless, she had Nick's full attention. He thought he heard a slight drawl, one he hadn't noticed during their previous encounter, but it only seemed to show itself in the use of specific words. Was it possible she was from somewhere else originally, he wondered.

"One of your smiles is all this old man needs," Bill answered slyly. To which the woman promptly grinned making the corners of her eyes smile too.

The sound of her throaty laughter had Nick's hand moving up of its own volition to rest over his heart, while Bill put in their usual order of Guinness and steak pies. His eyes continued to watch the new girl as she walked quickly to the bar in the middle of the pub, hips swaying in a steady rhythm.

Nick noticed her reflection through the bar mirror as she poured pints and interacted with the regulars seated there, greeting each person by name as she placed a small bowl of homemade crisps in front of them. He was still staring in her direction when Bill chortled directly into his ear, no doubt enjoying the spectacle of an awestruck Nick.

"Who's the new server, Bill?"

"As Frank once sang, she is "Pennies from Heaven," and you don't stand a chance of collecting."

With a wide grin, Nick looked away from the bar and turned to meet the man's stare. Frank was a reference to Bill's favorite crooner, Sinatra. And though he had a great appreciation for the man's voice, the song's title didn't answer his question. "No doubt, but what I meant was, what's her name and story?"

Bill met Nick's question with a twinkle in his eyes despite their rheumy quality. "You mean, is she taken?"

"Precisely," said Nick with a grin.

Bill didn't usually pay attention to Nick's love life. In fact, he often told Nick he was too attractive for his own good. He had inherited his mother's hair and olive skin along with his father's blue eyes. Combined with his easy-going personality and muscular physique, girls had started fawning over him before he'd completed his first communion. Bill had accused him once or twice of needing someone hanging on his arm, but Nick was only having fun. He knew what a man in love looked like, and up to now he had never been that man.

He smiled back at his grandfather's best friend. "Pennies from Heaven" might be good for him, not to mention amusing for Bill. Nick had few doubts this woman would lead him on a merry chase.

"Her name is Laura Howard, and she is Joe's youngest niece," said Bill, pulling Nick from his revery.

"She's Kate's sister?"

Bill nodded in the affirmative.

"That explains a lot," said Nick with an intrigued smile. He and Kate were acquaintances, and though Laura's sister was objectively attractive, he'd never been interested in anything more than the small talk they engaged in when they ran into each other at the pub. He assumed she felt the same way from her reserved nature around him.

Nick frowned in his water glass as he took a sip of the cool, lemon-tinged liquid. If Laura was as immune to his charms as her sister, he was going to have to work a lot harder to gain her attention than funny conversations and the occasional run in at the neighborhood deli.

Of course, Laura working at Walker's Pub increases the odds in my favor, he thought while humming a classic rock song under his breath. He could already hear the cheers of victory when he finally caught her attention.

"Well then, you know her family hales from a small town in Virginia, but Laura is also quite the world traveler. From the number of postcards Joe has collected over the last ten years, I would guess she's seen more of the world than you or I could ever dream of."

"No offense, old man, but that's not hard to do. Neither one of us has been outside the five boroughs in six months, and New Jersey doesn't count."

"Jersey never does unless we're talking about Frank, and I'm not old, just well preserved. And what you mean is, it's not hard when your whole family lives within a five-mile radius."

"Exactly," admitted Nick, resigned to his fate. Sometimes, he felt like his roots tripped him up as much as they sustained him. To say staying close to his family had not been his original plan was an understatement.

His mother had always wanted a lawyer in the family, probably because she thought it would help keep his older brothers out of trouble, and it was better than becoming a priest. It wasn't unheard of for a large family in the parish to dedicate a kid to a life of celibacy before they could even walk, let alone go through puberty.

"Nicky, there's no reason for you to join the family business," the Kelly matriarch had said, shaking her index finger in his face from her five-foot nothing height whenever he'd tried to argue in the contrary. "My baby's too smart not to use all of those brains God gave him."

When he'd started school at New York University fifteen years ago, he'd also planned to attend law school in California afterward, and eventually work for the District Attorney's office. Anywhere but the five boroughs would have been ideal. It felt like a lifetime ago now, and although he was helping people, he did it as a firefighter instead of as a prosecutor.

Like so many other people, Nick's future had changed on 9/11. His father and older brothers had all been first responders on the scene. Of them, only his brother Leo had come home. Law school, even a local one, didn't make sense when his family needed him more.

Even now, the events of that day still haunted the Kelly clan. Diagnosed with leukemia six months ago, Leo was currently on sick leave from the department. Treatment was difficult, but his brother was a fighter, and thanks to early detection the survival rate was better.

The best news had been the recent government health funds made available to first responders who served during 9/11. Unfortunately, it hadn't arrived in time for his sister Aria's husband, who had died of an exposure-related health issue two years ago, after a short, horrific battle.

Although Nick's dreams had taken a left turn, he wouldn't change the outcome. He liked living close to his mother. Well, mostly, if he was being completely honest. And staying near his siblings and their respective families had its rewards. It meant he made it to Sunday dinners when he wasn't on shift, and he got to be Uncle Nick on his days off.

Brooklyn was his slice of the world, which was more than enough every other day of the week. He couldn't change the losses of that infamous day, but he could find joy in the everyday, ordinary interactions and choices he made, living near the family he still had and a profession honoring those he'd lost. A certain green-eyed server only proved his point. All he had to do was walk into his favorite pub to find her.

Laura

Laura snickered as she left Bill and his companion, who clearly didn't remember her from Saturday's line at Ruth's Deli. She filled their drinks for Teresa and put the rest of the order into the kitchen. Bill was certainly a character. He had a zest for life at his age she was envious of as a young person. It was as if his perspective on life was to enjoy every moment, appreciating the simple things like lunch out, because he knew life came with an expiration date.

Sometimes Laura felt like she spent all of her time chasing after an elusive concept, as though finding the secret to a happy life for others would help her find what she'd lost when Drew died.

Looking from Bill to Nick again, she wondered what their relationship to each other was. They didn't appear to be related, but no one would assume she shared any genes with Uncle Joe either, not with her blonde hair and green eyes. Whatever their relationship, the younger man had hit the genetics jackpot.

He was positively drool-worthy, with hair the color of rich umber, bronze skin, and a square jaw. Nick Kelly was a masterpiece, which her peace of mind did not appreciate in the least.

Whatever, I'm sure he knows it. Besides, it's not like he remembers me.

With one last look at the back corner booth, Laura said a quick goodbye to Uncle Joe and Amir in the kitchen and exited through the backdoor of the pub. She took in the surrounding maple and oak trees lining the streets of the neighborhood. Despite the unusually warm weather, leaves had begun to wrap branches in a riot of colors lovelier than any gilded present. The air in her lungs smelled like sweet earth and she looked forward to the days of sweaters and pumpkin spiced lattes when temperatures finally turned crisp with the season.

When her alarm went off the next morning, Laura contemplated hitting the snooze button before giving in to self-discipline.

"I really should have gone without that second glass of wine with dinner," she mumbled sleepily. Laura had never been much of a morning person, but the extra glass of wine didn't help the whole early to rise gig.

Her brother called Laura a cheap date, but the fact of the matter was, she wasn't trying to be anything more than a lightweight. Though Lon had recently taken to drinking himself under the table, she had no intention of joining him.

"When did I start competing with my siblings for idiot life decisions?" she asked into the quiet room.

Flopping onto her back, she stared up at the ceiling. It was cerulean and dotted with wispy white clouds as though the guest room were a beach under the noonday sun. Her sister had hired a friend to paint the ceilings in the apartment to represent the daytime from sunrise to dusk. She claimed it helped her keep perspective, and remember no matter what the day held, tomorrow meant a brand-new beginning. It was a whimsical notion, and such a Kate thing to do, Laura's heart squeezed painfully.

She rubbed the sleep from her eyes again as they watered, refusing to acknowledge the moisture for what it was—bone-deep sadness.

Not that she thought God would suddenly start caring. As far as she was concerned, He hadn't cared ten years ago, but Laura still asked, "Where are You? Don't You care what happens to us?"

Laura didn't know why she even bothered. Her mother said God could deal with anything she wanted to tell Him, but if she wasn't ready to listen in return, it simply made for a one-sided conversation. She could live with being the only one who spoke; she'd been doing it for years.

Laura pictured God with a universal chess board at His fingertips, moving people around like pawns on a whim. Taught to believe otherwise, time and experience had proven those teachings wrong. Another silent tear slid from the corner of her eye. She had been living with their one-sided pattern for the last ten years, and hearing what God had to say wouldn't bring Drew back, keep Kate safe, or change Lon's self-destructive path. It was little wonder she and her siblings were stumbling through life, hurt and lost. The real miracle was that they were functioning at all.

Well, that was debatable where her brother was concerned. He was walking a fine line toward alcoholism and a sexually transmitted infection. Grief made for poor company, and a sad substitute for the love they had all once taken for granted.

"TLC had it right. No use chasing after waterfalls." Laura reached behind her to comb her hands through her bed partner's soft hair.

Regardless of her feelings, running was one of the few habits Laura kept no matter where she was in the world. She and Drew had been on their high school cross-country team together, and although her life had tipped upside down the day he died, she found comfort in doing something they once shared. Besides, the endorphin high was all natural, and an effortless way to order her thoughts before the day began.

"Come on, buddy; let's get in some mileage before breakfast," said Laura on her way to the bathroom. "Maybe Uncle Joe will let you hang around the pub today instead of going to daycare. Because what the health inspector doesn't know can't hurt us."

Micky barked in consensus.

Her mornings had developed into a pattern over the last few weeks: a quick three miler through Prospect Park followed by twenty minutes at the dog run for Micky. After which, Laura cleaned up, scarfed breakfast, and savored a cup of coffee courtesy of the roaster two blocks down, before helping Uncle Joe get ready for the lunch crowd.

Her hope was to add eclectic menu offerings to the standard ones of fish and chips or shepherd's pie with soda bread. Traditional pub fare was great, but Laura wanted to expand the pub's repertoire with representation from around the world. Unfortunately, her attitude about food didn't extend to her personal life. Love once was more than enough exposure for a lifetime.

Micky met her at the door, leash in mouth, and waited patiently for her as she put on an elastic headband. It was a steely gray to match her leggings—and her mood, if she wanted to own it.

"Good boy," Laura said, giving him ear scratches as they stepped outside into the pale morning light. "Let's run."

Chapter 4

Nick

Nick padded across his studio apartment, watching the sun make its lazy ascent into the sky from his third-floor windows. He was working a twelve-hour shift tonight, which meant getting in a morning run before doing yard work at his parents' house, instead of after. Normally, he worked a twenty-four-hour tour followed by two days off but had volunteered to take the half shift for a guy on family leave. He liked to think someone else would do the same for him if the time ever came.

He leaned over to tie his laces and glanced around at the place he'd moved into five years ago. A small, third-floor walkup, it wasn't anything special but contained a certain funky charm and the rent was cheap, so the rest of his money went to saving for a down payment on a house. He was almost ready to put in an offer on an old brownstone at the end of a block in Boerum Hill.

Located close to the engine house, his favorite farmer's market, and Walker's Pub, it was also a reasonable distance to his parents' house in Carroll Gardens. Nick had checked it out during an open house last spring, and while it would require a major renovation, he felt up to the challenge. So far, the owner had rejected any offers from other buyers, but the realtor assured him it had less to do with money and more about the plans a buyer had for the home. He was positive he could paint a vision for the owner if given the opportunity.

The house was perfect for hosting Sunday dinners, lessening the burden on his mother, and a place where traditions could crowd holidays with both celebration and the inevitable family drama that followed. It would hold his oversized family and more. While he didn't have a wife and kids yet, he hoped he would someday. Pop had always said the right person would come along when the time was right, so in the meantime, he'd keep moving toward the future. Nick wanted the brownstone to be the house he came home to after every shift.

He locked the door and jumped down the stairs, waving to Mr. Papovich at the mailboxes while holding open the door for Mrs. Papovich and their yappy Pomeranian.

"Hush now! You know you love Nick," she chided. "Sorry, Nick; Sergeant Pepper is a little out of sorts today." She leaned in, telling him in an overly loud whisper, "Between you and me, I think he's constipated." Then she looked directly at her husband before saying, "It tends to make a body cranky, doesn't it, George?"

"No offense taken," said Nick as he gave the little dog a quick salute and tried to keep from laughing at the disgruntled man buried beneath a stack of catalogues and envelopes.

By the time he reached the sidewalk, he was moving at a steady pace. His usual run took him to the gym where he worked out, but Nick decided he might need an extra couple of miles and turned in the opposite direction to gain mileage. With earbuds in and music blaring out dubstep from the iPod tucked into an armband, he focused his breathing and set his eyes on the leaves in front of him. If he had a favorite season in New York, it would be fall. It meant brisk mornings, cooler days, and holidays around the corner.

By the time he entered Prospect Park, he'd worked up a decent sweat and was contemplating which trail to take when he caught a glimpse of short, blonde hair. The petite woman wore leggings with a long-sleeve shirt, and what had to be the brightest tennis shoes he'd ever seen. But the best part was that she and her fuzzy companion were running in his direction.

Laura

Laura's eyes were focused on the trail in front of her, the beat coming through her earbuds helping her keep an easy pace. Micky made a good running partner, which was funny because she'd never known Kate to run anywhere. Her sister had the natural grace and body of a ballet dancer without any effort. She sashayed more than walked, even in the heels she insisted on wearing at five-foot nine. Laura didn't mind taking after her father's mother and was only a little envious her sister had inherited their mother's height and graceful manner of being.

Her father always told Laura she was cute, petite, and feisty; like dynamite, she packed a whole lot of punch into a small package. She could almost hear the warm rumble of his voice.

"Laura, you are exactly who you're supposed to be. Don't ever let anyone steal the truth from you, not even yourself."

She missed him. Her father always knew the right thing to say to reassure her, and while he was there to catch her if she fell, he never fought her battles for her. Unlike her mother, he didn't hover and worry, as if Laura's brokenness needed repairing.

Probably because there is no piecing me back together this time.

Lost in her thoughts, Laura didn't notice the other runner approaching until he was upon them. Trying to veer out of his way by taking a couple of steps to the right, she forgot to pull in the leash accordingly. Before she could correct the colossal mistake, her legs had tangled in the leash, and she tripped over Micky.

One second, Laura was running and in the next she found herself laid out on the pavement.

"Whoa, there. I've had women trip over themselves to get to me, but this gives falling head over heels a whole new meaning," said the man without a hint of seriousness, and looking a little sheepish for forcing her off the trail. Though he cut a large figure, she didn't get the impression he used his body to intimidate others.

Squatting next to his victim, intended or otherwise, the man took in the whole of Laura's body, checking for obvious injuries. Fortunately, she'd managed to stick her hands out at the last moment to help brace for the fall. It was the sole reason her teeth were still intact.

"May I?" he asked. She dumbly bobbed her head up and down in response.

He ran his hands gently along her arms. "Any pain when I do this?"

"Huh?"

He repeated his motions with her legs, taking in the scrapes starting to bleed through the fabric of her leggings, while he watched her as if she'd hit her head.

"I asked if you have any pain when I do this?" he said again, staring at her quizzically.

He was rubbing his hands along her limbs again. Laura shook her head to clear it, and he must have taken it for a negative, because he stopped touching her instantly. Why did she want him to go back to what he was doing, then? And worse, what was the foreign sensation in the pit of her stomach?

Wait. What was Nick Kelly doing here to begin with? Laura tried once more to gather her thoughts, recognizing the eyes staring back at her from beneath a New York Mets baseball cap for the first time. Of course. Nick must be the runner she'd tried to avoid. *Figures,* she groused internally.

"Can you stand?" he asked, extending his hands to help her up.

Laura accepted his help, placing her small hands in his larger ones. After all, it was partially his fault she was on the ground. A little zip of electricity shot through her at the contact, providing her with a small dose of adrenaline.

"Your face looks a little pale. Are you sure you're good to go?" he asked.

"Um…" she replied still searching for the words to extricate herself from the embarrassment of the moment.

"Did you hit your head? You might have a concussion," said Nick, taking her chin gently in his hand and tilting her face up to make sure her eyes dilated properly with the sunlight.

"No, I don't think so." Her whole body felt like one big bruise, but other than her stomach buzzing unsteadily, she'd live.

"I think there are bees in my stomach," she said trying to put a name to the sensation.

"Pardon me?"

"I have bees. Yeah, there are definitely bees swarming in my stomach."

His charcoal brows rose in surprise. "Oh. Not the effect I usually have, but I can work with bees. Bees are better than butterflies, right?" Nick asked lightly and chuckled.

She scowled in his direction. "Bees are not better than butterflies," Laura said flatly, looking from side to side. "Oh my gosh, Micky—"

"Is right here and appears to be fine."

Looking down, she saw him sitting next to Nick, practically plastered to the man's leg, hiding from her.

"Traitor."

Micky whined pitifully and lay down next to his new friend, the Hulk, putting his paws over his head before peeking up at her with his light eyes. Those puppy eyes were her undoing.

"I forgive you. Next time, try not to throw me to the ground, buddy." He jumped up, immediately coming to her side. With a wince, she leaned down slightly and rubbed his ears, patting his head in reassurance. "Yeah, yeah. We'll still go play at the dog run."

Nick watched the two of them interact, a smile forming at the corners of his mouth.

Laura knew she was a sucker for any animal, including her sister's dog. Raised on a horse farm, it was natural for her to bond with creatures of all kinds, but she could admit to feeling attached to Micky in a way that went beyond normal for the brief time they'd known each other. It was as if she knew him in her soul, like an old friend, except they'd only met recently.

"I think I should join you, in case you do have a concussion," said Nick, still watching her for any signs of a head injury.

Laura's eyes traveled up his chest and over the lines of his cleanly shaven jaw before landing on his blue eyes. They were the color of the sky between sunset and night, complete with twinkling stars every time he smiled.

Great, the behemoth has pretty eyes to go with all of his muscles. He really was too much of everything for her peace of mind.

Too good looking. Too friendly. Too capable. And he'd had far too much overlap with her life in a week's span for what was supposed to be another stop on her way to...well, somewhere. First the line at the deli, then Walker's Pub, and now the park. Was it happenstance, or was the universe trying to tell her something more important?

In any case, the other two places could be a coincidence, but Prospect Park wasn't in Boerum Hill or Carroll Gardens. Granted, the park was public, and she often saw different faces when she ran through it or brought Micky to the dog run. Laura decided she was overthinking the situation, and having a friend in Brooklyn might be nice.

"Fine. You can join us, but only because I need you to throw the ball for Micky-the-circus-dog."

Nick quickly scanned her arms as if he knew they must be throbbing from with the way she'd stopped her fall.

"Sounds good. Come on Eminem, let's go play while your aunt holds down a bench for us."

Laura laughed under her breath at the sound of the nickname.

Looking sideways at her, Nick said, "What? Eminem suits him

better. He has more personality than any Mick I've ever known, and this way there isn't any confusion about coning," he said, his brows waggling up and down suggestively. "Unless, of course, you want to revisit that conversation?"

Another laugh escaped, causing her to wince the teensiest bit at the end and reach for her side. She should have had Nick check her ribs, Laura thought. Shaking her head over the sensation the idea caused, she noticed a rosy flush creep into his cheeks.

Huh, it would appear I'm not the only one thinking about him checking me out more thoroughly. Or she really needed to get those bees in her stomach under control. They were causing hormone fluctuations she had no intention of actually indulging in.

When they reached the dog run, Nick silently directed Laura toward a bench inside the fence, taking the ball Micky dropped at his feet. It was still early, so the area was almost empty with only one other dog to play with. Watching their interaction, Nick leaned against the fence and asked, "Why did Kate name him Micky Mouse to begin with?"

Laura shifted, trying to find a comfortable position on the hard bench. Giving up, she stretched her battered legs in front of her and cradled her sore arms across her body before answering. "Kate thought having a dog would make her feel safer. Um, you know, living in a city," she said, catching herself before she said more than she should.

Nick's eyes tracked her as she stumbled through her explanation.

"She said he reminded her of a cartoon animal with human characteristics. I tried to tell her to name him after an intelligent book character, like Sherlock Holmes, instead of a talking mouse. It's not even spelled the right way," she finished with exasperation.

"Again, at least Eminem is a cooler name than Micky Mouse."

"I concede 'oh wise one.'" The quote rolled off her tongue subconsciously, one she hadn't used in years, but which had been a running joke between her and Drew. She waited for the guilt that usually came in such instances, but when nothing happened, she smiled softly. Sometimes the boy she had loved showed up when she least expected it—as though he were telling her it was as much her joke as his.

"Did you just quote Yoda?"

"Yeah, but don't get overly excited. This is more a fluke than the norm."

"I'm not buying what you're selling, Tink. I think you're a closet nerd."

"Is that supposed to be a compliment?" Laura asked, confused by the look on his face.

"Absolutely. An intelligent woman is always beautiful, but the all-out nerdy ones are hot."

He said it blandly, as if he hadn't turned her world upside down with his statement. Laura had enough life experience to know most men who looked like Nick did not fall for women who looked like her. Said category belonged to a group of women who were leggy, gorgeous, and oozed sex appeal. Not that she wanted to be anyone other than herself. Still, it was nice having someone who looked like he could grace the cover of a magazine compliment her.

Sheesh! How long has *it been since I glimpsed myself through someone else's eyes?*

"Wait. Did you call me Tink?" Laura asked belatedly.

"Yep. Now back to us spending time together soon—"

"We weren't talking about that."

"Of course, we were. Now that I know you like *Star Wars*, hanging out with you is a given."

"Um, I'm usually busy during the week," she fudged, searching for an excuse. "I work for Uncle Joe at the pub most days," she continued vaguely. "And taking care of Eminem is a full-time job. Obviously."

Chapter 5

Nick

Nick smiled, absurdly pleased over her use of the nickname, and glanced over at the aforementioned mongrel who was showing off for a labradoodle across the lawn.

Yep, pal, not much different than what's happening over here. Laura wasn't making this easy for him. He couldn't remember the last time a girl had turned him down, but he could tell she was wavering. Her sarcasm suggested as much.

"Perfect. I have this Sunday off, and the farmers' markets in Brooklyn are amazing. There's a large one a few blocks down from my parents' house. We can meet there at eleven."

"Meet at your parents' house?" she asked, her voice an octave higher than normal.

Laura looked slightly panicked. "No, the market," Nick rushed to reassure her. He had never taken any girl home for Sunday dinner. Every Kelly sibling knew you didn't bring someone to the table until they were joining the family. Sunday dinner was sacred, not to mention slightly dangerous.

The inquisition your significant other had to endure was no joke. Only those with a screw-you attitude usually survived. It was painful to watch, but once you were in the family, it was for life. Similar to *The Godfather*, but without the feuds and bloodshed.

Okay, sometimes there are feuds and bloodshed, conceded Nick. Still, family was family.

Nick's heart fluttered when a picture of Laura seated next to him at the crowded cherry-stained table filled his head uninvited, making him raise his hand to his chest.

He'd probably overdone his workout yesterday. A pectoral spasm could feel like flutters in the chest, right? He'd ask Leo the next time they met for a beer.

His older brother took perverse pleasure in knowing more than he did sometimes, but it was because Leo should have gone to med school. Though his brother didn't advertise his big brain, the guy geeked out over medical textbooks. Nick knew Leo had become a paramedic with the FDNY instead, for the approval of Pop and Donnie. It was something he could completely relate to. He would never stop trying to win their approval, even if it were never coming. The old guilt resurfaced for a brief moment until he pushed it back into the past and tried to focus on his present.

Nick could see the final rebuttal waiting to burst from Laura's lovely mouth and tried to prevent it by rushing in. "It's two people spending time together in a public place. Brooklyn is big enough I'm sure we could avoid seeing each other except at Walker's, if that's what you really want." Nick shrugged. "But what's the harm in seeing a friendly face now and again?"

Laura twisted her mouth back and forth, her eyes filled with secrets he wanted to know.

Noticing the earbuds hanging around her neck, he changed tactics. "We can listen to music, each bring a book, and ignore one another while our furry friend chases the birds and entertains small children with his antics."

She hesitated for another moment before saying, "Fine. Eleven o'clock sharp."

"Great. We can meet on the corner where Carroll Street intersects with Smith. And the park after?"

"Depends on how much I enjoy the company at the market," she said with a raised eyebrow.

"Got it. Come with my winning personality if I want to spend the afternoon with Tink and Eminem."

She is a total ball buster, he thought, which only made him like her more.

Though it doubtless hurt to laugh, Laura did so anyway. Hearing the sound made his chest flutter in the vicinity of his heart again. Once was a fluke, twice a coincidence, but three times made a pattern. Like a string attached between objects, Laura tugged, and his heart seemed to flutter on the receiving end. For the first time in his life, Nick realized, he had butterflies over a woman.

"You're so weird," she said with a snort.

"Yep. But you like weird," he replied with a winning smile, relishing those butterflies dancing within his chest.

"Maybe. But I do like to laugh, and you are sort of funny."

"At least you didn't say funny looking," replied Nick with another trademark smirk as he helped her into a taxi.

Nick kissed his mother's cheek and grabbed the key to the shed from a hook by the back door. "Sorry I'm late. My run took longer than I thought it would," he said, the corners of his mouth lifting as he thought about his time with Laura at the park. He'd seen her off by cab to keep her from walking home. She had tried to convince him that she looked worse than she felt but as a first responder he couldn't, in good conscience, let her walk home by herself.

Laura hadn't so much as blinked when he'd said the words, but then again, she hadn't noticed his uniform the first time they met. Either way, she didn't ask him anything about his job. She was different from the women he usually spent time with, and he liked her all the more for it.

The older he got, the less he appreciated women fawning over him or his career. They knew nothing about his decision to join up, or worse, they assumed they did. Not that it mattered, because he never talked about the job with anyone aside from his family and best friend, Dean Santiago.

Doorknob in hand, he glanced back at his mother, the heavy hair he'd inherited from her now streaked with silver. She had aged since his father's death, but the fire in her amber eyes remained a reminder of how age was merely a number. Luna lived her life with equal parts passion and love.

"Do you want me to edge this time or wait until next week?" he asked. "I have enough time to do the front after I mow. My shift doesn't start until six tonight."

"I thought you were on a twenty-four, forty-eight-hour rotation."

"Sawicki and his wife finally had their adoption go through. He's on parental leave for the next couple of weeks, so I'm taking his twelve tonight. But I have Sunday off for dinner."

Luna smiled and reached up to pat her baby's cheek. "Such a sweet boy, Nicky. Always willing to help others, including your old Ma. I still have bulbs to plant out front, so wait until after I've finished with the garden next week."

What she didn't say was even more critical. Nick knew she had every intention of winning this year's Carroll Gardens accolade for the best garden on May Day, a sign posted in the yard announcing it to every passerby.

"That uppity busybody, Vera Monahan, can stick it where the sun refuses to shine come spring," said Luna, an Italian accent appearing out of the ether.

It didn't matter that his mother was a native of Brooklyn; the accent developed every time she got upset or sentimental. She blamed it entirely on her grandmother, who had insisted Luna speak Italian at home. His mother had been closer to her father, who understood how she longed to fit in with friends who didn't have an Italian nonna. Nick knew she missed his Gramps every day, almost as much as she missed Pop and Donnie.

He also heard what she didn't say with her foot-tapping, fist-shaking, accented diatribe. Nick had better not scalp the yard, like he did when he was twelve, and his edge should be as clean and straight as his father's line—because Patrick Kelly had suddenly become a saint, who'd never committed any wrong, upon his death. Anything less than yard perfection would mean temporary banishment. Though he wasn't exactly sure what she would banish him from, she could be extremely creative when disappointed by her children.

"I'll drop something by the Sawickis' for dinner later this week. Are they still in Cobble Hill?" she asked, interrupting his wayward thoughts.

"Yep, except they moved out of the rental and bought a house on the same block as Dean's folks. He'll never hear the end of it from his ma now."

"Well, as Queen Bey says, he should put a ring on it. Women like C.J. are rare and she's not going to wait around forever."

"Trust me, he knows. We all know. I think it's only a matter of time. Anyway, I'll text you later tonight with the Sawickis' address. I thought I'd go with you to meet the new addition." Food was the way his mother took care of people. It never surprised him when she made a meal for someone in his Squad since becoming extended family was inevitable when you put your life in each other's hands every shift. He also thought it made her feel like she was still supporting the good men and women of the FDNY, despite his father and brother's passing.

His mother cocked her head and casually said, "You know, you could have a family of your own. Then I could cook for you and hold your bambinos instead of everyone else's."

"Ma, it's not like I don't want that to happen. But like Pop always said, the best things come to those who wait with busy hands and a sense of humor. I'm trying."

"Don't forget the full heart," she chided.

"I haven't. Cross my heart," Nick replied, crossing his heart with an index finger.

He kept the plans he'd made with Laura to himself. No sense inviting the drama, which would undoubtedly ensue once his family knew he was interested in someone, if it didn't go anywhere in the coming weeks.

"Oh Nicky, your father would be so proud of you. I'm sure it'll happen when the time is right," she said, taking in a quick breath. "Speaking of which, Jules called to tell me her feet are swollen, her back aches, and she has acid reflux. That girl is going to be the death of me with all her complaining. She's growing a child. Did she think it would be easy?" she asked in exasperation, the Italian accent present once more.

Julietta was the third of four girls born to Luna and Patrick Kelly, and Nick's older sister by almost three years. She was also the one who caused his mother the most heartburn, real or imagined.

Nick laughed. "I'm sure she did, but you'll still be the first one to the hospital when the baby arrives, regardless of her complaints."

"Of course. I'm Nonna," she told him, as if it made perfect sense to throw elbows to hold a baby, even when no one ever tried to stop her.

Nick kissed the top of her head. "And what an incredible one you are."

Laura

Laura captured her bottom lip with her teeth as she contemplated her last interaction with Nick. He had tucked her and Micky into a cab and handed the driver a twenty-dollar bill for the mile to her apartment, all while his new friend watched him like he'd hung the moon.

Looking down her nose at her companion she said, "He gives

you a stupid nickname, pays for a ride home, and suddenly he's your bread 'n butter. You are awfully fickle for someone who's supposed to be loyal."

Micky had simply licked her face in response. "Yeah, I know. He's attractive, funny, *and* kind." Plopping back in the seat, her head had landed on the headrest and lolled to the side where she watched the tree lined streets, people rushing from place to place with a purpose she recognized but lacked in her own life.

"I'm in so much trouble," she said aloud as she pulled herself back into the present. She turned her attention to the silverware from the industrial dishwasher, laying it on a towel to roll inside paper napkins for tomorrow's lunch crowd.

She was still sore, and her knees were raw and scabby but, overall, she was much better than she had been three days ago. Uncle Joe had sent her home after she'd hobbled into Walker's Pub in such a pitiful state.

"It's a good thing Pat's boy was there to take care of you," Uncle Joe had said.

"I'd hardly call it helpful when he's the reason I fell."

"I thought you tripped over Micky."

"I did, but I wouldn't have if a certain someone hadn't been taking up the entire running path. That man tips the scale of behemoth with so much height and muscle."

She sucked in another breath and rambled on, "And to top it all off, he runs like a svelte jungle cat despite all of his, his, his…."

Laura waved her arms in circles as she searched for the words to accurately describe Nick's physique.

"His large attributes?"

Laura stopped waving her arms around aimlessly and gave Uncle Joe the stink eye. "Ha, ha, very funny."

Uncle Joe had smiled and with a knowing look said, "I think the 'lady doth protest too much.'"

"It's not like that!" she exclaimed, stepping right into his clever trap. "You know I'm not interested in having a romantic relationship with anyone," she continued with more calm than she felt, trying to keep her emotions in check—or hidden, was more like it.

Uncle Joe weighed his words before he spoke.

"Honey, Drew passed away a long time ago."

"Ten years is a blink in a lifetime. Grief doesn't have a deadline," Laura replied automatically.

"No, it doesn't. But I don't think you're grieving anymore. It's more like you're trying to avoid any real happiness in case life pulls the rug out from underneath you again.

"Geez, don't pull any punches. Please, tell me what you really think. No need to consider my feelings," she said, sarcasm coating her delivery and stance. "I'm happy...enough," Laura finished when he raised his brows in disbelief.

Huffing a laugh, he threw the wet washcloth in his hands to the counter with a splat and pulled Laura into his arms. When she wrapped her arms around his waist, he gave her one more hard squeeze and released her.

"You are more like your mother than you like to think. She's always spoiling for a fight, sometimes over the smallest things. Only your dad knows what to do with her. He can soothe her hard edges with a single word."

"Sounds about right. It's not much different than the way he manages an unbroken horse no one else can ride."

"I probably wouldn't use that analogy in front of your mom."

Laura laughed, relieving the earlier tension.

"Come on, kiddo. You know I'm not trying to be cruel, but someone needs to be honest with you. You stopped moving forward with your life when Drew lost his. We both know that's a fruitless quest."

She hated how right he was. There were people who might choose the existence she led, but Laura knew she was stalling. She still wanted her own home and a family, but fear kept her from reaching for those dreams. She couldn't lose what she didn't have. Besides, being angry meant she could blame God, Karma, and even the universe for her circumstances instead of finding direction or a new purpose in life.

Her head fell back, and she looked to the ceiling for the answers she didn't have. "I know, I know. Traveling was supposed to help me figure things out—figure *me* out—instead, it's become an uncomplicated way for me to avoid everything," she mumbled at the end.

She took a seat at the stainless counter, laying her forehead on the cool metal. "I need to grow up, but I'm afraid to leave Neverland."

Joe sat on a stool next to her. "You're a little stuck, but not irresponsible," he said nudging her knee with his. "Kate would never let you stay in her apartment otherwise."

Laura smiled briefly. "True, and she left her dog with me," she said, catching an oddly sheepish look on his face for the conversation they were having. "Hold up. Why did she leave Micky with me instead of you?"

"Well, I think Kate thought getting a dog was a better idea than the reality of pet ownership."

Laura snickered. "Sounds like Kate and explains why she was so eager for me to meet him."

"I'm fairly certain she's hoping you'll want to take Micky with you when you leave. For his sake, doll, you should. Don't get me wrong, she takes care of him, but he needs to be with someone who appreciates everything he has to offer."

Laura swallowed down the knot of nerves the idea produced. "It's harder to travel with a pet, though."

"All the more reason for you to consider putting down some roots," said Uncle Joe firmly.

"I don't know if I can go back to Midwell. The farm will always be home, but I'm not sure if a small town is big enough now that I've seen more of the world." Or, if she could live somewhere with memories of Drew tucked into every nook and cranny.

Joe shrugged nonchalantly. "Then stay in Brooklyn. When you get an itch to travel—on occasion— I'll take Micky. You can continue at Walker's Pub as long as you like, and since an old man's got to retire someday, you could even work towards becoming part owner if the food and drink industry interests you. I've seen you talking to Amir about the menu, and I know you go home and cook every night."

"I'm messing around with the different foods and flavors I've had overseas. It's no big deal."

"You've got more talent than you give yourself credit for. Everyone loves the fancy crisps you make, and those spiced-fruit tarts sell like hot cakes to the late-night crowd.

When she merely stared at him, he held his hands up in surrender, saying, "No pressure. You and Amir have fun changing up the menu. But don't be surprised if word spreads and business picks up."

"That's a good thing, right?"

"As long as you plan to stick around; otherwise, don't mess with the low expectations I've already created for the customers. I don't want to deal with their disappointment when you leave."

"Please, you can't be serious. Walker's Pub is a time-honored establishment. Nothing I do will change that."

"I'm sure we'll all continue on the way we were before you arrived. But then again, no one can stay exactly the same after knowing someone. Life is a chain reaction of people and events."

Laura crossed her arms and gave him a pointed stare. "Waxing philosophical, huh? You sound like Dad."

"Doesn't make it any less true. You know this better than a lot of people do."

"Subtle, Uncle Joe. I'm fully aware I'm a shadow of the girl I once was," she said, grief sneaking in to weigh her down.

"Not a shadow, but you are a different person for knowing Drew, as well as losing him. If he had lived, you might be living an entirely different life. Would you trade the last ten years?"

She hesitated. "Thanks, now I feel guilty for attempting to move forward, if a bit lamely."

"You said it yourself; Midwell is small potatoes now. You've become an independent woman with a global perspective. While searching for a life without Drew, you became the woman you are, instead of the girl he knew."

"My dreams of becoming a wife and a vet weren't a whim. If Drew were alive, I'd be those today."

"Of course, honey. I don't doubt the love you had for him, or the life you dreamed of making together. I'm only pointing out that sometimes life isn't a straight line. There are curves, hills, and flash floods once in a while," he said with the conviction of experience. "We don't move on; we course correct. We survive, and sometimes we learn to thrive despite everything life throws at us. Drew will always be a part of your story, but he isn't the end of it."

"Says the man who's never had a romantic relationship in my lifetime," she said, accusingly.

"Doesn't mean I haven't been in love before."

"When? Where? Who?" burst from Laura's lips in quick succession. "Sorry, I assumed since—never mind, it doesn't matter."

Uncle Joe laughed under his breath. "It was a long time ago. Her parents didn't think I could give her the kind of life she deserved, not that I can blame them. I was eighteen and still lived at home. She asked me to wait, to give them time to accept me. I was angry when I should have been patient and things ended badly."

Laura didn't know what to say, but if he'd never had another meaningful relationship, did that mean Uncle Joe still had feelings for the mystery woman?

"We went our separate ways, and she eventually married someone else. See, I know a thing or two about the road of life. The pub helped me find my way, and it'll help you do the same if you give it a chance."

Chapter 6

Nick

Nick arrived on the corner of Carroll and Smith Street at five minutes to eleven on Sunday morning. He had no idea if Laura liked to be early, and he didn't want to risk her starting through the market without him. An independent spirit like her might fly the coop, with or without his sorry butt. He worried she wouldn't give him a second chance if he blew this one.

A song by John Mayer played in his ears while he took in the scenery surrounding him. The temptation to sing along with the words grew with every tick of the second hand on his watch. Nick observed the bustle of the market collide with the other shops up and down the street, wondering how many of those people waited for the world to change instead of being the change themselves. The crowds would swell even more once church services were over and brunch concluded at the nearby restaurants, but he was hopeful Laura would join him for sandwiches in the park before then.

"Hey, sorry I'm late," said Laura, a little breathless as she reached the corner. Micky barked a greeting and put his paw out for Nick to shake.

Not an early bird, Nick noted. "No problem. Hey pal, good to see you too," he replied, looking into Laura's eyes, framed by long lashes, for any sign that she wanted to back out, but all he saw were pools he could get lost in.

It's official. Light green is my new favorite color.

Dean's girlfriend, Chaucey, had called them peridot when he tried to describe Laura to them over a pint at the pub the previous afternoon. He had hoped he might catch a glimpse of her, but she'd been conspicuously absent after saying she worked most days.

"I went to early mass this morning at the church down the street, so I had plenty of time to get to the market."

"You're Catholic?"

"More than I'd like, sometimes. My Pop's Irish and Ma's Italian. There was really no way of getting around it," he replied with a small laugh.

She grinned. "Does that mean you also come from a large family?" she asked when he stopped to purchase some apples and pears at the stand of a farm from up state.

"Youngest of six. Seven, technically."

"Oh," Laura said and came to an abrupt halt. "I'm so sorry."

Her empathy was palpable.

"I never knew her. She came after my older sister, Jules, but Ma still feels the absence."

Laura nodded in understanding. "So, you're the baby?"

"Yep, and you?"

"Looks like we have something in common after all," she answered with a sideways glance he couldn't read.

"Are you also Catholic?" he asked, enjoying their easy rapport.

"No, but I went to church growing up. Mostly Methodist, but my dad says any denomination will do, so long as you show up."

"Do you still go?"

"Not really," she said, looking bashful. "I guess you could say God and I had a falling out. Something happened and we didn't agree on the outcome."

"Got it," he said, and let whatever that something was go unanswered for the time being. Nick was curious, but feared poking around might scare her off.

"How was the service?" she asked into the silence that followed, stopping to smell handmade soaps. When she reached for her wallet to purchase one made from oatmeal and goat's milk, he held out cash for the vendor, feeling like the man when Laura smiled and said a quiet thank you.

"The downside to the early service is listening to the mass in Latin. The upside is not feeling chastised since I don't understand everything the priest is saying."

"I can imagine that is quite the bonus for someone like you," Laura deadpanned.

"Oh, you wound me," he exaggerated, covering his heart with his hand. "I may not be a saint, but I don't necessarily qualify for the highway to hell…yet."

"Purgatory it is, then, huh?"

"Probably. Or a nice girl could come along and help me reform my wicked ways," he said suggestively.

"Well, then, I guess that settles things."

"How so?" Nick asked, unsure he wanted to hear the answer.

"No one has ever accused me of being nice."

Nick chuckled and started to lead them in the direction of an art display across the lawn. Laura grabbed his hand to get his attention and, taking her cue, they changed course to make a beeline for the vegetables brought in from local gardens. She let go quickly and turned away, but he still caught the faint pink on her cheeks. Good; he hoped the physical contact affected her as much as it did him.

Helping her stand the other day on the path had been perfunctory. He'd been concerned about her injuries, but Nick's heart had reacted in the same way: pounding so loud he could hear it, his palm seared as if he'd wrapped it around a lightning bolt.

Get a grip; it's not as if you've never touched a woman. Find your cool, Kelly, he told himself. But the shock of holding Laura's hand still ran through his body like an electrical current. He felt like he'd been sleepwalking through his life and was suddenly awake. Their chemistry was undeniable, but Nick suspected that it was so much more than purely physical.

Once Laura had her tote filled with fruits and vegetables, he led her back toward the art. Nick's best friend was sliding a print into a cardboard tube for a customer, while the artist spoke with another customer about the large painting behind her.

"Hey, man, thought we might see you today," said Dean as he pulled Nick in for a bro hug and smiled a little too brightly at Laura.

"Way to be subtle, dude." Nick mumbled. He trusted his best friend implicitly with his life at work, but outside of it the guy was more trouble than a wingman ought to be.

"Dean, meet Laura Howard. She's Joe Walker's niece."

"No way!" gushed Chaucey, as she joined their little circle. "You're Kate's sister," she accused in a British accent.

"Guilty," replied Laura.

"Our boy Nick neglected to mention your name when he said he was coming to the market with someone new in tow." She further chided Nick with a punch to his upper arm.

"Ouch," he grumped, rubbing his hand over his shoulder.

Chaucey could throw a punch better than most men he knew so he usually made it a point to stay on her good side, unlike Dean who spoke before he thought more often than not. Squad 2 took regular bets on how long she would put up with whatever nonsense came out of his mouth. His best friend had learned to beg for forgiveness like a gospel choir sang about Jesus— with fervor.

Laura looked back and forth between the other woman and the art behind them, bouncing on the balls of her feet in realization. "Oh my gosh! You must be Chaucey Jain. Kate raves about your art all the time and the ceilings in her apartment are gorgeous."

"Ahh, that's sweet. I spend more money than is good for my budget at your sister's boutique, but her lavender hair care line is to die for. And please, call me C.J. Only my mother calls me Chaucey. Thank Kali."

"I adore your name. Kate said your mother is a professor of literature at Oxford. Is it safe to assume she's a fan of Chaucer?" Laura asked with one eyebrow raised.

"Yes, Mum is positively obsessed with the old man. Frankly, my father isn't any better, despite his views on colonialism."

Laura's eyes went wide, and he stepped back to watch the two women interact. Accustomed to Chaucey speaking her mind, Nick had a feeling she and Laura would get along fine. If he secretly hoped helping the spunky blonde make friends meant her being willing to stick around, so be it. That he wanted her to stay long enough to figure out if the butterflies she caused were temporary or in it for the long haul went without saying.

Laura

Once Laura recovered from the initial shock, she let loose a loud laugh, admiring the moxie of the woman in front of her. Chaucey wore brightly colored, hand-painted converse high-tops with a pair of jeans torn at the knees and hugging her curves. A white smock billowed around her elbows and hung over her hips loosely. Copper bracelets layered each forearm, complimenting the golden hue of her skin and the highlights in her hair, tied back with a block-patterned silk scarf.

With another glance behind the other woman's shoulders, Laura asked, "Is this new?" Titled *Grace in Truth*, the piece in question was oil on canvas and large enough to cover an entire wall. "Oh, C.J., it's beautiful," whispered Laura in reverence.

Women in every shade, shape, stature, and stage of life stood shoulder to shoulder in assorted styles of clothing and coverage, their expressions ranging from sad, wary, and disappointed to fierce, proud, and satisfied. "I wish Kate had the space to hang this in her apartment," she said wistfully. Or, for the first time in ten years, she wished for a wall of her own on which to hang the provocative work.

What would the world be like if women spent more time accepting and supporting one another instead of comparing and competing? Laura asked herself.

Better, she acknowledged, *we could accomplish so much more together.*

Micky whined at her feet as he watched a couple of kids play catch in the middle of the market's chaos.

"You ready to get sandwiches and head to the park?" asked Nick, his fuzzy friend barking in consensus.

The guys said a quick goodbye, Dean winking at Laura and

ribbing Nick with his elbow, while Laura swapped phone numbers with Chaucey and promised to call her for a girls' night out.

Nick and Laura left Ruth's Deli half an hour later with Reubens on rye with pastrami, sauerkraut, Havarti cheese, extra dressing, and vinegar chips on the side, the way she preferred. Micky eagerly trotted beside them as they made the short walk into the Gowanus Hills of northwest Brooklyn and entered Green-Wood Cemetery through the 5th Avenue gate.

"Wow!" exclaimed Laura in surprise as she pirouetted to catch the back side of the brownstone, Gothic-Revival architecture. "I feel like we walked through the doors of a church."

"Well, we are on hallowed ground," replied Nick, looking pleased.

"Um, is it okay to have Micky in here?" she asked doubtfully.

"Service Animals are welcome."

"But he isn't one," she argued.

"I think he qualifies as an emotional support candidate."

Laura stopped short in the middle of the path and placed her fists on her hips in indignation. Unfortunately, she also pulled said candidate up short, forcing a yelp from him. "What exactly are you implying?" she demanded.

"Easy, Tink. All I meant was that our pal makes everyone he

comes in contact with feel good."

"Oh." Laura could admit she'd overreacted a tiny bit. Uncle Joe may have had a good point when he told her she was spoiling for a fight. Or, maybe she was feeling overly sensitive about her family's expectations to move past her grief, which Nick knew nothing about.

"Still, you shouldn't joke about people who need an emotional support animal."

"Again, I wasn't," he said placatingly, hands open in surrender. "I have a friend who's a former Marine, and his Dachshund, Bixby, goes everywhere with him. Having a fuzzy companion makes it easier for him to be in certain social situations. It also helps him manage the chronic pain he endures from shrapnel left in one of his legs."

"Oh," she said a second time. For someone who usually had more than enough words, hers had suddenly gone missing.

They started walking again when Laura stopped once more, careful not to pull on Micky's leash as hard this time around. "I'm sorry for assuming the worst. My dad is always telling me I need to do a better job of looking for rainbows instead of thunderstorms."

"We're good," said Nick, gently taking her canvas tote and Micky's leash from her. "Besides, a thunderstorm can be fun sometimes, depending on the company."

"In my experience, a thunderstorm means that I got caught in the rain, unprepared," said Laura. "And don't even get me started on the lightning. It'll knock a person right off their feet."

The ghost of a boy who lived on in her heart laughed. *You sure are cute, falling for me.*

Laura had fallen at Drew's feet on the first day of high school cross-country practice, when she tripped over her untied shoelace. It was a total cliché. Embarrassed and mad, she'd squinted up at the boy standing over her, prepared to give him a piece of her mind. In the next instant he'd extended his hand to help her stand and grinned even wider in the face of her scowl before he said, "Did it hurt when you fell from Heaven?"

She had laughed at his corny joke, and snapped, "Not really. Fallen angels grow fangs, or didn't you know?" It was a reference to her favorite vampire television series and made her feel slightly less foolish about the situation.

"Well then, that settles things," Drew had replied with a smile.

When she simply looked back at him blankly, he'd swung his arm around her shoulders. "I like a girl who bites back."

Laura couldn't help but think of how she'd also fallen at Nick's feet not long ago, but the similarities between the two ended there. Drew had always had a sharp edge to him, one that tended to make him callous to other people's needs, putting his own first. It was a topic they had quarreled over more than once. And though she didn't know Nick well, intuitively she knew he took care of others.

Nick chuckled, jolting Laura back into the moment, where they continued to wind through the cemetery's grounds, the red-and-gold-dressed trees as much of a reminder of how time marched on with or without a person as the stately mausoleums dotting the landscape.

"You're right; thunderstorms can be harsh, but if you get caught in the rain with the right person, they can also be exhilarating, and force you inside for shelter when you had other plans," Nick stated with a half grin.

"You do know I was referring more to life in general and not actual weather patterns, right?"

With another lopsided smile, he replied, "Same lessons apply."

"What happens when the lightning knocks you down, though?" Laura asked, curious about his response.

"Then, the person you're with extends a helping hand, and possibly CPR," he said, only half serious.

"But what happens if they leave?" she pushed further.

"Ahh. Well, if the worst happens, I think it's important to have family and friends who will help you remember why you can't stay on the ground," said Nick with solemn deliberation.

With those words, Laura realized the man walking beside her was a deeper well than she'd perceived at first and, like herself, might be speaking from personal experience. Did Nick also lose someone close to him? Or was it a hazard of the job?

When he'd mentioned it previously, he'd been so cursory it felt like an invasion of his privacy to inquire into the details. Instead of asking Nick what she wanted to know about being a first responder, she lost herself in the surroundings of the grounds. They were a veritable treasure trove of the past. Everywhere she looked she saw evidence of New York's gilded age, both in size and the opulence demonstrated by the final resting places of Green-Wood's prominent residents.

"Why come here and not somewhere more traditional, like Central Park?" Laura asked softly after a while, interrupting the reverie Nick had fallen into.

"For starters, it's on this side of the bridge, but this was actually here before Central Park existed. If anything, the park is a replica of what's in front of you. Before any of this was here, though, the land was open hills and the site of the Battle of Brooklyn."

"During the Revolutionary War?" Laura asked, surprise evident in her tone. She liked to research wherever she planned to visit, but finding out the battle had taken place where she stood was surreal. Then again, battlefields were whatever space an army used to make war.

"The cemetery didn't open until 1840, after Manhattan put limits on cemetery locations due to sanitation. Not to mention, land was at a premium in the city."

"So, someone brilliant had the idea to use the land across the way?"

"Kind of. Brooklyn was already under development as a suburb of Manhattan, when a man named Henry Evelyn Pierrepont started buying up parcels of land to use for a rural cemetery."

"He had the foresight to know if Brooklyn didn't plan

accordingly, it would have the same issues as the city across the water," Laura murmured with admiration.

"Exactly."

"Hmm. How is it you know so much about this place?"

Looking caught, Nick replied bashfully, "It happens to be my favorite park in Brooklyn. When I'm here, I can let go of all of the hard stuff in life. Being at peace—with myself, with the world—is the best way to describe the feeling I get."

Nick paused for a moment, debating how much to open up but finished when Laura continued to look up at him expectantly. "When I'm inside this place, where life and death coexist, I'm reminded how small I am when compared to everything else in the universe. And for all of the ugly, there is more beauty than I could ever hope to witness in my lifetime."

Chapter 7

Laura

Laura released the breath she hadn't realized she was holding. The man in front of her watched her intently, his soul laid bare in his blue eyes, before turning away and releasing his hold over her. She tried to ignore how attractive she found his vulnerability and debated swooning into his strong arms.

Wait, what? She shook her head and tried to find her common sense. It's not like it was a crime to enjoy someone else's company, even if it did lead to silly ideas like fainting over an emotionally available man. Why then, did it feel as if she'd betrayed Drew with a single thought? Okay, more than one if she was being entirely honest.

That's on you, firecracker, a voice she missed like a phantom limb whispered in the recesses of her head.

The swift reassurance surprised her, causing her guilt to recede with equal parts fondness and regret. Laura told herself Drew had only ever wanted her happiness, and had their situation been the reverse, Laura would have wanted him to find a way forward. Was it love that kept her holding on so tightly to the past? Or was she afraid to accept who she'd become without him?

Laura sighed and half jogged to catch up with her guide, and came to an abrupt halt when he stopped, nearly bumping into the solid wall of his back. She really needed to start paying better attention to where she was going when Nick was around.

He reached behind to steady her with a quick hand to her lower back and winked. "Careful Tink, I wouldn't want you to run me over again."

She blinked slowly, looking more like an owl instead of a woman in control of her senses, but Nick had her completely off kilter in every sense of the word. And to make matters worse, the beehive in her stomach had descended in force. She blamed it on his starry gaze and warm touch.

Scowling at his back for good measure, she asked, "Why did we stop?"

"I thought we could sit here for lunch, or read and listen to music if you want," he replied with a shrug of his shoulders, whose size were decidedly a little overkill for her liking.

No siree, she told herself. She was not at all interested in dating a man with so much stature. It was a neck crick waiting to happen.

Gaining a small semblance of equilibrium once more, her snarky inner voice decided to join in the fray. *Way to go; someday you might actually believe the lies you tell yourself.*

Laura joined Nick under the shade of a tree next to the large statue of a woman.

"I love the view," remarked Laura. "Very clever of the artist—Minerva, goddess of wisdom, justice, and war waiving to Lady Liberty across the water.

"An apropos reminder of how our freedom was won, and how easily it can slip away," he said absentmindedly. "We are a nation of individuals and agendas, yet our Constitution and the dream of democracy bind us together in one purpose."

"You talk as if it's something you've given a lot of thought to."

"I guess you could say I was on a different path once upon a time."

From what Uncle Joe had mentioned in a previous conversation, Laura knew Nick had decided to become a firefighter after 9/11, as though his life had been on a different trajectory before then. Laura couldn't help but wonder what that other path had been or why he'd chosen to abandon it.

"Were you in New York when the Twin Towers were hit?"

Well, that was certainly one way to go. Sometimes, she seriously thought supergluing her mouth shut might be in everyone's best interest. Nick was slow to respond, and noticeably caught off guard by her nosy inquisition.

"It's all right if you don't want to talk about it." Laura tried to backtrack and berated herself for being so insensitive. She never talked about 9/11, and her reasons had nothing to do with terrorism on American soil, let alone in her backyard.

"Nah, it's okay. I was in class at NYU and thinking about my law school acceptances when everything went to hell in a handbasket," he said, looking off in the distance, eyes squinting from the afternoon sunshine.

"Well, that explains your passion for democracy," she said, trying to lighten the mood, and not follow up with the dozens of questions bouncing around in her head.

"Want to listen to music?" Nick asked, effectively changing the subject.

Laura took the hint and tucked her earbuds into her ears in answer while he unwrapped a sandwich and snatched a pickle from the pile she'd requested at the deli.

When the same large hand plucked out one of her earbuds a minute later, casually placing it into his own ear, she refused to give him the satisfaction of a smile. If she was supposed to be a faerie, the man next to her was a unicorn, completely one of a kind.

The bees in her belly zipped and zoomed happily in agreement.

Stupid bees, go bother someone else with your notions, she berated her newly established hive.

Nick

"Let's see if you have as good a taste in music as you do movies," he said, watching Laura's reaction. She rolled her eyes and hit play on the music app, brushing him off. Nick laughed and moved in a little closer to her, using the excuse of the earbuds to shorten the distance between them until he could feel the heat from her arm causing goosebumps along his.

He swept his eyes over his surroundings, those of death and life alike, reminding himself that his faith in eternity wasn't dependent upon his circumstances. Some days it was a harder leap to make than others. Closing his eyes, Nick let the sounds of a familiar song wash away the awkwardness of talking about law school—not to mention the memories of fear and funerals followed by survivor's guilt, all of which had changed the entire course of his future. It had been his choice, and yet, sometimes it felt like there had never really been one to begin with.

Nick listened to the notes of an old blues tune flow into words about a famous highway, keeping his eyes on the horizon, and imagined what it would be like to leave everything behind for a new start. Or even a vacation that didn't involve camping with his sisters and their kids. As the last verse faded, he removed her earbuds from their ears, replacing them with his.

Most days he was proud to be from the Empire State, but sharing his favorite place only reminded him how much of the world Laura had seen, and how small his own was. When she started humming next to him, he leaned back onto his elbow so he could watch her at a distance, appreciating the view of her profile.

Laura sang quietly, almost shy at first. No one would mistake her for a professional singer, but he liked the husky quality of her voice and the way she got into the music. She nodded in time with the beat while she swayed back and forth in a steady rhythm.

When she looked back over her shoulder as the last notes of the song faded out, Nick pretended to be interested in the clover as Micky stretched out beside him in the sun to roll back and forth in the grass.

"Solid choice, Kelly. Of course, the verdict's still out about your book. What did you bring to read?" she asked, taking his earbud out and handing it back to him.

The light brush of her fingers caused a zap of awareness somewhere in the vicinity of his heart, but it wasn't why a flush crept into his face all the way to the roots of his hair. He'd brought two choices: one to impress, and the other because he had to be ready for book club with his nieces next week.

To impress, or be honest? A dilemma possibly faced by anyone when confronted with their reflection each morning, but wanting to impress someone didn't mean compromising authenticity. Or did it? Nick lamented the fact his father would've known the answer.

"Are you blushing?" Laura asked, slightly confused at first. And then she gasped.

Uh oh, thought Nick. She looked much too triumphant for his comfort. He started to squirm under the gleam in her gaze.

"Unless...Oh my gosh! Nick Kelly reads romance novels. Are they the kind with half-dressed pirates and women who strap daggers to their bare thighs on the covers? Please, please, please, tell me they are!" Laura exclaimed, trying to see the book he held behind him.

He scowled out at the distance and then looked back at her sheepishly. "First off, if I did read books like that, there is no shame in it. However, in service to men everywhere, there are scenes in those novels that might not be entirely realistic all of the time."

"Exactly which scenes are you referring to? I mean, are we talking about the ones in the bedroom or the ones where the guy saves the day?" she asked with raised brows.

"Both." Nick knew he was outing himself. Only a man who'd actually read a romance novel would answer so definitively. Still, Laura didn't need to know his sisters occasionally provided material from their bookshelves for his compulsive reading habit.

"Would you care to expound on your answer?"

"No."

"All right, but for the record, sometimes it's the girl who saves everyone."

"Agreed. Someone has to save the guy when he inevitably makes a stupid mistake."

She nodded in confirmation and rubbed her hands together in gleeful anticipation of his book choice.

"Of course," Nick interjected once more, "The best stories are always the ones where the protagonists rescue each other and save the day together."

Laura blinked. Clearly, she hadn't expected those words to come out of his mouth. Nick really hadn't planned to say them either, but they fell out of his mouth before he could think it through. He felt the heat creep back into his cheeks over the impulsive sentiment.

"Okay," she said slowly, as though she were sifting through his words to find the intention behind them. "Let's see the book you brought then."

Nick pulled the first book out of his small daypack.

"*The Pickwick Papers*, by Charles Dickens. What's the big deal about this?" she asked, unmistakably disappointed, and slightly exasperated.

Nick pulled out the second book and laid it next to the first. "In all fairness, I have read it, but I'm currently reading this one because my nieces are." A truth and an omission. He had started reading the series because of the girls, but it turned out he actually liked the story.

Laura looked back and forth between the book with a red ribbon set on a black backdrop for the cover and Nick, saying, "Well, the only important question remaining is, are you Team Jacob or Edward?"

Nick didn't even bat an eye. "Team Wolf all the way, though I'm only on book three, so the jury is still out."

"Hmm. I need to think about what this says about your character, but since you haven't read the whole series yet, I can excuse your misguided choice."

"Thank you for such a magnanimous offer."

"Never let it be said I'm not generous toward my lowly subjects." Wiping the superior look from her face she continued, "Seriously though, I think it's great you find ways to connect with your nieces. It shows that you care."

"It's no big deal. And if I'm being honest, I voted to read *Graceling* by Kristin Cashore for book club. At least it's a battle for good over evil in both."

"Both have a strong female protagonist. I can understand their interest in the paranormal though and I think it's cool how you want to be able to relate to them."

"You think I'm cool, huh?"

She pursed her lips. "Moderately," she conceded. "I wouldn't want to inflate your ego any more than it already is."

Nick grinned widely, causing his eyes to light up from within. "I'll take moderately for now and hope for totally amazing in the future."

Laura ignored his mention of the future. Flipping over onto her stomach, she pulled a small paperback out of her canvas tote. He watched her turn to a dog-eared page in the middle and chuckled when he caught a glimpse of the cover.

Dressed in Victorian clothing with a twist, the models on the front promised a good romp between the pages despite their lack of an eye patch or leg-strapped dagger.

Without looking up, she said, "It's Steampunk, which makes it science fiction. Or fantasy, depending on which side of the genre battle you're on."

Nick barked out a laugh of disbelief, rolled to his side to face her, and held up his book. "And this is only young adult."

Micky chose the moment to change locations, moving to fill the small space left between their bodies with his own. They both reached out at the same time to run their hands over his fur, barely missing each other's hands. Nick was keenly aware of Laura's nearness but let himself be content with the buffer of books and beast for the time being.

Chapter 8

Laura

"Yes, that is what I'm talking about! The extra chili sauce really kicks it up a notch." Amir grabbed a clean spoon to dip into the chicken satay and peanut soup again.

"Are you sure it doesn't overwhelm the curry and cumin? I want the heat to compliment the other ingredients," said Laura, contemplating her latest culinary experiment.

"I'm positive. This is the perfect amount of heat, but I can still taste the complex flavors on the back of my tongue when the heat begins to dissipate. Besides, your peanut sauce turned soup is fantastic."

"Enough to add it to the menu?" she asked, chewing her thumb nail with self-doubt.

Amir smiled widely, his chestnut curls sliding down to shade his mischievous eyes. "Definitely, and so is the rice pudding with almonds and plum sauce."

"Let's do it then. If it goes well, we can alternate with the split pea or barley vegetable on a more regular basis."

"I thought we were running a restaurant, not a social club," said Joe, pushing into the kitchen through the heavy swing door, his hands full of bussed dishes.

"Sorry, Uncle Joe. We were putting the final additions into our newest creation."

"So, what's the verdict?"

Amir jumped in before Laura could hem and haw anymore. "Perfect, and menu ready."

"Great! Let's put it on the chalkboard for today's special."

"The rice pudding with plum sauce is also done and makes a great side dish or dessert to the soup," stated Amir, a shameless smile on his countenance.

"No need to gang up on me," Laura grumbled, poking her elbow into his side.

He wiggled away from her and laughed at her scowl before ruffling her short locks. An easy rapport had developed between them as a result of their time spent in the kitchen, and Laura considered him a friend and co-conspirator in her creative culinary pursuit for the pub's new menu.

Though Amir was only twenty-one, he'd been working for Uncle Joe in various capacities since the age of sixteen. He'd grown up in the neighborhood and gone from grocery delivery and stocking to sous chef at eighteen. The pub's cook had then taken him as his official protégé before retiring last year. While he had no formal culinary education, Amir appreciated complex flavors, and had great instincts.

"I'll get another batch of this going and then start on the plum sauce. Persimmons might be fun to try next week if you can track them down."

"Ooh, persimmons would go well with crushed pistachios on top of an olive oil cake. Great idea, Amir. I'll add them to my list for the market and experiment with the recipe this weekend."

"I mentioned persimmons. You're the one who added them to cake, but I am completely on board with it," he chuckled. "Oh, and a reminder that I'm leaving a half hour early tonight. My parents are short staffed at the bodega right now. I told them I'd lend an extra hand."

"No problem. Micky is at doggie daycare, Teresa is training the newbie on closing this week, and Saint already asked Ronan to come in for extra hands at the bar. There are soccer games airing simultaneously on television tonight, but Uncle Joe and I can manage the kitchen until it closes at nine."

"Thanks. We've seen a little trouble in the evenings recently, and I don't like the idea of my sister working the register by herself. My brother gets home from visiting his in-laws tomorrow, so he'll be able to help out then."

"What kind of trouble?" Laura asked, concerned.

Amir tried to play the situation off with little reaction. "Nothing to worry about, just ignorant people who don't know anything about my family."

"Are the police involved?" Laura asked, concerned about the Zaman family.

"My father doesn't want to make a big deal about it."

"You know if you need anything, we're here for you." Walker's Pub was the kind of place where everyone was welcome, and family was less about blood or personal background and more about where you felt at home. Of course, Laura tried not to examine too closely what it meant for her.

Amir nodded solemnly and quietly turned back to the soup simmering on the stove.

Nick

By the time Nick arrived at his parents' house for Sunday dinner, three quarters of the family sat around the long table crammed into the dining room, while the other quarter finished dinner preparations. At twelve and thirteen years of age, Sofi and Eleanor were arguing the differences and similarities between wolves and vampires. To be or not to be a Cullen was the question at the center of the disagreement. His nephew ran circles around the table, pestering the girls with siren noises and toy cars darting in front of their faces, while Leo tried to slow the boy down with each lap.

"I blame this on you," said his sister Aria as she plopped a full bowl of pasta primavera into his unoccupied hands. "Put that on the table and come help me in the kitchen."

Nick obediently followed after her. His father used to tell him it was easier to go along with a woman than to argue with her, and she'd be more likely to feed him if he did. It had turned out to be sound advice in his experience. No sense in changing the system if it "wasn't broke."

"You can't be talking about Eleanor and Sofi's argument. You're the one who introduced them to the series. I only started reading it to find a way to relate to them."

"No, the girls are arguing for the fun of it. Who needs a sister when you have a cousin?" said Aria with a shrug of her shoulders. "No, I'm talking about my son."

"I have no clue what you're referring to," Nick replied, at a loss for what she was implying.

She swept her long wavy hair behind her shoulder and glared at him with the same eyes as their mother. "Seriously? You have no idea why my son is running around making siren noises, or why he's decided to join the FDNY like Uncle Nick?"

Nick watched her warily and chose his words with caution. "Finn is nine. He has plenty of time to change his mind."

Aria crossed her arms in front of her chest and tapped her foot impatiently.

"And I may have taken him with me to hang out with the Squad the last time he stayed over," he said, chagrined. "We were bonding, and they had come off a big situation. You know how it is."

His sisters had both been married to police officers. Aria's husband Miles had passed away a couple of years ago, but Nate left Gina shortly after 9/11. Post-traumatic stress had torn their marriage apart at the seams before anyone in the family knew what was happening. Preoccupied with Pop and Donnie's deaths, Nick had missed the other collateral damage happening so close to home. But the hits had kept coming, from Gina's divorce to his brother in-law's death and, more recently, Leo's diagnosis. Sometimes, Nick wondered how many knocks his family could withstand before they stopped getting back up. The idea left a bitter taste in his mouth.

"Fine, but no more visits to the station house," said Aria, interrupting his thoughts.

"You can't keep the kids safe from everything. We know better than most how one decision on any given day can change life in an instant." Nick understood where she was coming from, but control was purely a façade. No one could change the outcome of anything regardless of how often they asked themselves what if, and he'd done his fair share of it. He looked away when her anger finally gave way to pity as if she could sense the guilt gnawing away at his conscience.

Aria gave his arm a hard squeeze and nudged him out of the kitchen with an armful of garlic bread and a salad, signaling the end of the conversation.

"Everyone sit down. Leo, say grace," Luna commanded from the head of the table.

"Sure, Ma, but aren't we waiting for Jules and Dae?"

"I'll take them a plate later. Jules's feet are swollen. The doctor was worried enough to put her on bedrest until her appointment next week."

A cacophony of voices instantly filled the space with questions, concerns, and empathy.

Luna raised two fingers to her mouth and let out an ear-piercing whistle to wrangle her brood. "Enough. Your sister is fine; she needs to keep her feet elevated and soak them in an Epsom salt bath before bed."

"Ma, it might be the early signs of pre-eclampsia," said Leo as the resident medic. "It could be serious."

Nick's mother made the sign of the cross and kissed the gold pendant of Saint Gerard, patron saint of expectant mothers, resting between her collar bones. His father had given it to her when she became pregnant with his oldest brother. A veritable lifetime had passed since then.

"I am fully aware of how serious the situation might be, Leonardo Patrick Kelly. Now, say grace."

Leo glanced surreptitiously at Nick, who knew his concerns were valid, and obediently bowed his head, adding a prayer for his sister and her unborn child at the end. The Kelly family said a collective, "In the name of the Father, and of the Son, and of the Holy Spirit," crossing themselves with fingers to forehead, sternum, and then from shoulder to shoulder.

The ritual had always been soothing in its repetition, but Nick threw in an extra plea on his family's behalf anyway. *Please let Jules and the baby be okay.* A heart could only endure so much suffering before the scar tissue did more harm than good. Though his Pop had taught him to end with the words "Your will be done," Nick couldn't bring himself to say the words and hoped God would understand that his fear outweighed his belief at the moment.

An hour later, with dinner over and Monday on the horizon, his mother started giving orders like the general she was.

"Gina and Nick are on dishes. Eleanor and Sofi, go help them. Vinny, you take Leo home; he looks tired. And for heaven sakes, Finn, stop running through the house!" Luna yelled, sending her troops into battle. Everyone did as she ordered without any argument, knowing their mother was worried and hiding it with a stern countenance.

"Ouch! Mom, you don't have to do it so hard," grumbled Sofi when Gina swatted her bottom with a dish towel. "I'm drying as fast as I can."

"Which is what, slow as a sloth?"

"Geez, you don't have to—"

Gina released the towel in her direction again, narrowly missing Sofi as she stepped out of her mom's reach. "Don't you use that tone with me, young lady. I've had enough of your attitude for one night. Do as Nonna said so we can go home. I have an early shift at the hospital tomorrow morning."

"What else is new? You're always working."

Nick raised his brows at Gina, who looked away from him, the weight she bore as a single mother heavy upon her shoulders. It was a no-win situation. If she worked long hours, it was to provide her daughter with a better life, but Sofi only saw her mother's absence.

"Can Sofi stay over tonight, Auntie?" asked Eleanor to break the tension.

"I second the motion," said Aria as she entered the kitchen. "I'll take the girls to school tomorrow on my way to the bank."

"Please, Mom," pleaded Sofi.

"Actually, that would be great."

"Thank you, thank you, thank you!" exclaimed Sofi, dancing around the kitchen and kissing her mother's cheek.

Gina had gone from neglectful to hero status in the space of a second.

Nick watched as the girls chattered excitedly and bebopped out of the kitchen together.

When he turned back to the sink, Aria had wrapped Gina up in a hug, her shoulders shaking with emotion as she tried to hold all of her broken parts together and failed.

"We've got this, sis," comforted Aria.

Nick reached out and pulled them both into his embrace.

"Count me in. I'm not going anywhere. Promise," he said and kissed the top of each sister's head in turn. He couldn't take back his choices or the consequences of 9/11, but he could be available in the here and now, when his family needed him most.

Chapter 9

Laura

Laura reached for the phone ringing on top of the kitchen counter, securing it between her ear and shoulder while she chopped up a red onion, its potency threating to make her cry. "Laura speaking."

"I waited a whole week to call you, so I didn't scare you off. But I can't wait any longer. I need a wing woman, and I need her now," replied an inebriated British accent.

"You sound like you might need someone to cut you off at the bar and order a cab."

"I do not disagree with you in the least, darling," Chaucey said, sounding surprisingly sober this time around, until she ruined it with a giggled tee-hee.

"Where is Dean?" asked Laura, washing her hands thoroughly before wiping the tears on her cheeks with a clean towel.

"Dean shmean. I am not talking to him right now. He's a sore loserrr," Chaucey pouted.

Her newly acquired wing woman was most assuredly tipsy, if not drunk. "Uh-oh. Sounds like there's trouble in paradise. Tell me where you are, and I'll pick you up."

"I don't want to go home. I want to dance. Go dancinnng with me, bish" Chaucey pleaded.

Laura laughed at the slang for girlfriend. She had never been anyone's bish before. It was strangely endearing. Or it was simply nice to have another friend in her new home.

Hold up; Brooklyn is not home. It's a temporary place of residence. Those are mutually exclusive ideas, right? Laura asked herself, uncertain. No way was she going to analyze her thoughts about a second friend either, because that would mean acknowledging Nick as the first.

Without an immediate answer on the horizon, she returned to the situation at hand. "How about we start with where I'm picking you up from."

"Walker's, but Joe won't let me dance on top of the bar." She tee-heed once more, followed by an exaggerated hiccup.

"I'll be right down. Do not leave," Laura commanded and looked at Micky lying at her feet with his eyes closed. Not fooled in the least, she nudged him with her foot. Her furry companion merely pretended to be asleep until something more interesting came along, like food or a walk.

"Looks like we have plans tonight after all, pal."

Micky jumped to his feet, all pretense of sleep gone as he trotted after Laura to the door and down the steps.

The pub was in full swing when Laura stepped inside, a nippy breeze close at her heels, trailed by the warmth of too many bodies in a confined space. She immediately clapped eyes on the pub's dancing queen directly in front of the bar. Micky left her side for the kitchen and waited patiently for an opening, no doubt hoping for scraps from Teresa or Amir. She pushed her way through the cheering crowd when one of the teams on the screen in the corner scored a goal.

Personally, she preferred to watch America's favorite pastime. All of those men in tight pants and baseball caps, top specimens of athleticism and skill running around. *Hmm*, she pondered, wondering if the FDNY hosted a league. *It would certainly be entertaining to watch Nick play ball*, she mused. An image of him in a baseball cap wearing his classic smirk filled her head and a silly grin spread across her own lips, until she realized what she was doing, in public no less.

Snapping out of her daydream, she sauntered to the far end of the bar, where Ronan Bower dipped his head in acknowledgment of her arrival and walked to the other end to help fellow bartender Toussaint James with the crowd gathered around pints and shots. Ronan and Saint danced around each other, pints and shots sliding in front of customers at a dizzying pace, no one the wiser to their romantic relationship, which they preferred to keep out of the workplace. Laura was only aware of it because she'd overheard them arguing below her bedroom window after closing one night.

The way Saint pulled Ronan in until they were forehead to forehead had made her long for someone to hold as though the sun rose and set with him in her arms.

"Bish, you're finally here!" said Chaucey loud enough for Laura to hear her over a new round of cheering and expletives.

Laura grinned in response but reconsidered her previous notion. "I think if I get to call you C.J., we should come up with a different nickname for me other than the slang for—" the crowd drowned out the rest of her words.

"Sure, pet."

She cringed as soon as the word left her wing woman's mouth. Laura knew it was a common enough endearment, but it made her feel like someone's lapdog. Of course, this led to thoughts of Micky's new nickname and a certain gentleman with a penchant for doling them out without a by your leave.

"How about Tink? Nick already uses it, and besides, there's really no way to shorten my name without it sounding ridiculous."

"Tink, you're finally here!" exclaimed Chaucey, as though she'd hit the rewind button on their earlier greeting.

Laura laughed and took her hand. "Yes, I'm here to rescue you from yourself. Let's go upstairs to the apartment. We can eat copious amounts of peanut butter party mix while we watch an old movie."

"Is there chocolate in the party mix?"

Laura nodded in the affirmative.

"Fine, but Joe is still a party pooper."

Laura snorted. "I'll be sure to let him know tomorrow. Did you bring a purse or coat with you?" she asked, motioning the length of Chaucey's body. Dressed in tight, black pants and a graphic tee with Gustav Klimt's *The Kiss* stretched across her chest, there wasn't any space to carry a wallet, phone, or lipstick.

Like smoke and mist, Saint appeared out of the ether with both accessories. "Here you go, honey. Our dancing queen is a regular when she and he who shall not be named are in a tiff," said Saint with a reference to Harry Potter's arch nemesis. "She'll be glad there was no actual bar dancing, once the alcohol wears off."

"No problem. It's not like I had far to go anyway." And, oddly, she was happy about the change in plans.

Saint gave her hand a quick pat and watched Ronan pour another round for the party at the other end of the bar, remarking in a heavy New Orleans drawl, "Sometimes, a change in plans can lead to an unexpected adventure. Life would be boring without all those twists and turns of fate, don't you think?"

Laura didn't reply, but the thought of all those unplanned twists and turns caused her stomach to flip, and not in a way that made her want to ride the roller coaster. Ignoring her sudden case of motion sickness, she kept her eyes focused on Chaucey's combat boots as they stomped toward the front door and whistled for Micky to follow.

"How do you feel about Cary Grant?" Laura asked after handing Chaucey a bowl of peanut butter party mix and a large mug of coffee with a teaspoon of sweetened condensed milk. It was a time-tested tradition in the Howard household. Carbs, peanut butter, and decaf made for a magical combination and would help ward off a hangover come the morning.

"Depends. Are we watching *His Girl Friday?*"

"Sure, Kate has the whole collection of his movies.

"Tall, dark, and handsome sounds exactly like your sister's type," said Chaucey, sinking further into the couch cushions.

"I know, right? I never could figure out why she fell for her ex of a dirtbag to begin with." *Uh-oh.* Laura hoped Kate had mentioned her former marital status to her friend.

"That wanker deserves everything Karma sends his average height, mediocre jawline, ugly-nose way."

"The man looks like a modern-day Norse god with his flowing locks and hours at the gym. Unfortunately, neither his looks nor his money made him a better human being."

"Kate never said so outright, but I always got the impression he hurt her, and more than emotionally." For being tipsy, Chaucey was surprisingly astute about her sister's relationship.

Laura's lips twisted back and forth as she debated her response. "He was totally manipulative when they were dating. The verbal abuse started shortly after the wedding, but Kate didn't say anything until he started getting physical." Or so Laura assumed, since her sister had never clarified how long it had actually been going on.

She chewed on the inside of her cheek. Kate would be angry with Laura for telling anyone outside of the family, but it was better for her sister to have allies when her ex eventually showed up at her doorstep. Because he would, of that Laura was certain. It was only a matter of time before he found out where Kate was hiding.

Her ex-brother-in-law had treated her sister like private property, and Laura knew he still believed Kate belonged to him, despite the divorce. There was no reasoning with a man like Preston Toliver. He thought he could buy anyone and his way out of everything. Unfortunately for her sister, the judge overseeing the battery charges seemed to agree with his line of thinking.

Laura popped the DVD into the player and settled on the opposite side of the couch from her new friend, trying to lose herself in the film of a bygone era, instead of worrying about Kate. The story of a female reporter who refused to play by the rules society dictated was fun, if not unique for its time. Lois Lane had made her debut in the *Superman* comics two years prior to the movie's release in 1940.

Then again, it took Lois forty years to figure out that Clark Kent and Superman were one and the same, thought Laura. Why women were always the last to figure out the friend and the superhero are the same person was beyond her. Then again, it wasn't like she was killing it in the romance department these days.

Nick popped into her thoughts for the second time in as many hours.

Ugh. She couldn't remember the last time she'd had so much fun bantering with someone. Comparing Nick to Drew felt unfair to all of them, so she didn't. Instead, she told herself it was normal to enjoy another person's company, even if that person happen to be six-foot-something with muscles, a killer smile, and eyes that put the Mediterranean Sea to shame. It wasn't easy to ignore him when he had the whole brawny and brilliant thing working in his favor.

When Chaucey fell asleep halfway through the movie, Laura covered her with a knitted throw blanket, her unladylike snoring a solid match for Micky's. Leaving both to their dreams, she started for her own bed until a light wrap on the door stopped her in her tracks.

A look through the peep hole revealed Nick and his best friend, halfway draped over the banister.

"Hey, sorry to stop by so late," said Nick, an apology written all over his face as she opened the door wide.

Laura looked from him to Dean, barely propped up next to him at the top of the landing. He slurred a greeting in her direction, and Nick kept a hold of him when he lunged drunkenly to give her a hug.

She could smell the alcohol coming from his breath. "Something tells me your night was even more interesting than mine."

"I'm not sure I'd classify it as interesting. It was more of an intervention. Dean would only leave the bar if he could see C.J.," said Nick, followed by a brief shake of his head. "He freaked out when he couldn't find her at Walker's, and she wouldn't answer her phone. Dean said they had a big fight."

"How did you know she was here?"

"Doofus here finally called me five shots in. I spoke with Saint, who told me you'd come in a while ago and taken C.J. home with you." Nick shrugged. "Mystery solved."

"He looks heavy."

"Nah, but I wouldn't complain if I could leave him on your couch," he answered with a strained smile.

"Sure."

Nick half carried, half dragged Dean inside. The couch creaked loudly under the added weight.

Dean pulled Chaucey's feet onto his lap and closed his eyes, at peace with his destination for the night. "Sorry, baby. Imma a fool, butta fool in love which chew," he slurred.

Laura smiled and covered the squabbling lovebirds with a second throw, creating a cozy nest for them.

"Market and park again next weekend?" Nick asked quietly, walking towards the door.

Micky's ears perked up in interest, but Laura refused to acknowledge him. She had no intention of letting him influence her with his puppy dog eyes. This was her decision. Of course, looking into Nick's eyes were a huge mistake, and all the swaying it took.

"Sounds good."

He smirked and she considered a swift kick to his shins to remove it. Taking the high road, she closed the door in his face without another word. It made her feel slightly better until she heard his laugh coming from the opposite side.

"Sweet dreams, Tink."

Laura muttered something about overconfident men with too many muscles on her way to the bathroom. She took note of the half-moons beneath her tired eyes in the mirror. "Not that I care what I look like," she admonished her reflection while she brushed her teeth. It was a lie. She knew it and so did the bees that buzzed through her body after a minute in Nick's company.

Laura leaned in to further examine her face, checking out an angry pimple on her chin. Her mother would tell her to leave it alone. Not one to graciously accept advice, she popped the blemish, satisfied. "At least I didn't have spinach in my teeth."

The bees continued to swarm. "Fine. If I acknowledge I find Nick attractive enough to want to satisfy my reproductive urges with, will you turn the buzzing down to a low a hum?"

Laura rolled her eyes over how ridiculous she sounded, talking aloud to imaginary bees, but the fiery sensation of the past moment seemed to calm as she snuggled into the toile duvet Kate had picked out for her. Turning on her night light, she mumbled, "Go pollinate some tulips," and drifted off to sleep.

Nick

The call came in at five a.m., jolting Nick awake from a sprint with a pack of wolves as the engine house alarm blared inside the bunk room. An intercom announcement followed quickly on its heels.

"This is a fire emergency. Proceed to the bay."

He had finished reading the third installment of the *Twilight* series around midnight and fallen asleep with the book on top of his chest. It fell to the floor with a thump, which he ignored, shoving his feet into his boots. By the time he hauled himself into the truck he had his coat and helmet on.

"Here you go, Captain."

The promotion from Lieutenant to Captain was a recent one and a weighty responsibility considering the lives in his care each shift. Administration and station management were a natural fit for his analytical thinking, but he lived for the teamwork required to outsmart a fire and save lives. Squad 2 was a well-oiled machine, thanks to the work his crews put into each shift, and Nick made it a point to work harder than the rest to be worthy of the Kelly reputation.

He put his hand out to take the radio from his driver, and calmly relayed any pertinent information to the rest of the Squad. Familiar with the location and complications the fire might present, part of his job was to make sure everyone else knew and was prepared.

Every shift had emergencies, some more serious than others, but the last one had been bugging Nick ever since. It wasn't his job to investigate the cause of a fire, but something about it didn't sit right with him. He couldn't put his finger on why, but it had his Spidey senses on overload with this new one.

Both fires were within a couple of blocks from each other, each early-morning calls, but that was where the similarities ended. The first had been a fire behind an old strip mall and easy to contain, whereas this one was at an abandoned, two-story duplex with empty lots on either side and spreading fast due to the building's dilapidated state. Still, Nick couldn't shake the feeling that the fires were somehow linked.

First to arrive on scene, everyone else moved into position while Nick radioed the other engine company a couple of blocks out to let them know the plan, before joining the rest of Squad 2.

"See you on the flip side, Pop," Nick whispered reverently. Lowering his face shield, he grabbed the ax from Dean and kicked in the front door. Whenever possible, Nick tried to be the first in and the last one out. He'd be damned if he'd leave anyone behind on his watch.

Chapter 10

Nick

"Hey man, how's it going? I haven't seen you in a while." Nick watched his friend shuffle forward at a measured pace, his companion moving in time with him, the little whip of a tail waving until Bixby's whole bottom shook in happy greeting. "I was starting to worry that you and Bixby had moved on to better digs."

Nick bent down to pet the dog and stood to shake the hand of a man who had given his all in a desert across the world, receiving a purple heart as thanks in lieu of better government care. Though things were changing for veterans, the bureaucracy wasn't efficient enough for those who had sacrificed everything for their country, and its fight against terrorism.

Retired Sergeant Malcom Smith grinned, his teeth a startling contrast to his ebony skin, as he shook Nick's hand and ran the other over his bald head. "What, and leave your sorry self here to greet the newcomers? Nah, man, I had an appointment at the VA Hospital last week that I couldn't reschedule."

Nick grimaced, knowing if his friend had missed the appointment there wouldn't be another one available for months. Malcom had weaned himself off the pain meds shortly after his accident, terrified of becoming addicted, but he still needed other prescriptions filled to help him cope with his PTSD.

Bixby offered companionship and comfort, encouraging the former Marine's success, but as Malcom often said, "Every part of the pie counts in recovery." Most people would consider his friend's story a triumph, but Nick knew how hard he'd fought to come out mostly whole on the other side of a nightmare. He was tougher than nails and made every single day count, not only for himself, but for others in his situation. It was the reason he was in the serving line beside Nick, passing out rolls and soup to those who showed up for food and a little kindness in the back parking lot of Our Lady of the Bridge.

They were halfway through the afternoon when a familiar truck drove past the tented tables. Nick had called in reinforcements from Walker's Pub when supplies had dwindled quickly in light of the number of people lining up. Homelessness was a regular occurrence, and the need for food, warmth, and shelter would only increase with falling temperatures in the coming months. It was also becoming more prevalent in the families and veterans they saw each week.

Amir jumped out of the passenger side, and the person Nick had hoped would come with him, winding around to the back of the truck to unload large aluminum containers of stew, Irish Soda bread, beer-battered fish, and chips. And was that the pub's new blackberry-peach and ginger cobbler he smelled? Laura's additions to the menu made his mouth water. Okay, the woman herself did too, he admitted.

He watched her walk toward his table, arms laden, and a smile tugging at the corner of her mouth before she looked away quickly.

She was as cute today as she'd been last Sunday afternoon. He could hardly wait for their next park date.

What music will she choose? What book will she bring?

These were the thoughts crowding his brain when he wasn't at work, and sometimes even when he was.

"Hey, Tink, no Eminem today?"

"He's wrappin' it up in the truck," she said casually.

Nick smiled in response. "Very punny. Someone's on her game today."

Laura gave him a cheeky smile and whistled for their furry friend. Nick felt the familiar tug on his heartstrings, used to the feeling by now, though he'd be more comfortable if he were certain she felt something similar in return. He knew she enjoyed his company as much as he did hers and their interactions were easy, but he hoped the relationship would get the chance to grow into something beyond another casual flirtation.

Bees weren't butterflies, but they did produce honey. Nick hoped her swarm was as busy at work as the butterflies flitting throughout his entire body every time she came near. He took the stacked containers from her hands and laid them on the table before greeting Micky with a thorough ear scratch, introducing Malcom to Laura in the process.

"It's great to meet both of you. In fact, you look really familiar. Do you ever come into Walker's Pub?" Laura asked.

"No, I avoid temptation where I can," he replied with candor.

Laura nodded in understanding and introduced her furry companion. "This is Micky Mouse, or as Nick likes to call him, Eminem." Laura rolled her eyes for Nick's benefit, but it only made him grin wider.

Micky and Bixby sniffed each other's nether regions thoroughly, the scents which would tell them everything they needed to know about the other taking priority over everything else.

Relationships would be so much easier if people had the ability to sniff each other out. Nick shook his head over his weird thoughts. *Or, maybe that's what the pheromones are for.*

"Can Eminem stay with you and Bixby while we store the rest of the food inside?" asked Nick."

"Sure," said Malcom. "Looks like we have a new friend, don't we Bix?"

"Do you ever go to the dog run at Prospect Park?" Laura seemed certain she'd seen Malcom and Bixby before.

"We jog the trail every other day. I knew I'd seen your companion somewhere before. Those eyes of his are hard to miss."

"I swear, sometimes, I think he's human," said Nick.

Malcom looked at the dogs sitting at his feet. "I think you may be right. Far more intelligence shining in those eyes than several people I know."

Laura

Laura looked up at the stone façade reaching for the partly cloudy sky, its gothic spires stretching to touch the birds playing tag against its ornate cornices. The flying buttresses were insignificant compared with Europe's most famous masterpieces, but impressive to her, nonetheless.

"It's even more beautiful inside," said Nick, mistaking her hesitation for awe.

"Um," replied Laura, buying herself a second.

"I promise the walls don't bite, and Father Hugo won't make you go to confession," he said jokingly, and bumped her shoulder lightly when she continued to stand there like cement held her feet in place.

"Confession isn't really the problem. I talk to God all the time. It's…well, I haven't stepped inside an actual church for a while."

"I know, you mentioned you don't attend regularly. Exactly how long are we talking?" Nick asked.

Laura glanced up at him self-consciously and said slowly, "Ten years, give or take a few months."

"Wait. I thought you were quite the world traveler. I mean, I assumed you didn't go to service, but if you haven't stepped inside a church—"

She cut him off before he could say the rest of the embarrassing truth. "Yes!" Laura said, exasperated. "It means I didn't see the inside of Notre Dame in Paris or Westminster Abbey in London, or countless other architecturally inspiring, beautiful historic feats of engineering on my travels."

Nick's jaw hung slack as though he were waiting for the punchline. And he was right, it was a total joke—on her. She had deliberately avoided those opportunities, because they were houses of worship, and she had no desire to partake, aside from her one-sided conversations with the Almighty.

With a lift to her shoulders, she continued. "I told you I had a falling out with God."

"That is one heck of a misunderstanding," he said quietly. When she didn't respond, he conceded, "You don't have to come in. I'll put this stack inside and come back out for the rest."

Laura dawdled for a moment, before shucking off her pride. Her protest was nothing more than an attempt to lash out—an eye for an eye. Or in this case, one life for another. She knew it was juvenile, but she'd reasoned that if she couldn't have Drew, then God didn't get to keep her either.

"No. It's time to let it go. I'm not punishing anyone but myself at this point." She would decide later what the new concession meant. Was this yet another betrayal of Drew on her part since meeting the man beside her? Laura groaned internally.

Nick let her proceed him, holding the door open with his heel, and directed her down a short hallway into a square kitchen, done in the traditional 1970s decor common in old churches. Laura placed her burden on the orange-speckled countertop, taking note of the avocado-green appliances, laminate flooring, and cabinets in a worn, maple stain.

"Nothing fancy in here, but the nave is pretty spectacular. Want to take a peek? You can stand from the doorway if you want."

Laura recognized the offer for the challenge it was. She took a deep breath, looked her companion in the eye, and tucked her trembling spirit away into a corner of her soul. No one had ever accused her of being a coward, and she wasn't about to let Nick turn her into one.

"There was a time when I found it hard to step inside too," he said, giving her hand a faint squeeze.

Or he could simply be trying to help a friend out, interjected the voice of reason.

This was all Uncle Joe's fault, anyway. He was the one who had sent her in his stead. Never mind that she had offered to go when he mentioned Nick had called in a favor.

It had been a week since she'd last seen him, and he was the peanut butter left on a knife after making a sandwich, a temptation she couldn't resist. She felt the heat in her cheeks even thinking about it and hoped he wouldn't notice.

Deciding to be brave, Laura accepted his hand. Nick entwined their fingers, sending heat up her arm and into the pit of her stomach to join the warmth already in her face.

Weak knees are for twitterpated ninny heads, not grown women, Laura lamented. *Not true,* her ovaries decried.

Nick led her into the open space with soaring ceilings, reflecting the height she had observed from outside. Each stained-glass window displayed a different apostle, the vibrant colors muted in the late-afternoon light. The sanctuary around the altar was similarly ornate—polished and embellished with small touches of gold, wood, and carved stonework.

They sat on a worn pew in silent solace, his arm stretched behind her with parishioners scattered here and there in other pews. A handful kneeled at the front, while others lit prayer votives off to the side. Behind them, a small door creaked open, and Laura turned to see an older woman step out of a confessional, tucking a handkerchief into her purse as she walked to the candles nearest the exit.

A moment later, a priest emerged from the other side. Dressed in all black with the typical white collar, the Father wore the brightest-yellow cardigan she'd ever seen, glowing neon in the variegated light. The man had lines carved into his forehead and around his mouth and eyes. She wondered if they were the result of a career in God's service, or the life he'd lived before.

Each of those crevices contained a story, one Laura found herself curious to read. She pictured the man interceding for his flock on his knees, head bent in prayer, or solemnly caring for the sick and giving the last rites to those on the precipice of death. But what if those lines had started as something else? Had he always wanted to be a priest, or had his life taken an unexpected turn to bring him to this spiritual calling?

As she watched, he changed course, heading in their direction. Laura panicked, afraid he had somehow overheard her thoughts. Or it could be because she was openly staring at him.

Stop staring! Laura commanded her addled brain, but the Father had already taken a seat next to Nick and was reaching across to introduce himself.

"Hello, I'm Father Hugo. You must be Joe Walker's niece, Laura."

When she merely blinked in surprise, he laughed. The sound was musical and matched the mellifluous tone of his speaking voice. She could also detect a faint accent, but not enough to place where from.

"Joe comes to our rescue at least once a month. Whether it's hot meals for our Backdoor Dinners program or shoveling the walks out front before mass in winter, Joe is always willing to lend a helping hand. The fact that we play poker for pennies once a month might also mean I have the inside scoop on occasion," he said with a wink.

Laura couldn't decide which flummoxed her more, that a priest played poker, or that Uncle Joe had a life outside of Walker's Pub, one she'd been oblivious to in the month since her arrival.

"And I see you've already met our local Romeo."

Laura followed the length of Nick's jaw with her eyes until she met the vibrant pink on his high cheekbones. She immediately decided she liked Father Hugo, white collar and atrocious sweater included. Anyone who could make Nick squirm was all right in her book.

"More like Cyrano De Bergerac. A smooth talker, but not much to look at," she quipped, causing the Father to guffaw, the sound bouncing throughout the reverent space in echoes. She looked around, afraid to find everyone looking in their direction, but no one paid them any attention. It would seem booming laughter was a common occurrence at Our Lady of the Bridge.

Laura turned both her gaze and a slight smirk in Nick's direction where he watched her with a glint in his eyes, one she was beginning to recognize. She'd thrown a gauntlet down, a challenge, and one he planned on winning. Not that she could blame him, since she found herself sitting beside him in church. Her resolve to keep him at a distance was rapidly crumbling with each encounter they had.

Chapter 11

Nick

The bag slung over Laura's shoulder was a striped, heavy canvas, bulging with produce by the time Nick caught up with her at the farmer's market. Although it had been fun to see her at the church, he was excited to have her company all to himself today. She was standing in front of a goat cheese vendor, whom he promptly frowned at when he spied the pure delight on Laura's face, never mind the kid's high school status.

"Here, you have to try this! It melts in your mouth like an actual Brie," Laura said, shoving a small piece of baguette slathered in the creamy goat cheese toward his mouth. Nick reached for her bag, earning him a grateful smile, and instantly forgot about the gangly adolescent trying to win her over with cheese.

"It's good," he said around the food in his mouth. "We'll take one," he continued, motioning to the rounds on the table with one hand, and pulling out his wallet with the other. Nick liked seeing her flustered in general, but flustered over cheese was hysterical.

"I didn't mean to imply—"

"This is perfect. We can pick up beef salami and crackers from the deli. It looks like you already have fruit, which makes for an impromptu picnic if I've ever seen one."

She visibly relaxed and Nick slung his arm around her shoulders casually. "Come on Eminem, let's take your mom to the park."

Laura looked up. "Technically, I'm his aunt, not his mom."

"I think we both know Kate isn't really a dog person. I can totally see her with a cat, or a miniature Yorkie she can carry around in her purse, but not a dog like our pal."

"I think you'd be surprised. We did grow up on a horse farm."

"Which means she's probably a decent rider, but I'm not convinced she misses farm life," he said confidently.

"It's a little more complicated than her feelings about home. Sometimes, a person leaves because they need a fresh start, not because they don't love where they came from."

"Is that why you spent so much time traveling?" he asked, ignoring his resolve to let her bring up the subject. Laura had traveled for years, not weeks, or a gap year between schools. She had chosen to live among foreigners, rather than family, which he couldn't fathom. Not only that, but she hadn't been inside a church—not even for a tour—until Nick invited her. There was undoubtedly more to her story than purely a love for globetrotting.

Had Laura come to Brooklyn looking for a fresh start like her sister? If she had, Nick felt certain he could help her find one and, with any luck, she'd fall for him the way he was for her in the process. Bees and butterflies coexisted peacefully in nature, why not in an old house?

Laura

Nick had the strangest look on his face. Laura was busy trying to discern exactly what it meant when she realized they'd both fallen silent. She considered her options. One, she could respond to his question with an outright lie. Two, a lame excuse. Or three, a diversionary tactic. However, being vulnerable, the way friends are supposed to be with each other, would be a decidedly healthier approach than avoidance. Even if she wasn't overly familiar with the concept.

"Someone I really cared about died and I needed space to work through my grief." Although the words didn't begin to convey the way she felt about Drew—the person she was supposed to spend the rest of her life with—it was the explanation she could force past the sand coating the inside of her mouth.

Drew had been her first love, which was a powerful and life-altering experience without his death, let alone with it. In the space of one phone call, Laura had felt as though she'd lost everything, including her dreams and career aspirations. Looking back, it was easy to see how she had tangled up everything in her life with him and kept nothing of herself.

"Traveling was my way of trying to make sense of life after he died."

"Do you want to tell me what happened?" Nick asked, his voice tender, as though he understood how bruised her heart was even after so many years.

Laura glanced around at their surroundings where they sat at a picnic table ensconced between the Brooklyn and Manhattan bridges, overlooking the water. A breeze blew briskly through the channel, and she tugged on the peacoat she'd worn for the cooler October temperatures.

Keeping her eyes on the lower Manhattan skyline in the distance, she finally answered him. "Drew was in a car accident on his way home from school. He wanted to surprise me for my birthday."

Nick watched her with immense understanding brimming in his eyes, but she could also see the questions waiting there.

"Your brother?"

Evidently, Joe and Kate had never mentioned Lon by name. Laura tried to respond, but the words got stuck. She cleared her throat and tried again. "Drew," she whispered, "was my husband." The word still felt strange in her mouth, like molasses stuck to her tongue.

If Nick was surprised by her declaration, he didn't show it.

Instead, he stretched his hand across the table to take hers, his thumb stroking back and forth over the outside of her hand in a gesture of comfort while she watched, mesmerized. A lone tear rolled silently down her cheek, and though her voice remained soft, it didn't quiver under the onslaught of emotion the way it used to when she spoke about the boy she'd loved.

"He wanted us to say our vows without everyone within a fifty-mile radius watching on. It was our little secret. One I only needed to keep for six more weeks until our wedding in October." Laura pulled the chain holding a single thin gold band from beneath her t-shirt.

"I informed my family we were married in the same breath I told them I'd become a widow." Laura swallowed hard. It was the only time she could remember her father ever swearing in her presence. To this day, she didn't know if Cal Howard had forgiven Drew for what he saw as a betrayal, but she also understood it was easier to hold a grudge against a dead man than the daughter he'd give his own life for.

"I was going to attend the University of Virginia to finish my undergrad in Biology, and then go to vet school." What Laura didn't share was that she could barely get out of bed for months after Drew's death, her plans buried along with him.

"It sounds like you had a decent plan." His thumb made lazy circles on her hand, one-two-three—pause—he'd start all over again. Laura's shoulders relaxed and her breathing evened out.

"I wanted to open a veterinary clinic on my parents' property. Lon, my older brother, and I planned to work together. He would take care of the business side of things once my dad retired, while I took care of the horses. Kate thought she might join us and start a line of all-natural, organic animal care products. We were going to bring Howard Stables into the twentieth century. Guess it'll have to wait for the next generation."

"Why? You could go back to school and pursue your dream." Nick said it without accusation and Laura accepted the words for what they were, encouragement and support without all of the expectations her family held.

"Except I've been moving in the opposite direction for so long, I don't think it's what I want anymore."

"What do you want, then?"

Laura wished she knew how to answer his question. It was part of why she was here. Uncle Joe was certain working at Walker's Pub would help solve her dilemma if she gave it time, but she was no closer to an answer now than she had been when she arrived a month ago.

She stalled. "Today, I want to share a picnic with you and throw the frisbee."

"Done, on one condition."

Laura's eyebrow rose in question and a little apprehension.

Nick laughed and grinned in response. "You go first."

Her other eyebrow joined its companion as she waited for him to explain what he meant.

In response, he plugged his earbuds into the jack on her phone and tucked one into each of their ears.

Laura paused for a brief moment, opened her music collection, and tapped play on her choice.

"The force is strong with this one," Nick quoted, pleased.

Laura averted her eyes. "I think Drew would have liked you."

"Thanks, Tink. I think I would have liked him too."

"Yeah?"

"Yep. Call it a hunch, but something makes me think he was a *Star Wars* fan. And he had great taste in women," said Nick with a wink.

She blushed under his harmless flirting, crunching into a tangy apple from her stash of fruit, and waited for the song to end before speaking again. "Your turn."

He picked the first album in his list. Nick sang along, heedless of the other people around them. His voice was deep and steady, like the man it belonged to, thought Laura.

She opened her book, which Nick promptly snatched from her to study the cover.

"No Steampunk today."

"Nope. Tragedy is the theme of the day."

Nick nodded with understanding. "*Wuthering Heights* is good, but I like *Persuasion* better."

"Second chances and redemption are generally more tempting

than torment and despair, though I'm more curious about when you found the time to read the classics, Mr. Big Shot Lawyer."

"Never made it to law school, remember?" When she said nothing quippy in response, he continued, "As it turned out, I needed one more English credit to graduate with a degree in Poly Sci. British Lit fit into my schedule." He shrugged. "It wasn't so bad."

"Let me guess; most of the student body in the class was female?"

Nick smirked in answer and held out the book for her to take.

Laura shook her head but smiled back at him. "All right, Willoughby, what did you bring to read?" she asked, referencing the charming villain from *Sense and Sensibility*.

"Och, you wound me, lass," Nick said, looking appalled.

She laughed. "Your brogue is atrocious. Besides, who would you prefer to be? Darcy, the dashing hero of *Pride and Prejudice*?"

"No. I'm not broody enough to be him. I always preferred Colonel Brandon or Captain Frederick Wentworth. Proper heroes."

"The Colonel, though admirable, is a bit on the stodgy side for you. However, the Captain…" she paused and swallowed hard, hoping he wouldn't see through her words. "Well, you can always aspire." She looked away. There was no way Nick could know Captain Wentworth from *Persuasion* was her favorite book boyfriend. Still, she felt exposed under his gaze, and again asked, "So, what book did you bring?"

The familiar cover of a chessboard with a white queen and red pawn made its way into her line of vision. "Ahh, *Breaking Dawn*."

"Bookies Club with the nieces is this Wednesday. I have eight chapters to read between now and Wednesday."

"Interesting name choice."

"The alternative was Book Babes," he said with a raise of his brows.

"Bookies for the win. So, what's your final answer: are you Team Edward or Jacob?" Laura asked with a side glance, waiting expectantly for his answer.

"I'm still going to go with Team Wolf."

"But it isn't team vampire or wolf. It's about which guy. Come on, you have to choose."

"No, I don't. And it is absolutely about being a vamp or a wolf. No one wants to be a blood sucker, but a big, bad wolf holds appeal."

Nick caught her hand in his when she went to swat his shoulder, sending what was quickly becoming a familiar jolt to the center of her abdomen.

"Want to come to book club? The girls are certain to gang up on me and you can help them try to convince me why I should choose Edward for Bella. Especially, since he only ever hurts her."

"Does he really, though? And not that you care, but she wants to be with Edward and doesn't oppose the idea of becoming a blood sucker."

"That is exactly why she shouldn't be with him, though. Besides, Jacob can protect her better than Edward."

"How so?"

"First," Nick said raising one finger, "the dude is Wolverine, minus the whole skeletal surgery. And second, having a baby with him wouldn't endanger her life."

Laura rolled her eyes. "Oh, please. Technically, having a baby endangers any woman's life. Don't get me started on the maternal mortality rates of women in various countries, including this one."

"Third," he continued, raising another finger, "even though she wants Edward it doesn't mean she belongs with him."

"What chapter are you in?"

"Ten, why?"

It was Laura's turn to smirk.

"Look, I get it. The heart wants what the heart wants, but sometimes fate has something to say about it as well."

"I didn't realize Catholics believed in fate."

"Fate, providence, whatever you want to call it. We may have free will, but sometimes the circumstances are what they are. We can accept it or fight it, but in the end it's what you do with the hand you're dealt that counts."

Were God and providence the same thing? Was fate, for that matter? These were the questions circling the drain inside her head when she realized her hand still lay in his and he had started tracing lazy circles on her palm again, sending tingles up her arm. She shivered within her coat, but not from the cold this time. His touch was like a live wire running through her body and she struggled to keep up with the conversation.

"I think you should come to book club," said Nick softly to match his touch. "We're going to discuss the first eighteen chapters this month and the rest of the book next month."

She slid her hand out of his.

"Um, I don't know if that's such a good idea." The idea of committing to one meeting was inconsequential. A person could do anything at least once. But committing to two was purposeful. It suggested the intention to stick around and get involved.

"I'm watching the girls and Finn is going to my mom's so my sisters can go into the city for a night out. I'll cook dinner, and you can prove me wrong about fate over Bookies Club."

Laura stood up and reached for the frisbee. "Come on, Micky."

Fate, providence, or God? Did what she wanted matter at all?

Nick rose and followed after them, forming the last point of a triangle. They made for a funny little trio, thought Laura as she tossed the frisbee across the distance between them. Micky did a jump spin to catch her toss, making her look better than she deserved.

"What can I bring on Wednesday?" she asked, giving in to what was beginning to feel inevitable.

The man across from her didn't smile in triumph when she acquiesced to his invitation, and she almost wished he would. Then she could be snarky, instead of pathetically attracted to the muscles rippling over his forearms each time he threw the frisbee.

"Your company is more than enough," said Nick sincerely with another perfect release. It sailed through the open space between them until Micky caught it and trotted back to her, as though he agreed with Nick's assessment.

Chapter 12

Nick

The patterned knock on the door gave away who was behind it before the door swung open, tapping the opposite wall none too gently.

"Aria is going to kill you if you put a hole in the wall. She had it drywalled last week," said Nick, worried he would never hear the end of it if Dean damaged the newly textured walls.

"I know, I know," Dean grumbled as he unloaded a six pack of beer, books, and art supplies onto a small side table.

"Someone's feeling grumpy tonight."

Dean tried to shoot him the bird, only to drop the pile. Nick's hand shot out at the last second to catch the beer, his eyes conveying a WTF he didn't say aloud.

"Hullo, love," said Chaucey, kissing both of Nick's cheeks in greeting instead of helping her boyfriend.

"Why you gotta be like that?" Dean pouted. "You know how jealous I get when you do the whole French kiss thing.

Chaucey rolled her eyes in response. "A kiss to each cheek is very common in some places and Nick is Italian."

"He's also Irish. Are you gonna do a jig too?"

"No. Are you going to continue to act like a child about it?"

"Baby," pleaded Dean.

Chaucey turned on a heel and walked toward the sofa in the open loft, shooing his endearment away as she went. "Don't you baby me, Francis Dean Santiago."

His best friend winced. Dean hated his first name. It was his mother's maiden name, but not ideal for someone with his temperament. Dean's mother finally relented when poor "Franny" almost wound up suspended for fighting on his first day of kindergarten.

"This moronic behavior has to end. You cannot get into a fight every time another man looks in my direction, or you think I've paid someone else more attention than you."

"I know, sweet lips," he conceded.

"Uh-uh. No more sweet lips until you apologize to both me and Nick."

Dean looked at Nick and then back to Chaucey. "I'm pretty sure Nick doesn't care if I apologize to him," he said and sauntered her way to make amends.

Nick chuckled and left Dean to talk his way out of trouble, glancing at his watch. Laura would be here any minute now. He hoped she didn't feel ambushed, but at the time he'd thought Dean and Chaucey would make the book discussion more fun, though tortuous might be a better description if they kept bickering.

"C.J., Uncle Dean!" yelled Sofi and Eleanor trotting down the stairs Nick had recently built so his niece and nephew could finally stop sharing a bedroom. The loft, while large, had only been bare-bones construction with potential when Aria bought it after his brother-in-law passed away. The plus side was having them closer to him and helping her renovate the place. By the time Nick put an offer on the house he wanted next month and started renovations, his carpentry skills would be well honed.

"Uncle Nick, why didn't you tell you us they were here?" asked Sofi accusatorily with a glare. His sisters assured him it was a phase, but he had his doubts. There were days it felt like his niece had turned twelve and become an entirely different person overnight. If he actually believed in aliens, abduction would not be out of the question.

"We arrived all of five seconds ago, darlings," soothed Chaucey, winking at Nick over Dean's shoulder.

"Where are my hugs?" Dean opened his arms wide, to which the girls flew, laughing when he acted as though they'd knock him over with their exuberance.

When the doorbell rang, Nick left the antics, more than a little excited to see his next guest. He ran a hand nervously through his hair, let out the breath he'd been holding, and pulled the door open with so much pent-up energy he was surprised the hinges were still in place.

Laura's beauty wasn't the kind found on the cover of a magazine. Hers had a more natural quality to it in how the whole picture formed instead of individual features. And when she smiled, those whimsical butterflies inside his chest soared until the only thoughts left in his head were of her. Whether it was a laugh tugging at his heartstrings, or a snarky comment made in challenge, he wanted everything she threw his way.

If she was lightning, he wanted to be the weathervane. He pictured drawing her close enough to kiss and deepening that kiss until— Nick shook his head to wipe away the image and hoped Laura didn't notice the effect she was having on him. *Find your cool, Kelly.* He breathed in and slowly exhaled, thinking of his mother's lasagna burning to a crisp in his sister's oven, and the tongue lashing that would follow if it did. *Problem solved.*

Laura's confession at the park had made it apparent she needed time. He had a thousand questions he wanted to ask, but he also knew opening those old wounds might not be in her best interest. She would let him know when and if she was ready to be more than friends. The last thing he wanted was for a potential relationship between them to be a casualty of poor timing on his part.

Observation, patience, and listening to his gut had saved his life on more than one occasion, and they were the same skills he'd use to help navigate things with Laura. Nick would do everything in his power to make sure he didn't hurt her, but he hoped to keep his heart intact as well. In the meantime, they would continue to spend time together, getting to know each other without any pressure.

Laura shook the rain from her coat and propped a stylish umbrella next to the door, simultaneously handing him a container with some kind of salad he didn't recognize but was sure would taste good. Now that he knew who was behind the recent additions to the pub's menu, Nick ordered whatever was new during his weekly date with Bill. His stomach growled in anticipation, and he thanked his lucky stars for such a high metabolism.

"Not a drop of rain in the forecast until I left the pub and suddenly a deluge. I swear, the weather gets crazier every year. Thankfully, Kate keeps her apartment stocked for every potential disaster known to man."

"How was the drive otherwise?" he asked, hanging her coat on the rack he'd made from reclaimed wood and glass knobs.

"I'm glad you told me to leave early. I swear the cabbie took the long way during rush hour," said Laura with a shake of her head.

"Getting anywhere around here is absolutely horrid, but at least it's not Mumbai," said Chaucey from the couch.

"True. Maybe New York could implement rickshaws," she replied jokingly.

"Now that would be a sight."

Nick recognized when he was out of his depth. Laura and Chaucey were both well-traveled, while he and Dean had never been anywhere of real interest. Not that Dean cared. His best friend took pride in being a native New Yorker. As far as he was concerned, no other place compared to the Big Apple.

He left the trio to catch up and walked over to the hobbled-together kitchen Aria planned to remodel someday, like everything else about the loft. Twisting a corkscrew into the bottle of wine his sister had left for them, he tried not to let his feelings over past decisions gnaw at his confidence. Logically, he knew the decision to change careers and stay close to home had been the easiest way to help take care of his family. It was a decision he'd make all over again. But sometimes he saw the road not traveled all too sharply. He blinked, the vision of practicing law somewhere far from Brooklyn disappearing instantly, and poured two glasses of chardonnay into a couple of small jam jars.

Keeping it classy, Aria. He shook his head in dismay and added wineglasses to his list of housewarming gifts for his oldest sister.

As if to prove his point, he then popped open a couple of the beers Dean had brought using the bottle opener nailed to a saw table holding a temporary plywood countertop. At least Laura wasn't the kind of woman who seemed to care about such things. In fact, one of the traits he appreciated most about her was how down to earth she was.

When he finally joined the rest of the group in the only space with furniture, the girls were still busy swapping stories about India, while Dean doled out advice about boys to his nieces.

"The only boy worth dating is a fireman, and since none of the boys you know qualify, you don't need to date," he reasoned.

"But what if he plans to be one someday?" asked Sofi, already looking for a way around Dean's logic.

"Still doesn't count," Nick and Dean said simultaneously.

"That means no dating until you're at least twenty-one," finished Nick. On this specific topic, he and Dean were in step. Not that Aria or Gina would ever allow their daughters to marry a first responder anyway. But the point was moot for now, because neither he nor his best friend would let any boy near the girls for as long as they could get away with it.

Nick noticed Laura reaching for one of the beers and quickly reached for the other. When Dean raised an eyebrow, he shrugged and chuckled under his breath as his best friend reached for one of the tiny glasses of oaky liquid instead. Though Nick had never analyzed why his past relationships hadn't lasted long enough to call any of the women his girlfriend, he was beginning to realize part of what he appreciated about Laura was her ability to surprise him.

Laura

After trying on half of her wardrobe and raiding Kate's closet for any accessory left behind, Laura had finally settled on well-worn jeans, a boyfriend sweater, and infinity scarf paired with old school penny loafers. She'd hoped to achieve a casual, hip vibe that didn't scream "I'm terrified to meet two teenage girls," merely because their uncle had turned her world upside down in recent weeks.

Laura watched Nick from the corner of her eye, enjoying the view of his profile as he interacted with the group. Looking laid back and cool as ever, he wore dark jeans and a simple gray t-shirt, wrapped tight across his chest and shoulders. But the best part were the words scrawled across the front. She snickered.

"What's so funny?" Nick asked under his breath.

"Your shirt."

"Gandalf is always right."

"True."

"So, 'Use the force, Harry,' signed 'Gandalf,' is entirely accurate."

Laura belly laughed in response. "Whoever came up with that shirt is either really confused or a total genius."

"I know someone else who falls into both of those categories," he said with a charming grin.

Laura grinned right back. She'd been worried about feeling awkward after sharing her past the last time they were together, but all she felt was lighter. Nick really was beautiful to gaze upon, but he was so much more than his Michelangelo-worthy physique. He was intelligent, funny, and thoughtful. As if all of that weren't enough, she respected the way he loved his family and friends so wholeheartedly. Watching him with them made her want to be one of his people. She sucked in a sudden breath at the realization.

Nick turned to look at her, his customary good humor displaced by a soft look. Her hand moved closer to his of its own volition until their fingers seemed to brush lightly against one another without ever touching. Laura's stomach swarmed with the hive of bees that had become a regular occurrence in his company before droning drunkenly under the way he watched her, as if he were her personal beekeeper.

"Go brush your teeth and at least pretend to be asleep when your mom comes in," Nick told his nieces.

"Sure thing, Uncle Nick. Thanks for coming over. Book club was actually kind of fun."

"Did you hear that, Laura? Hell is freezing over."

"Whatever. We know what we said," said Sofi with a hard eyeroll.

"Night, Laura. Thanks for helping us win!" exclaimed Eleanor. The girls high tailed it up the stairs, their parting shot ringing through the loft and making Laura laugh.

Nick chuckled and let their declaration go. Turning to Laura, seated across from him on the couch, he said, "I second the motion, but we all know it was a close call."

"Was it, really?" asked Laura, smugly.

"Unequivocally. While Bella certainly loved Edward, she may have wanted to be invincible as much as she wanted to be with him."

"Perhaps." She wouldn't give him the satisfaction of conceding, but she agreed with his assessment. During those initial weeks following Drew's death, the idea of leaving behind her own human frailty had been an intoxicating proposition. In the end, she'd chosen life because the boy she loved no longer had the choice.

"Your closing argument is what sealed the deal, though," Nick complimented, drawing her back in from her bleak thoughts. "No matter how much Jacob loved Bella, he couldn't save her. He could only choose whether or not to accept her choice and move forward."

Laura had spoken from her own experience, but the sadness in Nick's eyes and voice was honest. Why did it seem as if he could relate to her and the characters, Laura wondered. She reached for him, not really thinking about her actions, but wanting to comfort him the way he'd done for her at the park.

As her hand cupped his jaw and she brushed his cheekbone with her thumb, she felt the familiar spark that always accompanied contact with Nick. He seemed to lean into her hand before turning his head to kiss her palm. His lips were soft and warm upon her skin. Her breath caught—there and gone so quickly Laura thought she'd imagined it—until Nick's eyes met hers. Her breathing became shallow and fast with an unfamiliar anticipation. She was suddenly desperate to know how those lips would feel upon hers.

In the next instant, a female voice came from the entry, followed by the sound of a door shutting immediately behind it.

"Hey, you're never going to believe who I saw. The train was behind schedule and that actress from Gossip Girl, you know, the one with incredible…"

Laura sprang away from Nick and almost fell off the couch trying to get her feet up under her. She was still shaking off whatever hormone-induced trance she'd been in when he finally came to stand beside her.

A woman with amber eyes and long wavy hair a shade lighter than Nick's, held out her hand to Laura.

"Hi, I'm Aria. I've heard so much about you," she said, smiling syrupy sweet in the face of her little brother's glower.

Chapter 13

Nick

"What is this I hear about the girls getting to meet your new girlfriend?"

Nick stopped in his tracks, slowly pivoting from the sink toward his mother, and finished gulping down a glass of water. Any sudden moves might mean his death or banishment. The reaction was a tad dramatic for the situation, but Nick reasoned it wasn't beyond the realm of possibility either.

"To which girls might you be referring?" he asked cautiously, trying not to blink. His mother could smell fear from a room away.

"Eleanor and Sofi. Why, did your sisters get to meet her too?" Luna asked indignantly.

"Nope." He decided to skate over the last part. She didn't need to know that Aria had met Laura, since she had asked the plural.

The least he could do was save his sister a tongue lashing for not disclosing his personal business. His nieces, on the other hand, had pinky sworn not to say anything to their nonna.

On second thought, Nick could hear Aria's evil cackle coming from a mile away. His oldest sister could be truly diabolical when she wanted to, and he had little doubt she had used his nieces to get him into trouble, in more than one way. Revenge was going to make him feel better, just as soon as he could extricate himself from his mother's laser glare.

She stared, silently waiting, the beams from her eyes pinning him in place.

Where was a Vibranium shield when he needed it?

Hmm, he wondered. Would Laura recognize the reference to Captain America if he brought it up, or did her nerd culture only extend to sci-fi and fantasy?

"Well?"

"Well, what?" asked Nick, startled from his reverie.

"Do you have a new girlfriend, Nicolas Kieran Kelly?" she asked, hands planted firmly on her hips.

Nick's head dropped until his chin nearly touched his chest. He was the baby, her favorite, and rarely the subject of her ire. His mother only pulled out his full name when he had utterly disappointed her. One might think she'd stumble over the mouthful of consonants, but each syllable was crisp, and suddenly Italian despite two of the three names being Irish in origin.

This was the perfect time to gird his loins, take no prisoners, and give no f—all right, he was getting a little carried away. He could do this. All he had to do was stick to the facts.

"No, Laura is not my girlfriend." *Not yet anyway*, he told himself. "She's a girl, and she's a friend." It was a technicality for the time being if last night's almost-kiss on the lips was any indication. He groaned internally over his sister's poor timing.

Nick hadn't planned to do anything except enjoy the touch of her hand on his face, but the temptation to place his lips to her palm had been too much, those silly butterflies flapping their wings and chanting, *Kiss her. Kiss her. Kiss her.*

His mother's disappointed voice cut through his flying cheer squadron.

"Don't use semantics with me. Why did the girls get to meet her? Are you ashamed of me, is that it?"

And there it was, Luna Ramono Kelly's favorite weapon to wield—guilt.

"Of course not, Ma," he assured her, but the fact remained that sometimes his life was easier when his mother didn't know the intimate details of it. He filled his glass again, thinking their conversation finished.

"Fine. Bring her to dinner then."

Water spewed from his mouth like the Trevi Fountain in Rome.

"And clean up your mess."

Nick wiped his mouth with the back of his hand and reached

for the kitchen towel.

"But—"

"No buts, Nicky. If you're not ashamed of your flesh and blood, bring your girlfriend to dinner."

"Ma, everyone knows Sunday dinner is for family," he groaned with apprehension.

"That was your father's rule, God bless his soul," said Luna, making the sign of the cross. "But sometimes he was wrong. I think it's time we made room at the table for more people."

Nick heard what his mother didn't say as if she'd spoken the words out loud. It was time to fill the empty chairs left behind by the others.

"Okay, Ma. I'll ask her," he agreed with a nod of his head.

He crossed his fingers, and prayed Laura wouldn't get cold feet about their relationship when he invited her to dinner. Maybe if dinner went well, he'd finally get to kiss her luscious lips.

Kiss her. Kiss her. Kiss her. Those butterflies knew what they were talking about, and he liked them all the more for it.

Encouraged, he slung an arm over his mother's shoulders as they walked out to admire her weeded flower beds planted with new bulbs for spring.

"You know, I think you're right. We should make room at the table for more people, and I know a guy who would be perfect for Aria."

Laura

Amir came into the pub's kitchen, head ducked, and hood pulled over his recently cropped curls. He usually entered with a story spilling from his lips, and a lightness to his step, but he'd been moody of late. Laura had tried to give him space when she could and usually had him joking around with her by the time he left for home, but today felt heavier.

"Everything okay?" Laura asked. He reluctantly looked up at her, the hood falling back far enough for her to get a full look at his face. "Amir!" His left eye was severely swollen with bruising across his cheekbone. "Who did this to you?" Laura demanded.

"It doesn't matter," he said, flinching as he sat down.

"Yes, it does. Please, tell me who did this to you," Laura pleaded, taking a seat beside him on one of the crates Uncle Joe used to hold produce in the commercial refrigerator. When he didn't answer immediately, she asked, "Are you hurt anywhere else?"

"My back, but I don't think anything's permanently damaged."

"What happened?"

"A group of guys showed up at the bodega late last night. I was closing up when I saw them spray painting the wall on the side of the alley. I went out thinking I'd scare them away, but instead of running off, they jumped me."

"Did you call the police this time?"

"No."

"What did your father say?"

"Nothing. He left me in my mother's care and went out at sunrise to paint over the wall, like he does every time someone covers it in slurs," said Amir with resignation lacing his voice. "He's right. The bigotry will never end, so what does it matter."

"I thought things were better now." Immediately following the events of 9/11, fear had run rampant, and the actions of terrorists became the mantle for an entire group of people.

Surely the situation has changed over the last ten years, thought Laura.

"You're kidding, right? How can you be so naïve?" Amir's voice rose with his feelings, frustration and hurt lacing his words. "It doesn't matter if I was born here or that my parents came to this country to find a better life. The only thing anyone ever sees when they look at us is a potential threat."

Laura didn't know what to say. He wasn't wrong. She knew not every Muslim was a terrorist, any more than every Christian was a pacifist. History was chock full of examples of prejudice, scapegoating, and abuses of power tearing humanity limb from limb.

Though she wanted justice for the Zaman family, she understood why they had stopped seeking it. Right or wrong, fear was a powerful motivator. It caused neighbors to turn against one another and created chasms between citizens and those who were supposed to serve and protect in equal measure.

Angry, Amir kicked the stack of crates in front of him, spilling the contents across the concrete floor. He and Laura knelt down to pick up the limes rolling in every direction. She reached underneath a stainless counter to retrieve the last one, uncertain about how to help him and his family.

Averting her eyes, Laura gave Amir a new recipe for the week inspired by Mediterranean flavors. He got to work, setting about his usual routine in the kitchen and assured her that he could see well enough not to burn down the kitchen.

"I'm sorry for what I said to you," he apologized quietly, the coriander sizzling in butter and permeating the air where his emotions still hung between them.

"You don't owe me an apology. I should pay better attention to what's happening in my neighborhood," said Laura, caught off guard by her own confession. But in the momentary silence she tasted the truth of it, if a little bittersweetly under the circumstances.

"Sometimes, it feels like nothing's ever going to change."

"You may be right. But I hope you're wrong," she said over her shoulder and pushed through the kitchen door.

Laura found Uncle Joe at the bar refilling the plastic condiment containers and putting lemon slices into a glass jar. She filled him in on the situation with Amir and kept her hands busy by wiping down the various surfaces with a wet rag and cleanser. "I felt totally helpless when he told me," she admitted.

"I'll touch base with Father Hugo," said Uncle Joe. "He has a few parishioners on the police force who are trying to create positive change through relationships with business owners, community groups, and neighbors."

Laura pursed her lips in resignation. "It's not an immediate fix, but maybe it'll be a start."

Uncle Joe smiled at her persistence. "In the meantime, we keep fighting the good fight by standing up for those who need it and refuse to give in to the hate around us."

It was the elephant in the room, but Laura knew the words were only so good as doing them. Her father was fond of saying good intentions paved the way to hell. What mattered was the follow-through but following through usually required sticking around long enough to invest. None of which was her strong suit these days.

A half hour later, Walker's Pub was officially open for business. They opened at noon on Fridays and Saturdays because last-call was at midnight instead of eleven on those nights. Laura usually got off work after the dinner crowd but had offered to stay so they could talk about Uncle Joe's plan. It also meant staying busy enough to keep Nick, and what had almost happened between them on his sister's couch, out of her thoughts. At least until he walked in at the end of his shift, dressed in his uniform.

Nope, she thought, *he doesn't need the baseball uniform to look good.* The one he wore worked more than fine.

"Hey, I was hoping I might catch you here tonight," Nick said by way of greeting and smiled. A group dressed in similar uniforms came inside behind him, but instead of coming up to the bar, they sat in a booth tucked into the far corner. Laura assumed they were a part of Squad 2, along with Nick and Dean, which they had explained to her during book club.

Sofi and Eleanor were debating the merits of being part of an engine company or a squad at the time. Of course, the men had instantly voted for a squad, but acknowledged both were important. The main difference, they clarified, was that a squad responded to more situations. They could do whatever an incident commander required of them when called to any level of emergency, but also served as an engine or ladder company in their primary district.

Laura had boiled it down to specialized training and a more versatile skill set. Nick had commented more than once during the discussion that Squad 2 was well prepared to oversee whatever came their way. The situations he'd described sounded more like a foreign language, or the stuff of fiction to her, but his passion for the job was admirable.

"Did you just get off shift?" Laura asked, nodding in the direction of the table.

"Yep, some of us wanted to grab a bite to eat and a pint before heading home."

"I imagine it's nice to wind down and change gears after all of the adrenaline," Laura mentioned casually.

Nick paused, eventually saying, "Depends on the person. Sometimes, it's necessary if the shift was hard. Usually, I pick up a book or go for a run with tunes."

"I can totally picture that," said Laura before catching herself. "Not that I go around picturing you in different scenarios." It was official: she should dig a hole and climb inside before she embarrassed herself any further.

When he seemed to hesitate once more, Laura worried that the situation was worse than she thought. Nick always had a comeback, especially if he could use it to make her blush. Had she gone too far by asking about his job?

He looked down at the bar as though he were debating his words. Definitely not Nick's modus operandi. He was usually direct and confident. What if he wanted to talk about the kiss?

Okay, almost-kiss, she corrected herself.

"Um, I need a big favor." Nick still wouldn't meet her eyes.

"What kind of favor?" Laura asked. *Please, oh please, let it be a kiss*, her inner voice begged, making her stomach muscles clench.

"Eleanor and Sofi spilled the beans about you to my mom."

"Oh? I mean, what did they say about me?" Laura tried not to panic, though she wasn't sure if she was more concerned about what the girls had told his mother, or the favor Nick had yet to request.

In the next moment he stood to his full height, seeming to have decided something, and pinned her with his gaze. Nick's confidence was something to behold and the buzz in her stomach, which had started with his arrival, intensified. Laura's mouth dried out.

"They told her you were my girlfriend."

Laura gulped. "Except, I'm not your girlfriend."

You want to be, shouted her gleeful internal voice. *Shush!* She tried to clamp down on her runaway thoughts.

It sounded like he mumbled, "Believe me, I'm fully aware," before speaking up. "I think she's confused by the whole you're a girl and a friend thing, but not my girlfriend."

"Why, exactly is that?" asked Laura, feeling a little confused about where the conversation was going.

"Because it's me," said Nick with his customary sardonic look.

Laura wanted to wipe it off his face. "You are not all that and a bag o' chips."

Nick chuckled despite her feisty declaration. "Again, fully aware, but Ma happens to be my biggest fan. She also knows I don't bring everyone around the girls." He spoke the last part softly, a concession of sorts.

Laura knew it was meant to be a compliment, but her own insecurity about how the evening at his sister's had gone crept in. The girlfriend, not a girlfriend convo reiterating how awkward—on her part— things had ended.

"It's more likely she knows you go around breaking women's hearts without a second thought," she said, using snark to cover up her discomfort. Too late, she realized how unkind her words were. They implied Nick didn't care about other people's feelings when the opposite couldn't have been more true. Though she didn't know his record with girlfriends, he spoke with respect about the women in his family. And any guy who could listen to her sad tale with compassion, wasn't a jerk. Still, she had painted him in that light.

Hurt shone in his eyes, but he didn't snap back at her. Instead, he did the exact opposite.

"Come to family dinner on Sunday afternoon. I can't promise everyone will behave, but I know you can deal with whatever the Kelly's dish out."

Laura simply stared. An invitation wasn't what she'd expected. Or another compliment.

Nick gently tapped the bar top with his knuckle twice when she still hadn't responded. "Think about it. Joe knows how to reach me. Text me and I'll get you the details."

He didn't smile at her like he normally would, reminding her she'd messed up. Uncle Joe coughed at the other end of the bar, raising a single eyebrow when she looked in his direction, his disappointment in her behavior apparent in the gesture.

She watched Nick saunter over to join the rest of his crew, enjoying the rear view immensely before dropping her head onto the bar with shame. A virus had eaten all of her brain cells. It was the only explanation for why she'd stood there in a zombie state, incoherent and speechless, when she should have apologized.

What is wrong with me? she asked herself. *You should start a list,* her snarky inner voice answered.

Laura looked to the man on her right filling pints and placing crisps in front of customers, her cheek still plastered to the bar, afraid to make eye contact with Nick in the corner. "Uncle Joe, I think I'm going to need that phone number." The least she could do was show up for dinner after her injurious behavior.

Uncle Joe didn't speak, but the look on his face said plenty.

Chapter 14

Laura

"Hi Kate, it's me. Again. I'm tired of talking to your voice mail. Call me back," whined Laura. "And call Momma. She thinks you're lying in a ditch somewhere." Laura hung up the phone and sat on the edge of the bed again. Micky put his head in her lap and waited expectantly. She ran her fingers through his fur and scratched behind his ears.

Her sister tended to lose herself in whatever project she took on, to the detriment of her familial relationships. Laura tried not to take offense; she knew Kate loved her fiercely, and the shop's success in London was paramount to her sister's continued happiness. Their mother, on the other hand, took everything personally on top of fretting about her children.

Laura glanced down at Micky. "What do you think; should I

wear the dress or the jeans to dinner?" Micky barked in response and trotted out of the room, presumably to find his own meal.

"Thanks for nothing," complained Laura. She debated for a moment before picking up the phone to call home. Not that she had any intention of asking her mother for advice. It would only invite unsought interference in the future, which would inevitably lead to her mother's disappointment when Laura didn't take kindly to it.

The line rang, once, twice, three times, before a voice on the other side said, "Hello, moon pie."

"Hey, Daddy," she said, relief lacing her words. The last thing she wanted to do was snitch on Kate about her unreturned calls, and their mother would ask if they had spoken recently.

"How's the Big Apple?"

"Not bad." She paused before saying, "I can see why Kate likes living here."

"Hmm," her father hummed.

"What's that supposed to mean?"

"Nothing in particular."

"It always means something. Go ahead and say it. You know you want to."

"It's nothing, really."

Laura might've believed him if he hadn't laughed under his breath afterward.

"Now you're having fun messing with me."

He chuckled again, this time a little louder. "I'm glad you like

Brooklyn. It's good to put roots down somewhere."

"You talked to Uncle Joe, didn't you?"

"Yes, ma'am. You have a steady job, a place to live, a new dog, and friends, I hear."

"I've had those before. Well, not the dog, but everything else. Besides, technically the dog belongs to Kate."

"Hmm," hummed her father once more.

"Fine. I like Brooklyn. What else did Uncle Joe tell you?"

"Oh, nothing much."

"Good, because it's not really any of his—"

"Though he might've mentioned a certain gentleman who works for the fire department."

"I knew it! Uncle Joe is a busy body disguised as a barkeep," she said, completely exasperated over her family's game of telephone.

"Now, don't go picking a fight with Joe. He's only looking out for your best interest."

"Well, he doesn't know what he's talking about this time."

"Hmm."

"Bye, Daddy," said Laura, disgruntled.

Cal Howard laughed, a rumble vibrating from his chest. "Love you, moon pie."

Laura glared at the phone she'd set down seconds ago and reopened the home screen. She tapped on the message icon and scrolled through the texts between her and Nick from yesterday, checking the address in her map app for the millionth time to calculate what time she needed to leave.

She looked back at the closet. Today's venue called for reinforcements. Dialing Chaucey, she bounced in place on the bed and prayed her friend would answer.

Nick

Nick was usually the last to arrive for family dinner, but today he'd made sure to get there early, thereby allowing his siblings enough time to harass him before Laura's arrival. And he could hardly wait to see the look on Aria's face when her dinner date showed up. Nick rubbed his hands together in silent glee.

When Laura finally arrived at a quarter to three, he raced his sisters and Leo to answer the door first. There might have been gentle shoving for his part, but his sisters weren't above torn clothing, and his brother had a mean bear hug. Leo could drop a person to the floor faster than a taser.

They'd always been a little overcompetitive, but he might need to add certifiably insane to the qualifier. In the end, his nephew managed to get there before any of them. Nick untangled himself from the wrestling match, tugging his dress shirt back into place, and tried to shoo the rest of them into the kitchen.

"I like the outfit. Very chic," said Sofi as she walked past them toward the table set up in the dining room.

Nick pivoted from the frothing horde of siblings to greet

Laura, his jaw promptly dropping somewhere in the vicinity of the floor. She wore a plaid mini skirt, a long gray jacket, and held a chocolate sheet cake with peanut butter frosting in her hands. He could smell the tantalizing goodness wafting from her direction. Her outfit choice and the cake confirmed what he already knew; she was officially the perfect woman for him.

"It's like that song you love, Uncle Nick," Eleanor chimed in.

The girls went back and forth with the verses until they came to Nick's favorite line, so he gave them what they actually wanted—his complete humiliation. At least he could do it with style. "I want a girl with a short skirt and a long jacket," he sang, taking the cake from Laura with one hand and spinning her around in a circle with the other.

Her smile lit up the room and his heart. She was the sun, and all he wanted to do was bask in her warmth for eternity. Except for the fact that his entire family was blatantly watching them. It killed the whole 'I want to worship and adore you' fantasy he'd been indulging.

"How did you know I love cake?"

"The dessert or the band?" Laura asked.

"Both," said Nick, grinning.

"Well, who doesn't love cake in all of its various forms?"

"Exactly. Before I introduce the circus, please know I'm incredibly sorry for subjecting you to this."

"And I'm sorry for what I said the other day at the pub. It was uncalled for," said Laura, contritely.

"You're here, which makes up for it," he said and winked.

Placing the cake on an antique sideboard pushed up against a wall in the cramped space, he said, "Laura, you know the girls and Aria already. This… is everyone else."

She laughed nervously. "Hi, it's nice to meet all of you."

They all started talking at once, until his mother jumped in, giving orders around the food and where to sit. "Laura, we're so glad you could join us today. Father Hugo speaks very highly of you."

Nick's head swiveled so fast he wouldn't be surprised if he looked like he needed an exorcism. "When did you talk to Father Hugo?"

"The man is my priest. I talk to him weekly. If you went to confession more often, you'd know this."

Nick wanted to roll his eyes but refrained. The last thing he needed was to bring out his mother's faux Italian accent. So, Luna Kelly had known about Laura for a while. His mother had pulled one over on him and managed to kill two birds with one stone.

"Let's say grace. Nick, it's your turn," his mother directed.

"Wait, why is there an empty seat next to me?" asked Aria. "I thought Jules was still on bed rest."

"She is. You can take her and Dae leftovers on your way home. I invited someone else to dinner. Nick thinks he'd be a good match for you." She smiled beatifically, with zero shame for her sneaky plans.

His oldest sister gave him her best death stare from across the room until the doorbell rang, causing her to practically jump out of her seat.

Leo and Gina laughed like hyenas, while Vinny tried to hold herself together until a loud snort broke free.

"Sorry, Aria. I tried to change their minds," she said, tucking a piece of hair back into her tawney braid.

"Oh, that's great. Thanks for nothing."

"Don't just sit there, Aria. Answer the door," said Luna, irritated with her brood of unruly children.

The girls and Finn were smart enough to keep their mouths shut as Aria marched across the dining room, smacking the back of Leo's head as she went.

"Ow!"

"That's nothing. Wait until I get ahold of the demon spawn who's plan this was to begin with."

Nick laughed obnoxiously in response. "Bring it," he said as she opened the front door, effectively preventing her from making any more threats.

Laura watched on in shock, while Nick sat back to watch her.

Mission accomplished, he thought. Not only had he gotten Aria back for her part in this charade, but he'd made it possible for the beautiful woman sitting beside him to avoid a Kelly family inquisition.

By the time they'd finished dessert and cleanup, the sun was setting over Brooklyn. Everyone had behaved admirably for the most part. It helped that Aria's dinner date was a teacher at the school her daughter attended. Eugene seemed like a nice-enough guy, and Nick thought he had guts to show up to a family dinner, but no one wanted the Kelly brand of crazy bandied about the fancy private school, especially Eleanor and Sofi. He had a fifty-fifty chance his stunt would come back to haunt him, or his sister and nieces would take his warning shot and think twice before betraying him in the future.

Nick helped Laura into her coat, offering to walk her home, and giving himself an excuse to leave before his sister could murder him. The November twilight was crisp and dry, the leaves underfoot a crunchy russet, rather than the newly fallen ones that swished with every footfall. They walked in companionable silence until they came to a café with wrought iron tables and chairs cloistered together beneath outdoor lights strung for evening ambience.

"Any chance you'll let me buy you a hot drink, and myself a little bit of time?"

Laura smiled. "Sure. Once your sister gets ahold of you, I may never see you again."

"If it was anyone else, I wouldn't be worried, but Aria will hide the body where no one ever finds it." He shivered to emphasize his point.

In honor of the season, Laura ordered a pumpkin spice latte with whipped cream and nutmeg sprinkled on top. Nick ordered a drip coffee to which he added four packets of raw sugar.

"Do you actually like coffee?" asked Laura, eyeing his twelve-ounce cup as they left through the side door.

He shrugged. "Not really. I usually get a matcha green tea latte with almond milk, but they were out of matcha," he explained.

Laura's eyes opened wide in surprise. "I did not see that one coming. Next time, try a chai tea latte. I feel sorry for your coffee."

They sat down at one of the tables and Nick crossed his legs at the ankle before sliding them out past her own. Laura let out a chortle, causing his aerial squadron to flap excitedly around his heart. Their flittering presence had become such a common occurrence; it was more normal than the absence of them at this point.

"What's so funny?" he asked, already knowing the answer.

"You, in a dainty chair."

"Have no fear, I can perch with the best of them."

Laura squinted at him, her eyes glimmering with humor in the warm light above them. "You do sort of remind me of a preening bird.

"Want me to fluff my pretty feathers for you?" he asked with a lift of perfectly straight brows.

Laura laughed unabashedly in response. "You're incorrigible."

"I am totally encourageable," said Nick, deliberately misinterpreting what she'd said.

"That isn't a real word."

"Yes, it is. It means I'm able to be encouraged. Thus, you can encourage me to fluff my feathers."

"Ha, ha." said Laura, holding her cup tightly for warmth, her teeth starting to chatter every now and again. "I wish I'd remembered my scarf today."

Nick reached over and pulled her chair closer to his. "This way we'll create more heat between the two of us," he said unwinding the navy wool scarf at his neck and gently wrapping it around Laura's.

"Thank you," she said, burrowing in for a moment. "Mm, it smells like cedarwood, cloves, and a touch of grapefruit."

Nick chuckled. "You're welcome, for both the scarf and the scent." When she took another sniff and hummed again, he teased, "Good enough to eat?"

"Can I ask you something personal?" she asked, ignoring him.

But Nick was still thinking about what they could cook up together. And not in the kitchen. "I thought we already covered this. I'm happy to fluff my feathers for you," he said, flexing his biceps playfully.

He chuckled again when she merely rolled her eyes at his antics. "Fine, no fluffing, but it's your loss."

Chapter 15

Laura

Laura watched him from beneath her lashes for a second, took a breath, and jumped into the deep end. He might not be ready for this conversation, but her intuition said it was important to their friendship.

"When did your dad pass away?"

Nick cocked his head and appeared to weigh his reply before asking, "How'd you know?"

"I noticed he was missing from the more recent family photos on the mantel. Gina was excited to show me what a chubby toddler you were," she explained.

"Makes you want to kiss my cheeks, doesn't it?" he asked, deflecting with his usual good humor.

"Maybe then, cherub, but they're not so cute now," heckled

Laura before coming back to the original subject. "Since your momma still wears her wedding ring…" Laura trailed off.

"Sometimes, I actually forget about the last ten years, and how many missing pieces there are in my life. Not that my family's anything special under the circumstances."

"We don't have to talk about it if you don't want to," she rushed to say, afraid she'd overstepped.

"Nah, you were honest with me about Drew and, I want to tell you. I want you to know who I am."

The regret in his eyes stole the air from her lungs. Reaching for his hand to offer a small measure of comfort, as he had done for her not so long ago, Laura waited for him to find his words.

"I told you I was in class at NYU the day the towers were hit."

It was less of a question and more of a statement, but Laura nodded in confirmation anyway.

"What I didn't tell you is I left the city for home immediately after."

"I'm sure that was for the best; it must have been total chaos." Laura reassured him.

He went on as though he hadn't heard her. "I thought the first tower was a fire. I didn't realize what was actually happening."

"No one did," said Laura confidently.

"By the time I got home, Pop, Donnie, Leo, and my brother in-laws were all on the scene, while I was stuck watching the rescue efforts from the safety of my parents' living room."

"Nick, you were a college student, not a first responder," she said softly. Laura had been so consumed with Drew's death at the time she'd never seen much of the news coverage from those awful days, but Nick would've had a front-row seat, all the while hoping the people he loved would somehow come home in the end.

"I know, and at the time I believed it was better to steer away from whatever rescue efforts were under way." He seemed to struggle with his next words. "It doesn't change the regret I carry or—"

"Or?" she prompted when he stopped short.

"Or the shame I feel for not being there when my family needed me."

"Oh, Nick," Laura whispered in understanding.

"Pop and Donnie never came home. Sofi is about the only part of Gina's marriage she doesn't regret. God knows, everything else was a shitshow after 9/11." Nick shook his head in the negative as if he still found it hard to believe. "Aria's husband Miles died from a stroke two years ago. Whether it was a biproduct of exposure is still a gray area for compensation as far as the government is concerned, but the guy was only forty years old. And after surviving everything else, Leo's fighting leukemia."

Laura had wondered if his brother might be sick. He seemed so full of life, yet the bruised smudges under his eyes told a different story, as did the skull cap he'd worn, even though the house had been a toasty seventy-two degrees. Leo put on a good face for everyone, including Vinny. A person would have to be blind not to see the love he had for his wife, but the shadows in his eyes gave away his fear about how long he'd be around for her.

Laura took Nick's hands in hers, giving them a gentle squeeze.

"Is that why you joined the FDNY?"

"At first. I could soothe my guilty conscience and honor the fallen all at the same time. But it only lasted a short while. By the end of training, I loved the job for itself."

Laura felt a twinge of resentment over the courage he'd had to tread a new path, while she'd spent so long being afraid of what the future held for her.

"And Jules? Aria mentioned she's on bed rest."

"Six months pregnant with pre-eclampsia."

Said matter-of-factly, Laura almost missed the undercurrent of anger in his voice. It was reassuring to know Nick was as rattled as she would be if it were Kate in the same situation. She leaned forward, taking his face into her hands. Brushing her thumbs over his high cheekbones, she took a moment to soak him in and acknowledge the pull toward him she was tired of fighting. With only a look or a touch, Nick centered her in a way no one before him had ever done. It was as though she'd been waiting for him to stop her merry-go-round all this time but didn't know it. Until now.

Nick met her eyes and bowed until his forehead touched hers, placing his hands on her hips to steady himself, understanding what she offered in the moment.

"I wish I could take away every loss...all the hurt you've endured," she whispered. "But if you had been there, you might not be here with me, and I can't imagine being with anyone else in this moment."

It wasn't absolution. Laura didn't have the power to take away his guilt, but she could help share the load and make it a lighter burden to carry.

They stayed that way for another minute, their breaths mingling together as one in the chilly air. Nick rose, kissing the top of her head as he went. His absence was brief as he reached for one of her hands, tucking it securely through his arm for the rest of the walk home. Laura tried not to snuggle in and failed. She told herself it was because of the temperature, but she knew the truth and so did her beehive.

"So, let's talk about how your brothers share names with ninja turtles…"

He laughed, carefree once more, causing the bees in Laura's stomach to zip and soar in response. Having successfully returned the gift of laughter that Nick had given her so many times before, Laura walked with a buoyancy in her step and a tiny spark of hope in her heart.

Nick

Nick realized whatever transpired between Laura and himself post-Sunday dinner translated to some sort of barrier breaking down between them, but he still didn't know whether to attribute the changes in their relationship to her feelings for him as a friend or something more. They texted back and forth every day and made plans around work, sometimes doubling up with Dean and Chaucey for a night out to the movies or a gallery showing. He and Laura never seemed to run out of things to discuss, whether it was books, music, movies, her travels, or their families. The list went on and on.

Nick wanted her more than he'd ever wanted any woman, but he let her set the tone. Unfortunately for him, it was currently at a glacier pace. Eventually, he hoped he'd get to kiss those rosy lips calling to him like a siren at sea.

Preferably, without the whole shipwreck scenario, he thought. For all intents and purposes, they were dating, but something held him back from crossing the line officially. And kissing her would be crossing a line—one he wasn't sure they could come back from if she didn't feel ready to step over it.

By nature, he was affectionate with the women in his life, and his playful temperament came with the territory. Second guessing his next move wasn't something he usually did, and he didn't intend to start now. He figured the more he was himself, the more Laura would feel free to be herself, until she realized how great they were together.

Nick worked Thanksgiving while Laura spent the day with Joe at the pub, which hosted an annual Friendsgiving for any available staff and regular patrons. Everyone brought their favorite food to share and, according to Laura, it was the most random assortment of holiday fare she'd ever eaten. Apparently, Dorito chicken casserole had yet to become a classic across the globe.

Bill made sure to give him a tough time over their weekly lunch dates, insisting Nick only came into the pub to see Laura these days. Since she was more fun to look at than the old man, he happily took the razzing. It didn't matter anyway; Nick knew he was hers, lock, stock, and barrel. He only hoped Laura realized it sooner rather than later.

Nick pushed his hair off his forehead and glanced down at his watch. Eight more hours until he saw Laura. They had plans to meet up at the dog run in Prospect Park and grab coffee together before her shift at Walker's Pub began.

The last sixteen hours had been relatively calm in the scheme of things. Squad 2 was playing backup as an engine company due to the increase in calls recently—not an uncommon occurrence when temperatures began to drop. Overworked heating systems, poorly maintained chimneys, and cooking inside all contributed to winter being a prime time for fires. At least it wasn't cold enough for the pumps to freeze yet, and snow wasn't in the forecast. Firefighting during a blizzard with freezing temperatures was the only time he ever wished he'd chosen law school instead.

Nick had spent his day checking equipment, working out, and catching up on his reading for next week's Bookies Club. A four-alarm call came in around four o'clock, and the stillness which permeates an engine house on a slow day immediately gave way to adrenaline and discipline.

Half of the warehouse district must be on fire, thought Nick. Multiple crews were on the site when they arrived, the majority of them from Brooklyn, but he recognized two engine companies called in from Queens. He'd never hear the end of it from Dean if they missed the action, but he knew better than to bypass command and went to find the fire warden assigned to the situation.

Two hours later they had the fire mostly under control, with the exception of a few flare ups, when Nick looked around to ask Dean if he'd seen the chief. He wanted to run his arson suspicions by him. Not spotting him where he thought he'd seen him last, Nick moved to avoid one of the engine companies folding a hose away into a familiar accordion pattern, readying it for future deployment.

"Hey, anyone seen Dean?"

"I think he's still inside. There was a flare up in the back. He went to check it out."

"Did anyone go with him?"

"I assume so. Rookie 101—if you're going to be a maverick—"

"Take a goose with you," said someone else nearby with a grin, the two firefighters bumping fists over the *Top Gun* reference.

Nick took off at a sprint for the back of the warehouse, where a crew had finished dousing the last of the flames seen from outside.

He came to stop, making sure to look in every direction, but Dean was nowhere in the vicinity. With a glance at the warehouse, he knew in his gut his best friend was somewhere inside. Pulling his respirator back over his face, he ducked into the cavernous space and scanned the smoke with the light on his helmet, his worst nightmare becoming more real with every passing second.

"Dean!" Nick yelled through his mask. "Dean!"

By the third call, he'd resigned himself to the situation of an injured, unconscious Dean, and what that would mean for getting them both out of the compromised building quickly. Nick refused to consider the alternative or leave without him. Even if they hadn't been best friends since kindergarten, he was Squad, and that made him family. And you never left your family behind. He had little doubt it was the reason his father and brother never came home.

A heavy haze filled the space, causing him to stumble over Dean's body, debris littered everywhere around the vicinity. The beams overhead creaked ominously in warning. With no time to waste, Nick hauled Dean over his shoulder like a sack of potatoes, and hoped he wasn't making any injuries worse in the meantime.

Counting back the turns, going left where he'd gone right, he exited the building with only seconds to spare. Behind Nick the roof groaned loudly, rending at the seams, and buckling into the pit of the warehouse with finality. If he'd waited any longer to go in search of Dean, one or both of them might not be going home.

Nick kept moving despite the chaos, a cloud of dust washing

over the two of them as he made his way to the rest of the Squad and the paramedics, who rushed forward to take Dean. Within seconds, the sirens blared as they headed for the nearest hospital, and Nick jumped into the cab of Squad 2's truck.

Exhaustion coated the familiar faces around him, and their collective silence echoed what no one dared speak aloud; mortality had come calling for one of their own. Nick shut the thought down. Thinking about the risks they took day in and day out was a slippery slope, and an easy one to fall down when dwelled on. But all that lay that way was a bottomless cavern, and the last thing he wanted to do was make the climb back up if he fell.

Chapter 16

Nick

Laura slammed the door of the taxi and ran straight into Nick's arms where he waited at the entrance of Brooklyn General. He'd called her as soon as he'd gotten to the hospital to update her on the situation.

"How's Dean?" she asked, sounding breathless, and interrupting his musings on the finer aspects of her anatomy pressed to his body.

He lay his head atop hers, holding her tight. "A concussion, minor smoke inhalation, and a severely sprained ankle. They're keeping him overnight for observation." He swore out of frustration. "I told him not to go inside without backup." It was hypocritical, considering he'd done exactly the same thing in order to find Dean. Nick shirked the thought off, telling himself the ends justified the means.

"And you?" she asked, worry evident in her voice.

He went to kiss the tip of her nose in response, pleased with her concern, but she retreated from his embrace to rake her gaze over him from head to toe and back up again. He still wore his uniform and needed a shower.

The corners of his lips quirked up. "Still good enough to ogle I see," Nick said flirtatiously. "Which is crazy under the circumstances. The entire roof collapsed immediately after I evacuated the building with Dean."

Laura winced, and he used the excuse to pull her close again. He should have left that last part out.

"Chief thinks it might be arson, same as the last two. It's why we're spread thin. We don't have enough crews to answer the multiple alarms and the usual situations, thanks to the recent budget cuts to emergency services.

"I hope they catch whoever it is soon."

"Me too. Our jobs are hard enough without someone starting fires on purpose."

"They're going to get someone killed."

"Let's hope they get caught before that," he said and released her, shaking off the kernel of fear trying to bury itself within. He wasn't invincible; no one was, but suddenly it felt like he had more to lose than it did yesterday.

Laura took his proffered hand and followed him off the elevator, down a long, sterile hallway filled with hospital staff and stations.

Nick led her past the Squad, huddled in a small, windowless room to the right. Some of the crew said hello, to which Laura smiled, but Nick didn't slow down long enough to introduce her. He told himself it was because he was tired, but the truth was more complex than he was ready to delve into after the stress of the day.

When it was Nick's turn to say goodnight to Dean, Laura hesitated, pulling against his grip.

"I should wait out here. I'm not Squad or family."

"Come on. C.J. will be glad to see you, and you're with me, which is all that matters," he said, leading her into the room. In the end she went with Nick, albeit reluctantly. "Besides, they think C.J.'s his fiancé, which makes her the gatekeeper."

Other than an oxygen cannula in his nose, Nick thought his best friend looked like his normal self, minus his usual yapping. Fortunately, the exposure to smoke had been minimal. Dean would be out for at least a week with the concussion or until the doctor cleared him to ride a desk. The sprain would take longer, but overall, the damage was less than Nick had expected when he'd carried him out of the warehouse.

"The pain meds finally kicked in, but the anti-nausea drug made him sleepy. He'll be out until the nurse comes back in," said Chaucey quietly, standing to greet them both with a kiss on the cheek. "I got a hold of his parents. Pam and Carlos are trying to catch a flight home tomorrow. His sister and the kids will drive down the day after."

"Perfect. Carlos can feed everyone while Pam chews Dean out for being foolish. Why is Aimee coming with the kids by herself?"

"Mac has term papers to grade but promised to join them by the weekend." Chaucey rolled her eyes before laughing. "You know how they are."

"Mac won't last twenty-four hours in a silent house, but it's nice of Aimee to play along."

While they droned on about Dean's family, Laura sat quietly, her knee bobbing up and down, fingers tapping the arm of the chair. Nick knew something was off, but he couldn't quite place what, or why. When she finally jumped into the conversation, it was too loud and upbeat for the situation, the smile on her face forced instead of the carefree one he'd become accustomed to recently.

"I'm going to give you guys a minute," she declared and leaned forward to hug Chaucey goodbye. "I'll call you tomorrow to check in."

Chaucey grabbed her hand and cocked her head in question before letting her go when Laura said nothing more.

When Nick joined her a short while later, she still seemed restless, eyes downcast as she paced the hall. Fortunately, the Squad had left, leaving the two of them alone.

Nick gazed at her with concern, but Laura wouldn't return his stare.

"You up for an outing?"

"Tonight?" she asked incredulously, finally meeting his eyes.

"Why not? I don't have anywhere else to be. And I know a place to get a great slice of pizza on the other side of the bridge."

She shrugged her shoulders as if to say okay and let him drape an arm over her shoulder as they headed for the parking garage. Nick tried to take solace when she didn't shy away from his touch, but his gut said something was seriously wrong.

He handed her the smaller helmet he'd bought a couple of years ago. At the time, he'd done it thinking to transport a kid here or there for his sisters. He should've known Aria, and Gina by extension, would throw a hissy fit about keeping the kids in a safety bubble at all times. His heart had been in the right place, if not his parental radar.

Laura slipped the helmet on and took a seat behind him, leaning in as she wrapped her arms around his waist. She fit perfectly against him, precisely the way he'd known she would. He took the Brooklyn Bridge toward Manhattan's financial district, the sun disappearing behind the city's formidable wall of real estate, and painted lines blurring beneath the wheels of the bike, until his worries dissipated with the wind in his face and Laura at his back.

Decorations covered every square, plaza, and major venue in festive colors and holiday displays, while a million twinkling lights tried to outshine the rest of the light pollution ever present in a large city. A slice of margarita pizza from a nearby food truck in each of their hands, they walked across the street to the World Trade Center Plaza.

The city was full of life: horns honked, people crowded crosswalks, and a hundred smells collided in the air. Yet, there was peace, a sort of stillness, surrounding the Memorial. Nick led them past the Survivor Tree toward the pools with their surrounding parapets engraved with the names of those who had perished on 9/11.

Only two other people lingered at a distance. The couple were a distinct pair. Dressed in trousers, chunky heels, and a fedora, the woman looked like she'd stepped from the pages of a vintage catalogue, except the camera she held was modern. Her partner, on the other hand, looked dressed to the nines in an expensive three-piece suit. Nick would almost bet the guy worked on Wall Street and made more money than he could ever dream of.

Looking down at the woman next to him, Nick smiled, not envious of the other couple in the least bit. He had everything he could ever want in the woman standing beside him. The thought sent a jolt of longing through him, but it didn't frighten him. Whether it was because of what had happened earlier in the day, or because they were at the Memorial, he was tired of playing it safe. Laura was the kind of woman any level-headed guy would want to be with, and he was getting ready to say those exact words when she broke the silence they'd slipped into.

"My birthday is September eleventh."

Laura said the words so faintly, he almost missed them.

Nick stopped dead in his tracks and turned slowly to look at

Laura. "How is it everything about you seems to redeem that awful day for me? You are a constant surprise in the best way."

She finally cracked a smile. "No pressure though, huh?"

"Nah," he scoffed. "Just because I now have an excuse to celebrate the one day of the year I dread more than going to the dentist means absolutely nothing," he said dryly, but Laura didn't respond with her typical humor. He wondered what he could've said wrong, until something she'd mentioned weeks ago came to the forefront of his thoughts.

Nick blew out a quick breath, shaking his head from side to side. "I don't know how I could be so thoughtless," he said, instantly repentant. "Drew died on your birthday." The words were barely audible to his own ears, and his heart rebelled at the pain they must cause her.

"It's not your fault," she said, looking away from him. "Why should I feel sorry for myself? At least I'm still alive."

Reaching the South Pool, Nick said quietly, "I couldn't bring myself to come before now. Seeing the names of all these people… it somehow makes everything real all over again." He ran his hands over the letters and swallowed hard. "Pop and Donnie deserved more than an unfinished life. They all did."

Laura placed a hand on his back, and he took comfort from the weight of her presence.

"We buried Pop in the cemetery at Holy Cross close to Gramps, but Donnie's remains are still in a repository waiting to be identified. Ma says it doesn't matter because they're always with us in here," he said thumping his chest over his heart.

"Does it matter to you?" Laura asked into the ether, the sound of falling water and a steady hum of traffic the backdrop in an otherwise surreal moment.

"I'm not sure anymore. I ride my brother's dream bike because he'll never get to and everywhere I go in Brooklyn contains a memory of Pop. It's part of why I couldn't bring myself to leave back then; I wasn't ready to say goodbye to them."

"And then you joined the department."

"I thought I could honor my family and maybe save others the heartache we live with. And to be here now, in this place with you, ten years after the unthinkable, feels…like everything has come full circle." He watched her, his eyes skating over her features, a look of awe in them. "None of these people will get a second chance, but you and I are still standing, despite our losses."

"Except, I don't need saving," said Laura, abruptly.

Nick flinched in surprise. He wanted to reach for her but worried she'd retreat if the anger in her voice was any indication. His feet rooted to the concrete, he gripped his chest with both hands instead and prepared to plead his case. Somehow, in this crazy world where everything could flip upside down without a moment's notice, they had found each other. If anyone understood the idea of how fleeting life was, it was Laura.

"This isn't about saving you or anyone else," Nick said,

uncertain how they'd gone from him trying to tell her how he felt, to this strange thread. He deliberately steadied his voice, confused by her accusation. "There are days I feel more broken than others, but I'm still here, and so are you. Any cracks left behind are how the light gets in until it can shine out again," he said, gazing tenderly at her.

Laura

No, no, no, thought Laura as panic sent ice through her veins and a need to flee became the forefront of her thoughts. Logically, she knew Nick wasn't trying to save her, or even fix her the way her mother was always trying to do. From the beginning, he'd seemed to accept her jagged edges and scar tissue for what they were: a living, breathing part of her. Rather than judge her choices, he'd walked beside her as she continued to find her way, offering support and empathy.

Seeing Dean in that hospital bed had only reminded her why she and Nick could never be anything more than friends. *Okay, touchy-feely friends,* Laura conceded to the bees swarming her stomach in rebellion.

Laura knew she wasn't being fair to him, but her fear of what the future held was stronger than her faith in the here and now. She had to make him stop looking at her the way he was, like she was the answer to every question he'd ever had. Laura didn't want to want more with him, and she could save them both the heartache of goodbye when she inevitably moved on, because she would, like she always did.

Then why did she suddenly feel so uncertain? It had never been a question before coming to Brooklyn.

At her continued silence, Nick took a step closer, taking her hands into his strong, calloused ones. Her bees droned with contentment at the renewed contact.

"Don't you see, everything—those awful events, and the decisions we made afterward—has all led to right now. This is our fork in the road."

Laura hesitated. Nick deserved someone who had plans to stick around. It would hurt to lose a friend, but it wasn't the same as losing the person who held you in their gravity. So, they would be friends, and she would keep her superglued heart intact when she left, while Nick moved on with another woman.

Thinking of Nick with someone else made her queasy, but this was best for both of them.

Nick took a breath before asking, "Is this about Dean's accident today?"

She swallowed thickly around the knot in her throat. "If only it were that simple."

"I know I can't ever take Drew's place. He's a part of you and you'll always love him. I'm not asking you to let him go, I'm asking you to move forward...with me."

How had she let the last month come to this, Laura asked herself. She'd let her feelings and attraction for Nick override her common sense. She'd taken the affection and attention he doled out so generously, because being with him made her feel like who she wanted to be for the first time since Drew. But now it was time to pay the piper and their friendship would be the cost.

"Look, if this is about today at the hospital, we can work through it. My job comes with certain risks, but crossing the street does too."

He's not wrong, said a ghostly whisper from the recesses of her heart. Laura hadn't heard Drew's voice in a while, not since she'd let herself get caught up in Nick. Even now she wanted to lose herself in his eyes and smile, to take refuge in his arms until the world retreated. It terrified her.

Might as well burn the whole house down, thought Laura. It wasn't rational, but she was beyond being reasonable right now.

"It's not only about the job, Nick. You're attached to your family at the hip. Everything you do is for them, which I admire, but I'm not like you."

She pulled her hands from his to place them on his broad chest and slowly lifted onto her tiptoes, the temptation of those firm lips more than she could ignore any longer. *One little taste.*

Laura touched her lips to his timidly, waiting for him to push her away. When he didn't, she swept over them again, seeking more, wanting something she had no right to ask for under the circumstances. Nick's hands rose to hold her jaw, teasing the short hair at the nape of her neck and sending a thousand tiny sparks throughout her body. She moaned softly, her skin pebbling from the contact. He groaned in response, deepening the kiss with a tilt of her head as she gripped his shirt with her hands, clinging and desperate for more of him.

Heat bloomed in her stomach and spread throughout her body. She wanted to drown in the fire that was Nick. Being with Drew had been sweet and filled with firsts. But Nick wasn't a boy on the cusp of manhood, and she was no longer the innocent girl she'd been ten years ago.

Desire washed over her in waves, until all she could think of was getting closer, and throwing caution to the wind. This is where she belonged.

The intrusive thought was enough to douse her passion with cold reality.

Laura tried to step back, pushing against Nick's chest. "I... have to go," she stammered, ignoring the fear in her voice. Looking dazed and confused by the sudden change, Nick reluctantly released her.

Ashamed of the coward she'd become, too frightened to take a second chance on love, Laura ran until her side cramped and her chest heaved with painful regret.

Chapter 17

Nick

"Hi Pop. Sorry I didn't come to see you sooner, but life's been busy. Yep, I know, isn't it always," Nick said from where he stood under a bare maple tree, the branches casting shadows over his father's grave in the waning sunlight as a cold breeze ruffled his hair in greeting. He shoved his hands into his winter coat. Come the spring, daffodils would replace the withered grass over his father's grave. They were a symbol of hope and rebirth, according to his mother, but today there was little sign of them in either his soul or the barren ground.

"I bought a house yesterday. It's a real fixer, but like you used to say, busy hands keep a man humble." He'd planned to tell Laura about his offer on the house, but the opportunity had gotten lost in the middle of everything else the night of Dean's accident.

Nick sighed in disappointment. *So much for future plans.*

"Truth is, I finally met someone worth my time. Her name is Laura and she's Joe Walker's niece. Funny, huh?"

Nick dropped his gaze to the ground and hummed in agreement. "I knew you'd get a kick out of that. Turns out, all I had to do was walk through the door of our favorite pub to find the right girl." His hand moved up over his chest. "She's a total spitfire like Ma. But she's also sweet and smart." Laura tugged the strings of his heart solely by existing in the world.

"And her laugh—her laugh makes my heart want to jump out of my chest every single time I hear it. I know you'd like her as much as I do," said Nick, trying not to despair over his last interaction with her.

Sure, his ego was a little bruised. He had never had a woman run away from him after a kiss, let alone the kind of kiss that bent a man's will, shattered all his preconceived notions, and made him want to go to war over the woman in his arms. The idea of not kissing Laura again felt tragic, somehow, like a book where you find out the love story was an alternate reality plot line, when in real life the characters never met. Nick swallowed hard past the lump in his throat at the thought.

"Pop, I think she's afraid to be with me because of the job." Nick paused a second before saying, "This is where you make a wisecrack about hazard pay and how no amount is ever enough for what we do or what our families give up," he said, coat straining against his shoulders as he shrugged them. "I know, right. So how do I convince her I'm worth the risk?"

"If you think you might love her, little brother, you fight like hell until she realizes you are," said Leo, dropping an arm around Nick's shoulders. "Because Kellys hold onto hope even when all hope is lost."

His father's familiar words calmed Nick's soul as he joined in the call and response Patrick Kelly had taught every cadet who joined his crew.

"We go where others fear to tread."

"I will stand in the breach."

"Though I may fall."

"My family will see me home."

Nick turned to meet his older brother's eyes, grateful to see him.

"Ma told me I'd find you here. Not that I wouldn't have figured it out eventually. The old man is a good listener when life is in the toilet."

Nick nodded in agreement. "I thought you had a round of chemo today."

"I do. Vinny's in the car. She wanted to give us a minute alone. You know, if you come with me, she can get a pedicure instead of holding my pitiful hand."

"And you know you're married to a rockstar, right?"

"Luckiest man alive right here," said Leo with complete sincerity.

Lucky was not something Nick usually attributed to his brother. The man had survived the front lines of 9/11 only to contract cancer from it ten years later. However, his brother did have Vinny and those two shared the kind of love people wrote about in novels, for better or worse, in sickness and in health.

"You sure are, brother." Nick glanced back at his father's headstone one more time before following his brother to the parking lot. Hopefully, his old man would put in a good word with the man upstairs on his behalf. Winning Laura over was going to require an act of providence.

Laura

Laura shoveled another spoonful of Ben and Jerry's into her mouth. Nothing beat Chubby Hubby's vanilla malted ice cream with pretzels and swirls of fudge and peanut butter goodness for heartache. Uncle Joe had left half an hour ago on a mysterious errand. Laura couldn't be sure, but she thought he might have a secret sweetheart. He'd disappeared multiple times in the last week, and always came back smelling of cheese and salami, or freshly baked bread. Why she associated the smell of a deli with dating, she refused to acknowledge, but more than likely it had something to do with Nick.

Everything reminded her of him these days. Every trip to the park with Micky. Every time she heard a song with a catchy tune.

Every bookstore she passed with book displays perfect for Bookies Club. Every Sunday she ate dinner by herself instead of with the Kelly clan. They were her favorite brand of familial crazy and loyalty all tied together in the man who'd cut through her razor-wired heart with his wit, humor, and affection.

You're totally pathetic, said her inner voice. "I know," she said aloud to the empty bar.

Micky barked and nuzzled her hip with his snout, sitting obediently at her side. He'd become clingy recently. Or she had. Whatever the reason, he seemed to think she needed him close by at all hours of the day. The doggie daycare attendant said he might be depressed, but Laura was fairly certain he was projecting her feelings.

"I miss him too, buddy."

The bell chimed, announcing a customer, and Laura tried to pull her "pathetic" self together, pasting on a smile for the newcomer.

"Are you okay? That smile looks intensely painful, like you've had a root canal without any anesthetic."

Laura let her attempt to look happy wither into a scowl. "Your accent may be sublime, but it doesn't mean your words don't cut deep."

"I take it you've seen neither hide nor hair of Nick yet?" Chaucey asked, eyeing the ice cream container sitting on top of the bar.

"Nope. Honestly, as much as I dread seeing him, I'd still give up the rest of this pint to lay eyes on him."

"Well, that's saying something. Dean mentioned Nick's had a full plate lately. He could simply be busy."

"Busy avoiding me. It's all my fault. If I hadn't kissed him, I could've salvaged our friendship, and none of this would be such a big deal." Laura heard the lie leave her lips, but it made her feel better to pretend the kiss was the only thing standing in the way of her friendship with Nick. Her cowardly heart had absolutely nothing to do with it.

"Hold up. You kissed Nick?!"

Laura cringed. "Um, did I leave that information out of the original telling? Oopsies."

"Okay, wait. If you kissed him, then why aren't you together?" C.J. paused to take a quick breath. "He's not a bad kisser, is he? Don't get me wrong, gorgeous men can be as bad at kissing as anyone, but I never really pictured it being an issue for Nick."

"It's not. He's yummy and delicious and, *really, really* good at it." The bees in Laura's stomach dive bombed her gut in angry retaliation. Her hive was severely disappointed there wouldn't be any repeat performances.

"Good enough to climb him like a tree?" C.J. asked knowingly.

"Yeah, but I didn't, just barely," said Laura rolling her eyes. "You know, it being a public place and a memorial. It seemed a little inappropriate at the time."

"Again, why aren't you two together?"

"Because I'm a coward. But it doesn't matter. I ruined everything with that kiss and now we can't be friends either." Laura seriously didn't know what she'd been thinking at the time. Oh right, she wasn't. Her flight or fight response was severely effed up. "Ugh," she said, planting her forehead on the bar.

"Ahh, Tink. That's cute. You were never going to merely be friends. Americans make everything so complicated."

"Maybe I should move to Britain."

"You could, but it won't solve your problem, so you should probably woman up instead."

Leave it to Chaucey to call a spade a spade. "Here's to big girl undies," toasted Laura as she slid a full wine glass in her friend's direction. Micky barked to mark the occasion, while she wondered when her path would cross with Nick's again. Because she had no doubt it would. The creator of the universe totally had it out for her.

"How's Dean?"

"Healing nicely, and very appreciative," said Chaucey with a naughty gleam in her eye.

"La, la, la," said Laura, putting her hands over her ears. "I do not need to hear the intimate details of your relationship."

Chaucey laughed wickedly in response and took a sip of her pinot gris. "What's with all of the mix-and-match decorations?" she asked after a little while, her eyes roaming the dining room.

"I thought it might be fun to incorporate Hanukkah and Kwanza into the usual Christmas ones this year to better reflect the pub's growing global menu. It's a little much, huh?"

Chaucey shrugged. "Everyone has an opinion these days, but I think it says a lot about a person who can acknowledge their traditions aren't the only ones."

"These are tame compared with some of the ones I witnessed while living abroad," said Laura with a hushed chuckle.

"I bet. Did you ever get to experience Holi when you lived in India?"

"The Festival of Color was my absolute favorite," Laura gushed. "I looked like a human rainbow at the end of the day!"

By the time Uncle Joe returned, C.J. had left for a weekly art class she taught at the local community center for elementary students.

"Uncle Joe, how come you smell like a deli every Thursday and sometimes Tuesdays?"

"Because I'm helping out at Ruth's Deli. I found out her regular delivery guy had to take time off to care for an aging parent who has dementia."

"Oh," said Laura, a little disappointed. Evidently, neither one of them was dating.

Which is what I chose, she reminded herself.

"How'd you find out about the delivery guy? It's not like

Brooklyn's a smalltown gossip mill."

"You'd be surprised how interconnected we are, especially as a local business community. It's like the guy who has six degrees of separation between him and everyone else." Uncle Joe snapped his fingers a couple of times. "His last name is Pork."

Laura laughed at the reference. "You mean Kevin Bacon?"

"Yeah, that's the one!" he exclaimed. "Anyway, I went to one of the neighborhood meetings Father Hugo hosts. He asked if anyone had a need, and I volunteered to fill it."

"It sounds like everyone is involved except me."

"Don't worry, I signed you up to deliver meals to Our Lady of the Bridge this Saturday," said Joe, backing into the kitchen with a tray full of bussed dishes.

"Perfect," said Laura after he'd left. Perfectly awful: church and a potential Nick sighting. She looked down at her furry friend. "Well pal, looks like it's time to put my big girl undies on."

Micky covered his eyes with a paw.

"Well, that concludes this week's community meeting. Remember, if you see something, say something. Look after each other and stay safe," said Father Hugo in closing.

Laura watched from the doorway of one of the Sunday school rooms as Ruth Abrams stood and ambled across the room to sit down in a metal folding chair a short distance from Amir. She waved in their direction, and though Amir returned the gesture, she could tell his thoughts were elsewhere. Or he was still upset with her. They hadn't spoken about anything meaningful in the last few weeks. The kitchen forced them into close proximity, but they were still a little broken by her careless words.

Moving quickly toward the kitchen after saying hello to those she recognized from the neighborhood, Laura drew up short, almost plowing into Father Hugo in the doorway.

"Oh! Sorry, Father."

"No problem. Here, let me take those from you," he said, smiling as he reached for the containers of hot food stacked high in her arms.

Each time she entered the church it became a little easier, if not completely comfortable. Laura would always be grateful to Nick for helping her through those initial visits. It seemed like she belonged anywhere he was. She shook her head to dispel the silly notion.

"Is Nick with you?" he asked as though he could read her thoughts. "You two are inseparable lately."

"We must've missed each other," she fudged, trying not to give away the current state of their relationship. At least she didn't need to worry about running into Nick right this instant. Her big girl undies weren't quite big enough for that yet. Probably because seeing him would make her want to see more of him. She missed her friend.

Fine. My really attractive friend, she conceded to the bees who perked up every time she thought about Nick in any capacity. It was really annoying since she thought about him twenty-four hours a day, seven days a week.

"Well, if you're in town for Christmas Eve, I hope you'll join us for Mass," said Father Hugo before disappearing into the kitchen.

Laura blinked back to reality. "When pigs fly," she mumbled.

"Mind if I sit here?" Ruth asked Amir, while her arthritic knees begged for relief and Bengay. Though she was proud of the deli's success, every year she worked felt more like ten. She should look into those knee replacements her sister had suggested. Then again, with no one to run the deli in her absence, her old knees would simply have to keep holding her up.

Amir nodded respectfully in her direction. "It's good to see you, Mrs. Abrams."

The young man had been her neighbor his entire life. She could remember when his mother would try to scold him, only for his impish grin to gain her laughter instead of her wrath. Ruth had thought him a delightful handful, with his almond-shaped eyes and bouncy curls.

"You're a grown man now, yet I still see the boy who left a note on my door every day for a year after my Ezra passed away. You did not forget me in my grief," she said with a brief pat to his arm.

Smiling at the recollection, he commented, "Mr. Abrams used to sneak me sweets when my mother wasn't looking."

"He always was fond of children. Ezra would have made a wonderful father. Alas, there are certain things that are out of our control," she acknowledged sadly.

Amir's gaze returned to the linoleum floor. Ruth could see the world resting on his shoulders, its weight too heavy for one still so young. Sometimes life came knocking before a person was ready to answer though.

"May I tell you a story?" Ruth asked, not waiting for his response. "My mother came to the United States as a young woman shortly after World War I. She worked as a housekeeper for a rabbi and his family when the offer came to join them and start a new life. Her family urged her to take the opportunity, partially because antisemitism was already on the rise. Of course, she stayed connected with them, reading about their lives from afar—marriages, births, and deaths—until one day the letters stopped coming. All because of one man's desire for power and a Jew-free world."

Amir's head snapped up, and she could see him trying to find the right words to say in the face of such evil. In the end, no platitudes left his lips, for which she was grateful. She had heard them all before anyway, and actions were more important in her experience. "My people are no strangers to prejudice or being the scapegoat for other people's fears. It's like a festering wound that never quite heals. About the time you think it will close, it becomes infected all over again, spreading like wildfire through the rest of the body."

"How do you deal with it?" asked Amir, watching her with something like hope.

She swept her hand toward the rest of the room. "I refuse to give up and I come here. Education is the antidote to ignorance, and I hope it will prevent history from repeating itself."

Amir chewed the inside of his cheek before saying, "With all due respect, Mrs. Abrams, I think it might be more complicated than a few community meetings."

"It is," Ruth acknowledged. "But the truth and dialogue are as good a place to start as any. Silence and isolation have never changed anything."

He nodded solemnly and Ruth continued, "We all come from diverse backgrounds and experiences, our ethnicity, race, and beliefs an integral part of who we are. But so too is our humanity. Surely, this must count for something."

Chapter 18

Laura

Pigs were flying somewhere.

Big, pink, hairy ones, Laura acknowledged with dismay.

She was supposed to be driving to the farm with Kate and Uncle Joe for the holiday. Instead, Uncle Joe had the flu and the airline had cancelled Kate's flight due to severe weather. Her parents were understandably disappointed but agreed with her decision to stay in Brooklyn since the pub would open back up a couple of days after Christmas anyway.

"Are you sure you're okay by yourself, Uncle Joe? I could stay and watch a movie with you while you fall into a medicinally induced sleep."

"Ha, ha," he half coughed from his oversized recliner. "What I need you to do is make sure Father Hugo gets those cookies for his parishioners tonight. Micky will watch *Die Hard* with me, won't you, boy?" Micky lay down at Joe's feet, eyes obediently on the television.

"Okay, but eat the chicken noodle soup I brought. It has extra garlic to help clean out your sinuses. I'll come by after the service to pick up Micky. And no more Nyquil," said Laura, snatching the bottle of flu medication. Uncle Joe would be asleep before the hero of the movie was down to his undershirt.

When Uncle Joe had asked her and Amir to make twelve dozen cookies, she'd assumed they were for the pub, not Christmas Eve Mass at Our Lady of the Bridge. She'd chosen Czech gingerbread cookies decorated like ornaments, snowflake-shaped Italian pizzelles, Greek butter cookies rolled in powdered sugar and, her personal favorite, peanut butter cookies dipped in Belgian chocolate with crushed candy cane.

Laura placed the large cookie tins on a table tucked to the side of the cold sanctuary and snuck into one of the last pews as the children's choir began to sing "Do They Know It's Christmas?" with the lyrics tweaked to match up with current events in the world. She relaxed against the wood at her back, taking in the soft candlelight and tree decorated with colored lights, paper garland, and homemade ornaments. The rest of the service was a simple affair with scripture readings by the kids, several of whom she recognized from the Backdoor Dinners program. After a closing song led by Father Hugo, he called each child forward by name, handing them a beautifully wrapped gift the size of a shoebox.

Walker's Pub, Ruth's Deli, Lavender Honey & Co., and Zaman's Bodega had each contributed to the items within, as had New York's finest and bravest, thanks to the Kelly family's connections. Everything from toiletries, art supplies, and warm socks to toys, books, and fidgets filled every available space and beyond in those boxes. Laura was certain they had needed duct tape to keep them closed. Extras were available for new families following the service, along with a warm welcome.

Laura made small talk with those she recognized from the pub and surrounding neighborhood. If she discreetly kept an eye out for Nick and the rest of the Kelly clan, she was disappointing no one but herself. Father Hugo approached the cookie table, greeting those within earshot jovially, and sporting the gawdiest holiday sweater she'd ever seen in orange, red, and electric blue. One thing was certain; the priest loved his eighties' apparel. She wouldn't be surprised if he had a pair of Hammer pants in his wardrobe.

"I see you were able to come after all. I wasn't sure you would when you mentioned pigs flying first," he said with a knowing twinkle in his eye.

Heat flared into her cheeks. The man might have poor taste in sweaters, but he could hear fine.

"It's got nothing to do with you, Father," Laura said bashfully.

"Then it must be God," said Father Hugo with another knowing look.

"Something like that, but if it makes you feel better, I was pleasantly surprised tonight."

He led her to a nearby pew and looked around the suddenly quiet space. "We used to hold a formal midnight mass for Christmas, but fewer people came with each passing year, until I realized this church would dry up like so many others if we didn't change."

"How so?" Laura asked, thinking of her own relationship with God.

"People don't need fancy decorations and eloquent liturgies; they need a refuge from the world and a community that cares about their daily bread. They *need* to know God loves them."

"Does God love us? I mean, I know the Bible tells me so and all that, but how do we really know?"

"Hmm," he hummed, reminding Laura of her father. "You mean aside from the whole cross and grace scenario?" he asked, half serious. "Maybe we should start with why you doubt God's love."

"He took someone from me. Someone I loved very much," said Laura, swallowing the old grief for Drew and their future. The absence of Nick in her life had given it room to grow, and the holidays added to the heavy feeling of someone missing. Or two someones. "Don't get me wrong; it's not like my situation compares with human trafficking or the atrocities of war."

"Free will is certainly doing a bang-up job of it these days," he acknowledged dryly.

"I thought God was supposed to be in control of things

down here." Rationally, Laura knew Drew's death had been a freak accident, and playing the "what if" game never changed the outcome. Still, her heart wanted someone to blame for its wounds and scars. "Is everything up to fate?"

Father Hugo shrugged, the patterns of his sweater shifting in the overhead lights. "Fate suggests a destiny you can't change no matter what choices you make. I choose to believe in providence instead."

"How is providence any different?"

"Providence is God's provision, regardless of everything else."

"Just not always in the way we want," said Laura, resignation in every word.

"No. But sometimes we get what we least expect—a miracle, a second chance."

"Or a fork in the road," grumbled Laura, thinking of Nick, with his starry eyes and perfectly kissable lips. Of course, there was also the community she'd found because of the pub.

Father Hugo smiled gently as though he could see the distance between her head and her heart as she tried to come to terms with the concept.

"Sometimes, providence is found in how we respond to the suffering around us—a kind word in place of anger, food instead of an empty belly, justice over corruption."

"So, what you're saying is, we love because God first loved us," she said in conclusion, impressed with his ability to deliver a sermon in less than three minutes.

"Now you're catching on," said the priest with a wink.

The end of the year came and went with little personal fanfare. Walker's Pub gave its patrons a low-key celebration with a televised countdown from Times Square, and in the spirit of Auld Lang Syne, horns to blow while friends and strangers alike kissed at midnight. Dean and Chaucey stopped in for a quick drink and well wishes for a happy new year, but still no sign of Nick.

A week later, Bill came in for his weekly lunch without Nick, sitting at the bar to talk with Uncle Joe instead. Laura served him a Spanish seafood paella topped with shrimp, clams, and mussels and a scoop of homemade green tangerine sorbet on the side for dessert, earning her a smile of appreciation. He never implied he knew anything about what had taken place between her and Nick, leaving promptly at one-thirty to catch the bus at the corner.

By dinnertime, the pub was in full swing, the usual patrons and several new ones from the looks of it sat at the bar and in the dining room. Laura glanced out at the corner booth and quickly ducked back behind the kitchen door again.

"Teresa," she hissed at the server loading a second tray with food, "When you said table six, you failed to mention who was sitting there."

"I didn't think it mattered. What's the problem—afraid to meet the in-laws?" Teresa teased, her hazel eyes conveying what her words didn't; Laura was already too involved to chicken out now.

It was her own fault for not telling anyone, aside from Chaucey, about her and Nick's…well, it wasn't exactly a breakup. Her heart shuddered and begged to differ. And the bees who had once annoyed her with their zippy excitement lay motionless in her stomach like baby bumblebees squished in her careless hands.

"Ugh."

"What's up?" asked a male voice directly into her ear.

"Shitake mushrooms!" yelped Laura, jumping a vertical foot. "Uncle Joe, you shouldn't sneak up on a woman like that," she whisper yelled, but he was too busy laughing at her to worry about her reprimand.

"You should see the look on your face right now."

"Yeah, yeah, real funny," said Laura, standing on her tiptoes to peek out at the pub's main dining room through the round window in the door this time.

"What are you doing skulking back here? We have a full house tonight, and Teresa could use help on the floor."

"I know." Laura huffed in defeat. Time to come clean. "The Kellys are at table six."

"So what? You've already met Nick's family."

"True, but I haven't seen them in a while," said Laura, stalling.

"So, you've missed a couple of Sunday dinners. Who cares?

Bill said Nick's been working overtime."

"Oh?" asked Laura, nonchalantly.

"Yeah, the house he bought is a total fixer and he could use the cash. Wait, why does it seem like this is news to you?"

"Uncle Joe, I think I screwed up." Laura quickly filled him in, starting with the night of Dean's accident, leaving out the juicier tidbits, namely the kiss still haunting her dreams and lady parts.

"Let me see if I've got this straight. You broke up with Nick because he's a firefighter, and you're afraid of losing him?"

"Well, technically I didn't break up with him because we were never dating."

"Semantics. You spent all of your free time together, correct?"

"Yeah, I guess so."

"And you're attracted to one another?"

"Um…" she said, not wanting to give him any ammo for his argument.

"Let me rephrase. Are you attracted to him? Because it's obvious to anyone within a ten-mile radius how Nick looks at you—like a starving man sitting down to a steak dinner."

"Eww. Gross, Uncle Joe."

"It's simply a fact, doll. So, is he the butter to your bread or what?"

Laura rolled her eyes. At least he hadn't asked her if she wanted Nick to butter her bread, even if the answer was a resounding, "Yes, please!"

Joe must have seen it in her eyes because all he said was, "Kids these days. What are you waiting for, a sign from God?" he asked, exasperated, as he pushed open the kitchen door.

Laura crossed her arms defensively. It wasn't as if she were entirely to blame. For as much as Nick loved his career, he'd been careful to keep her at arm's length from it. She was sure the only reason he'd called about Dean's accident was for Chaucey's sake. He hadn't even taken the opportunity to introduce her to the Squad when they'd sat mere feet away.

Feeling justified, she conveniently ignored her own reasons for freaking out. Laura relaxed her stance and, finding a semblance of gumption in the pit of her stomach, prepared to follow Uncle Joe into the dining room. When he stuck his head back inside, catching her unaware yet again, she let loose another expletive, this time without the reference to fungi.

Joe grinned. "Come on, doll. There's always a fork in the road on the menu at Walker's Pub."

Nick

Nick looked around the expansive living room taking up the front of his new house. His realtor had called in a couple of favors in order to finalize all of the paperwork in time for the end of the year. After signing away what felt like his life and that of any future children, he'd gone back to his tiny studio apartment, handed in his keys, and loaded the boxes containing his small life into the back of Dean's hatchback. They filled all of one closet in the sole bedroom with any furniture, which wasn't much. A double bed, secondhand dresser, IKEA bookshelf, and reading lamp assumed all of the recently cleaned space.

What was I thinking, he asked himself.

This had to be the worst idea he'd ever had. Nick knew he'd be fortunate to fully renovate the house in the next ten years. The lath and plaster cracked across the walls, resembling the San Andreas fault, and the ceiling was falling down, its light fixtures dangling precariously.

He'd cut the electricity to every space except the kitchen, a bathroom, and his bedroom upstairs to prevent any electrical fires. The old knob and tube fuse box was a disaster waiting to happen. Thankfully, the heat produced by steam radiators used a gas boiler, or living in the house that winter would be unbearable.

His mortgage loan contained a remodel portion and he'd lined up a plumber and electrician to come in when the holidays were over. Nick would stay with one of his sisters if the water needed turning off for an extensive period of time, or he could shower at the station during his shift. It would be money well spent, and once those items were complete, Dean and a handful of the Squad had offered to help put up sheet rock to cut costs. Until then, it was demolition derby time.

Nick double checked the pile of tarped trim he'd removed over the last week to make sure it wasn't anywhere close to the mess he was going to make and swung the sledgehammer over his shoulder until he had the wall down to its studs. It was a sorely needed physical release for the disappointment caused by the green-eyed pixie who haunted his dreams and consumed his waking thoughts. The worst part, though, was his family's intervention.

They had taken it upon themselves to help with his love life by casually running into Laura at the pub. His family was anything but subtle. It was both embarrassing and endearing all at once. None of which mattered if Laura didn't have any romantic feelings for him, despite the kiss she'd laid on him suggesting otherwise.

Nick's conversation with Laura in front of the Memorial had made it glaringly apparent her family wanted to use Brooklyn as a sort of intervention in her life. Loving to travel wasn't unheard of, but she had plainly used it as a crutch. Not that he could blame her. She'd lost the person she was supposed to spend the rest of her life with at a critical time in her own development as a young adult. Running away had become her fight-or-flight response in the face of emotional attachment.

Helping her overcome any concerns around his job was one thing, but helping her hurdle the risks of being in an intimate relationship might be a race only Laura could run. It also meant being friends may be all they ever were, even with their crazy physical chemistry. At least he knew where he stood now and friendship with Laura would be a better alternative than her absence from his life all together.

Nick popped an old CD from Donnie's collection into the bright-pink boom box he'd bought from Gina for three dollars at her yard sale last spring. The La's sang "There She Goes" into the dusty space, and with every swing of the hammer into the plaster, he took out his frustration until he'd let go of the things beyond his control. By the time he'd started on the next wall, his dreams for the future were firmly back in the hands of the universe, or at the very worst, his family's interference.

Chapter 19

Laura

Laura tucked the business card Father Hugo had given her back into her pants pocket and flipped the lights on as she walked through the pub and into the kitchen. At the priest's gentle suggestion, she'd made an appointment for the following week with a counselor who specialized in grief. Chaucey had been a little less subtle in her enthusiasm over Laura's personal growth.

"I'm so proud of you! You're so incredibly brave. Here's to taking steps towards a more fulfilling life," she'd toasted with a mimosa the previous Saturday. Brunch was a new concept Laura was trying out at the pub and hoped to put it into full swing by summer.

The surrounding silence was a balm for the noise in her head as she pulled flour and salt out from their various resting spots, lining them up on the stainless counter. She tucked a towel in at her waist and opened the sourdough starter Mrs. Abrams had gifted her in the spirit of Hanukkah.

When Amir came into the kitchen shortly afterward, she was preparing to knead the bread before setting it aside to rise. Pulling the dough apart for two smaller loaves, she passed him one. Kneading was free therapy and as she worked the dough, she thought about Father Hugo's ideas on providence. Next to her, Amir hummed a tune she didn't recognize, his hands folding and stretching the dough in time to the music on his lips.

"So," she started awkwardly, uncertain how to ask if the situation at the bodega was any better. "How are the community meetings going?"

He shrugged. "They're okay."

"Father Hugo seems like he'd be…a good group leader," Laura finished lamely, dipping her toes in to test the waters. *Group leader?* Subtlety had never been her forte. She blamed it on her mother.

Amir raised one brow in response and then promptly laughed. "You should stick with being blunt."

"I know," she said nodding her head in apology. "How are you doing? For real."

He peeked at her through the fringe of his long dark lashes, his hands still working the dough.

"Things at the bodega are quiet for now. I'm getting to know some of the other group members," replied Amir with another faint shrug of his shoulders. "We don't see eye to eye on everything, but it's a place to start."

"And your parents?"

"They don't want to create any rips in the space-time continuum. You know, in case it could actually change the future," he said sarcastically.

Laura chuckled at his reference to her favorite sci-fi movies from childhood. "Progress can be hard, but anything worth changing starts with a single voice, until there are too many to ignore."

"Mrs. Abrams said something similar."

"Sounds like she knows what she's talking about," said Laura, bumping his shoulder with hers. He bumped her shoulder in return, restoring the easy rapport between them with the silly motion. Laura almost purred with contentment. At least she'd repaired one broken relationship.

Now, if only she could figure out how to make things right with Nick. She may be too much of a coward to be romantically involved with him, but they could still be friends. All she needed to do was keep her hormones under control. Surely, she could refrain from kissing him again.

Putting the bread into a proofing drawer beneath the warm oven, Laura removed her apron and ran her slender fingers through her hair. She needed a haircut if she planned to keep the bedhead look to a minimum, but it would have to wait until Chaucey's stylist could fit her in at the end of the month. Maybe adding highlights would brighten up her mood and appearance.

When she emerged from the kitchen, Teresa was busy setting tables in her typically methodical manner, while Ronan opened the cash register for the day. Lost in her personal musings, Laura almost missed the silent presence sitting at the bar.

"Hi there. Sorry, it seems we're a little behind the eight ball today," said Laura, grabbing one of the weekly paper menus from behind the bar. She'd never seen him at Walker's before, but he reminded her of the lead actor in a K-drama Chaucey had recommended. Laura had binge watched the series the previous weekend and wondered the entire time what Nick would've thought of it.

She missed him, which wasn't a new feeling in and of itself, but for the past ten years the only other person she'd allowed herself to pine for was Drew. Laura had convinced herself being independent and strong meant foregoing other meaningful relationships. It was only recently she'd begun to realize those perceptions might have been at the expense of everyone else who cared for her, let alone herself.

"No worries. I'm putting in an order to go anyway," said the distinguished-looking stranger. The man stood, leaning slightly more than casually on a cane she hadn't noticed until then. He was tall and lean, his jet-black hair lightly peppered with silver at the temples, and the warm smile he flashed her direction caused his eyes to crinkle at the corners. She guessed he was in his early forties, much too young to need a cane for support, unless it was due to an injury or onset of disease.

Whelp, there goes my theory, thought Laura, not in the least bit disappointed.

Celebrities weren't really her thing. A real-world hero, on the other hand, gave her all sorts of uncontrollable urges, including kissing a man she couldn't be anything except friends with. Besides, his job was part of the reason she'd completely freaked out, she reminded herself.

"What can I get you?" she finally asked, feeling ridiculous over her internal monologue.

"My wife loved the dumpling soup you had on the menu last night. It was even better than my mother's, not that I'll ever tell her."

Laura smiled over the compliment. "Thank you. I promise to never tell your mother either," she said with laugh. "I'm sorry but I don't remember seeing you…"

"Actually, neither of us were here. Jules is on bedrest, but my mother in-law brought it by."

"Oh my gosh, you're Dae?" Laura asked, putting two and two together.

He chuckled softly. "DaeSeong Park at your service," he said with a bow of his head.

Laura bowed politely in return. If nothing else, she'd learned to parrot respectful cultural norms on her travels.

"You must be Joe's niece, Laura."

She nodded dumbly. Uncle Joe had taken pity on her and seen to the Kelly table last night, while she ran interference at the bar with Saint. By the time Nick's mother and sisters had paid their check, Laura was back in the kitchen helping Amir.

"You seem to have made quite the impression, which is no easy feat when it comes to Luna. Believe me, I know."

Laura relaxed at his words. Dae had come in peace, it would seem. She was more than a little relieved to find an ally in another outsider.

"She's a tough cookie for sure, but I can't imagine Luna not liking anyone who loves her children," she said, a little worried about what hit list she might find herself on now that she'd demolished her relationship with Nick and disparaged his choice of career—the same career Luna's husband and son had died in service to.

"True. But now that there's a grandchild on the way, I've cemented my place in her good graces," he said with a low chuckle.

"I bet," Laura grinned, picturing the family matron. Luna made for a ferocious parent, doling out sharp words and endearments in equal measure, but she only ever appeared to dote on the girls and Finn. "Give me five minutes and I'll have your order."

"Sounds good," said Dae with another friendly smile. She was almost through the swinging door when his next words reached her. "I know it's not any of my business, but Nick is one of best guys I know."

She glanced over her shoulder to acknowledge his words, then ducked into the kitchen.

The following day, Nick's oldest sister stopped in with a co-worker for a quick bite to eat on her lunch break. They shared a brief but pleasant interaction while Laura nervously took their order and delivered their food.

Wearing her big girl undies paid off when Uncle Joe smiled proudly.

"Way to take the fork in the road, doll," he said as he walked by her on his way to the other end of the bar.

Laura still wasn't exactly certain what he meant by those words but was happy to play along. When Nick's oldest sister approached the bar on her way out, Laura waited on tenterhooks for the condemnation she deserved. Instead, Aria said the last thing she expected to hear.

"I get the whole not being interested in a relationship with a first responder," she said, sounding sad enough that if the situation had been any different, Laura would've hugged her.

Instead, she burned with embarrassment. "Nick told you what happened?"

Aria watched her for a moment, potentially taking stock of how damaged Laura must be to let go of an incredible guy like her brother.

"Not everything, but enough for me to get the gist. Believe me, I understand where you're coming from more than most. If anyone is worth the risk, though, it's Nick."

The pattern of Kellys coming into the pub continued for the rest of the week. The next day it was Leo and Vinny for a cider and a Guinness at a cozy two top in the back room. His smile reminded Laura so much of Nick, she thought her heart might give out from the way it clenched. The couple said hello and goodbye and the one indication they knew anything were Leo's parting words: "He's worth the risk, sweetheart. No one is more loyal than a Kelly."

Obviously, Laura bemoaned. In fact, she'd never met a family so dedicated to each other. The question was, were they coming in on their own accord or was Nick trying to get her to lower her defenses against him? Laura wasn't sure if she wanted to know the answer.

Gina came in with the girls on Friday night for dessert. Laura was fairly certain the only Kelly to come into the pub regularly before recent events had been Nick. He remained missing in action, but his relations were very vigilant and unafraid to speak their mind.

"Hi Laura!" Eleanor and Sofi said in unison.

"Hi girls," Laura replied, past the point of feeling anxious when anyone from the family came in. They were on a harmless mission to change her mind, not that she could blame them. She knew how amazing Nick was, and for that reason alone she needed to keep her distance. Falling for him meant eventual heartbreak for both of them. Brooklyn was still her temporary home, and Laura would never dream of asking Nick to quit his job or leave his family.

"We missed you at Bookies Club last month," said Sofi, looking disappointed. "We finished *Breaking Dawn*."

"I'm really sorry," said Laura. And she was. She felt guilty for abandoning their small group as much as she missed debating with Nick the pros and cons of a plotline.

"Maybe you could come this month," said Eleanor, hope shining in her eyes. "You could make it up to us."

"Um, I don't know. What book are you reading?"

"Uncle Nick is going to pick it out this weekend. He could drop off a copy for you."

"I don't want him to go to any trouble," said Laura, trying to back pedal.

"Oh, it's no trouble at all," said Gina, joining the fray of sharks circling Laura with devious grins. "I'm sure Nick would be more than happy to come by on the girls' behalf."

"Okay," Laura squeaked. She'd worry about it in real time if Nick actually stopped by with a book, which he wouldn't, because there was no way he wanted to see her. He would've come by the pub by now if he actually missed her half as much as she missed him. She rubbed the spot above her heart, where Nick had taken up permanent residence. Her memories of Drew hadn't even bothered to balk at the intrusion. They'd simply made room for their new companion.

Luna was the last of the Kelly clan to make an appearance the following Wednesday, and she wasted no time with pleasantries as she slid onto a stool at the bar.

"Diet Coke, a lime, and extra ice please," she said, all business.

"Coming right up," said Laura, glancing back and forth between the glass she piled ice into and the head of the Kelly family. Luna didn't seem mad per se, but she also didn't seem like she wanted to chat it up either. Laura gave her a wide berth. Well, as wide a berth as she could manage while working behind the bar.

Luna was three quarters of the way through her drink and waiting for the food she'd ordered when a familiar face walked in and instantly matched stares with Laura.

"Ma," said Nick, kissing Luna's cheek and meeting Laura's eyes again before trailing them over her frame to take inventory of what he'd missed during his absence.

Laura shivered involuntarily in response, feeling as though he'd trailed his hands over her bare skin instead. She gulped as warmth engulfed her in the most delicious way.

"Hi Nicky," said Luna with a pat on his cheek. "I'm glad you're here. I've got to run, but your food is coming."

"I thought we were having an early dinner together."

"You're having an early dinner. I have other plans," she stated without further comment, giving Laura a quick wink.

What a sly minx, thought Laura, taking note for future reference. She would make sure to never underestimate the Kelly matriarch again. Luna was positively wily.

"Okay, here's your book," he said, removing a paperback from a non-descript, white plastic bag, still watching Laura from beneath his baseball cap and long lashes.

"It's not for me," she said, her smirk so much like Nick's that Laura did a double take.

"Then who's it for?"

"Laura. She told the girls she'd be at Bookies Club this month." Luna moved to pat Laura's cheek the way she had Nick. "I'll see you at Sunday dinner this weekend. Nick has the day off." It was neither a question nor a request. Laura dumbly nodded in the affirmative, her mouth ajar in astonishment.

Chapter 20

Nick

Nick removed his New York Mets cap and ran his hand through his hair, keeping his eyes glued to his shoes, mostly so he could keep from staring at the beautiful woman in front of him. "It would appear we've been the latest victims of my mom's scheming."

"Yeah, but in all fairness, she isn't the first Kelly who's ambushed me this week."

"About that," he said, embarrassment over his family's interference creeping into his cheeks. He was starting to realize there might be some truth to what Laura had said about his family ties being a little too tight. Being available to help his family didn't mean foregoing a life outside of them. His next vacation would be sans relatives, and somewhere far away from New York instead of camping. "I swear I didn't ask them to. I've been busy and they decided to take matters into their own hands."

"Your momma totally slipped past your force field. Next time, Captain America, try using a Vibranium Shield."

Nick's head flew up at the reference. Laura grinned back at him, her left eyebrow arched in challenge, and suddenly the balance in his world righted itself.

"I can live with superhero status if you're handing it out."

Laura laughed, and his heart tugged in response, sending his wilted butterflies soaring through his chest.

Keep your cool, he reminded them, reigning in his air show.

He sat down on the stool his mother had vacated, tapping his fingers nervously on the bar when Laura disappeared into the kitchen. When she appeared a minute later carrying a plate filled with coffee and chili-rubbed pot roast, an assortment of roasted seasonal veggies, and Moroccan couscous, he almost drooled. So much for his New Year's resolution to eat less red meat.

He picked up his fork and dove in. "This right here is worth every bit of sneakiness on my mom's part. I can't believe I almost missed pot roast," he said around the tender meat melting in his mouth. He'd never had anything so perfect. Except Laura's lips. He inhaled the piece in his mouth at the thought.

"I'm glad you like it, but there's no need to get choked up over it."

Laura pounded his back as he tried to dislodge the piece stuck halfway down his throat.

"Funny," he said hoarsely. "Where did you get the idea for the roast rub?" he asked, his voice turning to gravel as he thought of Laura's hands rubbing him down, and where else he'd like to have her put them on him.

"My dad and I share a love for coffee, and the espresso in Italy is incredible. I was drinking a cup after dinner one night in this little square in Florence and I started thinking about how I could incorporate it into a recipe. It's like taking a piece of wherever I am with me when I go."

Nick continued to shovel food into his mouth and tried to focus on what Laura was telling him instead of where his imagination kept trying to take him.

"I want to add penne with brie as a substitute for the couscous once I get the proportions worked out for the prosciutto and truffle oil."

"Sounds like a good French-Italian combo."

"Precisely. I was looking through photos from my time there, and inspiration struck."

"I have to admit, I'm actually a little surprised you're still in Brooklyn. You sprinted away from the Memorial so fast I expected you to be halfway across the world by now." It wasn't what he'd planned to say, but now that the words were out there, he didn't want to take them back.

Self-consciously, she tucked a piece of hair behind her ear and kept her eyes on the bar. "Honestly, I considered it, but since I have Micky…" she trailed off, worrying her bottom lip.

Nick took pity on her. She obviously felt bad about how

everything had played out. There would be a time and a place to get into this conversation but right now wasn't it.

"Don't forget Joe, C.J, and Dean," said Nick.

"True," she said with a sadness that crushed him.

"And then there's me. I mean, who else are you going to totally geek out with?"

The paltry smile on her face grew into a full grin, making the beats of his heart trip over themselves in response.

"I've missed you," she admitted softly, the brightness in her eyes giving away the truth.

Every good firefighter knew when to call it. There were times when you had to admit you couldn't do anything more. You could only hope to keep the damage to a minimum and everyone safe, including yourself.

"I've missed you too. Friends?" he asked, before he could chicken out.

"Friends," she replied, beaming broadly.

So much for playing it safe, Nick thought. At least he wouldn't have to spend Purgatory wondering what he'd missed. His butterflies consented wholeheartedly, taking flight past his defenses.

Laura

Wearing an extra top layer and gloves, Laura pulled the zipper up on her lightweight peach fleece and stared up at the cloud-laden sky.

Snow was in the forecast, but she hoped it would hold off until the afternoon.

"Come on, buddy, let's get in some more time this morning in case we're snowed in tomorrow." Micky padded beside her, content to follow her lead.

She forced her breathing into a nice, even pattern and relaxed her hand on the leash as she took the path for Breeze and Sullivan Hills. The loop was a familiar one she and Micky had taken over the past few months. It was a little longer than her usual three miles, but she figured she could use the time to sort out her swirling thoughts.

Laura had shown up for Sunday dinner as commanded by the Kelly matriarch, dessert in hand, this time with homemade fluffernutter cookies and mocha ice cream. If she was going into battle, she may as well have emotional reinforcements at the ready. To her relief, both were a big hit, and the girls had requested she bring dessert for their next book club. She was planning to use lots of peanut butter. Desperate times called for desperate measures.

Nick had been the very definition of cool, calm, and collected, keeping his affection toward her entirely platonic, sadly. As it turned out, Laura had missed his friendship, but she'd also missed his touch, teasing flirtation, and everything else she'd had access to before making a total ninny of herself.

Chaucey was right about making things overly complicated. In retrospect, she could've handled everything in a far less dramatic fashion, but panic can be a powerful propeller of stupidity. Instead of communicating to Nick what was going on in her brain, she had ripped their entire relationship apart at the seams, when she'd only needed them to sew on a few more buttons until her head could get in sync with her heart.

Asking for a takeback after her behavior felt lame, so she stuffed her face with Luna's superb Bolognese Ragù and tried to behave as if everything were normal between them. Except she'd had to use her napkin to wipe the drool from the corner of her mouth repeatedly. Nick made a t-shirt look better than cotton deserved, and she staunchly refused to acknowledge how good he made a pair of jeans look from behind.

At this rate, she'd be lucky if she didn't spontaneously combust before leaving Brooklyn in her rear-view mirror—though exactly when she would do so, or where she would go, had become a bit murky. Originally, she'd planned to leave when Kate returned from London. Central America had moved to the top of her bucket list over the course of her research the previous summer, but her list for sticking around was steadily gaining precedence.

One, Uncle Joe had officially made her the pub's manager, with an offer to buy in whenever the whim struck her.

Two, Chaucey was a better wing woman than Kate, whom she'd only spoken to through voicemail in the last month and a half. Granted, Laura had never made the effort to stay in touch on a regular basis before. It was usually her sister's job to check in. Still, Kate was officially on Laura's hit list, but only the one that started with a lower-case s.

Three, keeping Micky was a non-negotiable. *See point number two.* Besides, if she was going to be her own superhero, Laura needed a sidekick, and Micky made for a formidable one. He loved her unconditionally, never questioned her judgment (though maybe he should), and he liked to eat as much as she did. It was a match made in heaven.

And last, but worthy of an Adonis award for his good looks, was Nick. He had a gift for making her feel as though she belonged wherever he was. Yet again, another turn of events she hadn't expected when she'd tried to ditch him from her life. It didn't matter whether it was the inside of a church, Walker's Pub, or his parents' home, she fit solely because he did. The idea was both preposterous and exhilarating.

Preposterous, because she couldn't remember when she'd last felt like a fixture instead of a visitor. And exhilarating because there was hope for her yet. No matter how many times she tried to convince herself otherwise, Nick was enough to make her consider growing roots beneath the Brooklyn concrete.

Laura almost laughed. Nick Kelly had managed to accomplish in four months what her parents had been trying to do for years. Her hibernating hive perked up, giving her an extra boost of energy.

"Oh yay, I didn't kill you!" she declared loudly, causing Micky's head to whip up and look at her. "Not you, buddy. I was talking to the bees." He cocked his head again before returning his gaze to the path in front of them as though her outburst were an acceptable occurrence instead of signaling a need for a psychiatric visit. Yet another reason she was keeping him. She added it to her mental tally.

I'm so glad you were only hibernating, she said internally this time, happy to know she was capable of more than killing relationships and innocent bees. Well, the bees anyway. Her friendship with Nick said more about his ability to forgive and his family's determination than it did about her.

Seeing him walk into the pub had been…transcendent. As if time had come to an abrupt stop. The rest of the world went on spinning, but Nick was all there was for her at that moment. Where there had been churning chaos before, she'd felt a steady sense of peace roll over her. She was the sand, and he was the waves pulling her closer with every glance, every word.

Laura was halfway through her run when her sixth sense kicked in, dragging her from her dopey thoughts. Her father had taught her to always trust her intuition. If something felt wrong, then it most likely was. She looked around, trying to figure out where the possible danger could be coming from, but the lone person behind her was a walker who didn't appear to be in any hurry to catch up. Still, the sensation of someone watching her from afar hit once again as the hairs prickled along the back of her neck.

The trees to her right weren't dense enough to hide in, but the ones on the left might provide a good place to watch from a distance. She had decided to wait and take her chances with the walker when Micky started barking at the trail ahead. Coming over the next small rise, a familiar looking dachshund and his owner were doing a half jog, half shuffle in their direction. Relieved, she and her companion met them halfway.

"Hey, fancy seeing you two here. It's a beautiful morning for a run," greeted Malcom cheerfully, despite the gray.

"Yeah, we were planning to do the loop, but I think we'll turn around here. Any chance we can join you and Bixby?"

"Sure, as long as you don't mind the slow pace," he said.

"My hamstring is happy for the rescue," she fibbed. "This is perfect."

"Okay, let's shuffle."

Laura slowed to a minimal jog, the dogs trotting between her and Malcom. She kept an eye on the trees, occasionally looking back over her shoulder. She was beginning to think it was nothing but a self-induced freak out when the leash went taught, and Micky bared his teeth. He growled low in his chest at the woods they had recently passed.

Malcom came to an abrupt stop next to Bixby, who'd joined his canine friend; whether out of solidarity or because the threat was real, she couldn't discern. It was unlike Micky to behave in such a manner, which merely added to Laura's unease.

"It's probably a stray animal, or someone who's decided to camp out." Malcom pulled Bixby along by his harness until the dog's tiny legs pushed him over the trail in a jaunty waddle once more.

"There are homeless camping in the park's woods?"

"Until the city moves them on," Malcom said, without any judgment.

"What about the local shelters; can't they stay there?"

"The shelters are usually pretty crowded in winter, due to the frigid temps, but some of the people I know find the rules hard to follow, or mentally can't deal with the close quarters and concrete walls."

"Because of what they experienced overseas?" Laura asked, assuming he was referring to other veterans.

Malcom nodded in confirmation. "Sometimes. Financial help is rarely all that's needed."

"I imagine mental health is a part of the puzzle too," said Laura gently.

"For sure, and then there's rehab and recovery for those with chronic pain or addictions."

"Sounds like a complex issue."

"It is, but at least programs like Backdoor Dinners provide a meal and a little dignity. You never know where a brief moment of connection could lead."

Laura's head bobbed up in down in agreement, thinking about how to make the pub a regular partner of the program instead of an emergency fill in. She already knew Uncle Joe would be happy to help, and maybe Father Hugo could find a way to encourage more veterans like Malcom to get involved.

By the time she'd cleaned up and found Uncle Joe and Amir in the kitchen stocking the produce delivered mid-morning, she'd forgotten about the incident in the park, telling them about her new mission for the pub instead.

Chapter 21

Nick

"I mean if Rachel and Ross could be friends, then so can Laura and I," said Nick, referring to the hit television series *Friends.*

"Except Rachel and Ross were never really just friends," said Dean, holding up a piece of sheet rock while Nick screwed it into the studs. "They were always in love with each other, even when they were with other people."

"Stupid break," mumbled Nick. Anyone who was a fan knew how Ross had ruined everything by sleeping with another girl when he and Rachel were on a break but hadn't broken up.

"They were on a break, man."

Nick stared at his friend.

"I'm kidding, dude. Thanks to Ross, everyone in our generation knows a break is not a breakup, which means no hookup."

"Now you sound like Joey."

"Thanks. He was my favorite character."

Nick moved his head from side to side, at a total loss for words, and pulled another sheet from the pile. They'd been putting up sheet rock for the last couple of hours while the electrician worked on the opposite wall. "Ma invited her to dinner last Sunday, and she's coming to the next Bookies Club, so at least I get to hang out with her again soon."

"How come your mom never invites me to dinner?"

"Because you're you. But maybe if you finally propose to C.J. you'll earn a place at the table."

"Done. I bought the ring last week."

"Seriously?" asked Nick, flabbergasted by his best friend's announcement.

"Mm-hm. No point in waiting, once you know, right? Besides, no one else is going to put up with my stupidity."

No joke, thought Nick, feeling a little jealous. He pushed away the notion, stuffing his misplaced feelings behind him. "Did you know before the accident?" he asked, switching gears.

"Contrary to popular belief, I'm not a total idiot, but the accident helped put things into perspective. Feels like I'm seeing things clearly for the first time in a while."

"Congrats, man."

"Don't congratulate me yet. She has to say yes first."

"What's your plan?" asked Nick, getting excited for his friends and the life they were building together.

"No idea, but I thought a big gesture might help my cause."

"I've got you covered," said Nick grinning ear to ear. "Here's what we're going to do."

....

Nick stared down the old-school rotary phone on his desk. He shook his head back and forth. Why no one had replaced the outdated piece sometime in the last thirty years was beyond him, but his bet was on budget cuts.

Technically, he wasn't on shift but had plenty of paperwork to catch up on and a schedule to make. Distracted by thoughts of last Sunday night's dinner with Laura, he wasn't making any progress. Nick had been one hundred percent on his best behavior. He didn't hug her like he wanted to when she'd arrived, looking amazing in a floral dress, feminine wiles calling for him to make physical contact. *Any kind would do,* his addled brain had shouted. Okay, it hadn't been his brain, but all those urges had a purpose, and it was to desire the woman in front of him.

At dinner, he'd sat on his hands when he wasn't stuffing his face, to keep from holding her hand or putting his arm around her chair. Affection was a slippery slope he couldn't afford to slide down. Frankly, he deserved an Emmy for his stellar performance. If friendship was what Laura needed, then he would be the best friend she'd ever had, even if it killed him.

A grin slowly made its way across his face. Since he'd declared himself her official bestie, he really should call to remind her they were meeting at his place for Bookies Club on Tuesday. It seemed a little unorthodox to host on Valentine's Day, but his sisters traditionally did a Galentine's in the city instead, depending on Gina's schedule at the hospital. Finn was going to have a movie and pizza night with Nonna, but the nieces had requested to meet up with him for their monthly book discussion and toast marshmallows over the gas camping stove.

It was as good an excuse as any to talk with Laura and this way his imagination was the only thing he had to contend with. Unfortunately, his imagination was an over achiever, and he was already picturing her lips, hips, and rump. Then there was her waist, and—

Nick forced himself to focus and ended the self-torture. He dialed the pub, watching the digits go around one after the other and waited eagerly for someone to pick it up on the other end. Glancing at his watch out of habit, he tapped out a beat with the pen in his hand, while a song played on repeat inside his head. He'd almost given up when someone finally croaked, "Walker's Pub."

"Hey, this is Nick. I was calling to speak with Laura, but Kermit the Frog will do."

"Ha, ha. I'm sick."

"I can hear that. You sound like you should be in bed. How

come you're working today?"

"Uncle Joe sent me packing two minutes ago. I was on my way out, but someone was calling."

Nick chuckled over how disgruntled she sounded. "I won't keep you then. Get some rest," he said and hung up.

Who am I kidding, he asked himself. There was no way he was getting any work done now. He left the engine house five minutes later, stopping to grab a small bouquet from the shop on the corner and pick up soup from the deli. He was bounding up the stairs behind the pub when the door opened, revealing a red-nosed Laura and a rear-end wagging Micky.

"I think he must have Nick radar, because he started for the door before your feet hit the first stair."

"Dogs have superior hearing," he said, looking her over with concern as he stepped past her into the apartment.

Nick took in her glassy eyes, pale face, and the box of tissues next to a bottle of acetaminophen on the coffee table. He used the back of his hand to feel her cheek and forehead.

"Yep, you're rocking a fever. Did you already take these?" he asked, gesturing toward the bottle.

"I was going to, but someone showed up at my door," she complained. He smiled, amused, and walked toward the kitchen to find a vase for the flowers. Laura followed him and sat in one of the woven grass chairs to watch him search for something suitable in size. He noticed she wore an over-sized chunky sweater with a pair of leggings and merino wool socks. Cozy, natural, and still capable of turning him on even though she was sick.

"I like your hair. Did you get it cut?"

"Yeah, and highlights. This dreary weather is killing my mojo."

Nick thought her mojo was working fine. No matter how often he told himself she was only his friend, his heart proved him wrong.

"Snowdrops are my favorite," she rambled while he arranged them into a squat, square vase he'd found beneath the sink. "They look so delicate, but they're actually really hearty, blooming at the end of winter before all of the other spring flowers have the courage to come out."

Nick thought she could be talking about herself even if she didn't how true it was yet. He made a mental note to thank Chaucey for the insider info and snagged a spoon from a drawer, taking the paper bag from the deli back over to the couch in the living room. Laura sat at the opposite end and opened the container he handed her.

"Mm, minestrone. This looks amazing even if I can't smell it. Ooh, and you brought bread too." Laura bit into the miniature loaf, taking a huge chunk out of it. She groaned with pleasure.

He chuckled and grabbed her feet off the couch beside him, placing them over his legs so she could stretch out. Then he pulled a thick blanket over her to keep her warm until the meds had a chance to kick in.

"Want to watch something?" he asked while she shoveled soup into her mouth using the bread. She barely stopped long enough to bob her head up and down. Nick grabbed the remote with one hand and popped off one of her socks with the other.

Laura groaned again when he started massaging the arch of her foot. "Oh my gosh, who taught you how do that?"

Nick lifted an eyebrow.

"Oh right, three older sisters."

A half hour later she'd fallen asleep, mouth wide open with an intermittent congested snore. Nick thought it was cute, which proved yet again that he was a total goner where she was concerned. Gingerly removing himself from beneath her legs so he wouldn't wake her, he gave Micky a quick ear scratch, checked his food and water bowls, and left.

Laura

"Wait, let me get this straight," said Chaucey on the other end of the line.

Laura switched the phone from her left to right ear, holding it against her shoulder while she held up one of the recent sweaters she'd purchased and then another against her chest in front of the floor-length mirror. Chartreuse to compliment her eyes or teal for a more subtle but chic vibe? Laura rolled her eyes at herself and followed up by sticking her tongue out at her reflection.

"Nick brought you flowers and soup when you were sick, tucked you in on the couch, and massaged your feet until you fell asleep like Sleeping Beauty."

Laura held up the sweaters one more time, gave her reflection the stink eye, and tossed the clothing to the bed to free up her hands. "I never said I was Sleeping Beauty," she argued, pacing the plush oriental rug and what little hardwood floor it left uncovered.

Micky opened one eye from where he was napping, yawned, and stretched until he'd officially taken up a good portion of the bed as if to say, *I don't care which sweater you pick so long as they don't interfere with my plan for today.*

"That is beside the point," Chaucey chided.

"I know," Laura said, twisting her lips back and forth in defeat. "Nick is the kind of man who buys tampons for the women in his life."

"As he should. Menstruation is a completely normal occurrence."

Laura could picture the annoyed look on her friend's face, prompting her to ask, "Does Dean…"

"Buy feminine hygiene products for me? For all his machismo ways, he's actually great with all that. He also shows up with wine, fancy chocolate, and an Agatha Christie—I love her books. He calls it my monthly care package."

"Wow."

"You didn't think I kept him around for his looks alone, did you? Despite how it might appear sometimes, he's really a sweetheart. Anyway, have fun at Bookies tonight and call me tomorrow, Sleeping Beauty."

Laura threw the phone onto the bed and snatched up a sweater and a pair of jeans before heading for the bathroom to freshen up. She didn't bother to lie to herself about whom she wanted to look nice for.

• •

Snow fell in fat flakes, sticking to and accumulating quickly on concrete and nature alike, despite Punxsutawney Phil's spring prediction on the first day of February. Laura had left Micky sleeping on her bed. There was no point in dragging him out into the frosty weather with her. She tromped through the snow, leaving prints in the mounds of gathering white fluff as she tugged her knitted cap back into place over her ears.

She should have spent her money on a proper winter coat instead of the sweaters. The one she owned had worked well enough until now, but with the wind chill, the only warm part of her was her feet thanks to the waterproof, lambswool-lined boots Kate had left behind.

She sighed, sending a puff of warm breath into the cold. Valentine's Day had never really been her thing, even when Drew had been alive. Money had been a source of disagreement between them on multiple occasions, primarily because she came from it. But while Drew had lacked certain financial means, he'd always made up for it with creativity. It was something she'd appreciated, and encouraged by downplaying the gifts and fancy golf club dinners other couples they knew did to celebrate.

As usual, her sister had acknowledged the date with full fanfare, all the way from London. Kate had sent her a homemade Valentine card shaped like a heart, layered in construction paper, lace, and ribbon with a poem from Byron scrawled across the front of it in her sister's perfect calligraphy because, in spite of everything she'd been through, her sister remained a total devotee of romance. Sometimes, Laura envied her ability to be so optimistic. Or she was simply too pragmatic to engage in what she considered a commercialized opportunity to express feelings for someone who might not always be around.

Never mind, she told herself. She had reached a whole new level of jaded in recent years. Just call her a Valentine's Day killjoy. Except spending the evening discussing a book with two teenage girls and eating s'mores sounded like the ideal date at the moment.

Probably because it also involves Nick, quipped her inner voice.

She picked up her pace, not even attempting to squash the excitement of the bees buzzing in her stomach over the thought of seeing him.

When she arrived at his front door a short distance later, Laura had to admit she was a little impressed. She'd expected to see something more run down when Nick mentioned buying a fixer upper. Raising her hand to the knocker on the door, which could've used a new coat of paint, she looked up and down the row of brownstones and smiled.

If the house only needed minor repairs and cosmetics, then Nick had done well for himself. The neighborhood was centrally located and an ideal place to raise a family. It was the kind of neighborhood Laura would've chosen to settle down in. Not that she currently had any plans to move in such a direction, but the thought of "someday" had potential. She was still considering the prospect when the door opened to reveal a very apologetic-looking Nick.

Chapter 22

Laura

"Hey, I tried to reach you before you left."

"I was helping Uncle Joe prep for the dinner crowd and my cell phone is buried somewhere in this bag," she said as she handed him a reusable bag with everything they needed for s'mores. "Why, did you need me to bring something else?" Laura asked as she pulled off her insufficient coat.

"My sisters decided not to go out at the last minute because of the weather. They're going to do Galentine's at home with the girls instead, since Finn is already with my mom for the night."

"Oh," said Laura, feeling awkward—less so about spending time with Nick alone and more because of the holiday.

"Look, I know this is a little weird, but the fourteenth is only a number on the calendar. If you want to hang out, we can still do s'mores before you head home."

Laura hemmed and hawed in her head for a minute, but in the end decided there couldn't be any harm in dessert. Besides, his attitude about the day seemed to mesh well with her own. Even though couples like Chaucey and Dean made it a big deal, it didn't mean everyone had to. And she and Nick were friends.

Friends, she repeated the word to herself. Her heart lurched in disappoint at the label, but she said, "Okay."

Yippee! buzzed the Nick fan club within her stomach. Who was she kidding, Laura thought. Her heart was doing a full-on dance to *Stayin' Alive* by the Bee Gees as if the man standing so close to her was its sole reason for beating.

"Really?" he asked looking a little surprised, but then he said, "Right this way."

Laura was glad she'd worn a sweater. The house was on the chilly side, but the real shocker was the disastrous state of the first floor. In need of a dumpster fire didn't begin to cover it.

She had always thought of Nick as an optimist, but he might be delusional if this is what he considered a fixer upper. Granted, part of why the formerly elegant house looked so pitiful was because he'd stripped the entire downstairs to its bones. The huge pile of lath and plaster on top of a tarp in the center of the living room didn't add to the aesthetic either.

The kitchen looked intact, but the cracking plaster and peeling linoleum supported her overall first impression.

"I know it looks bad," said Nick.

Laura's eyes widened at his declaration.

"All right, really bad."

"Yeah."

His shoulders drooped in defeat at her confirmation.

"But at least we have s'mores," she said looping her arm through his in consolation and maybe because it was as good an excuse as any to touch him. "A peanut butter cup, toasted marshmallow tower of perfection, with the teensiest drizzle of caramel between the graham cracker layers and all of this will melt away. At least for tonight."

His smile reflected back at her was all it took for Laura to fully relax. Whatever the calendar's date, she was more than happy to spend it with Nick, crumbling house and all.

By the time they'd finished their s'mores the snow had tapered off, but with the accumulation, Brooklyn appeared to have come to a standstill. Peeking through the front window, Laura took note of the cars parked at the curb, buried in layers like a bride's wedding gown, the train formed from drifts against the tires.

"Looks like there's at least a foot out there," said Nick, rubbing his hands together now that they were away from the camping stove. "Sorry about the cold in here. The radiators run off a gas boiler, but they've been a little finicky lately."

"One more thing to fix, huh?"

"One of a growing list," he said, looking bashful.

It was completely endearing on a man who usually had the confidence of ten, and caused Laura to feel a little swoony until she remembered that she'd have to walk home in the snow if she couldn't hail a cab. Turning to Nick, she was getting ready to ask if he'd be willing to walk with her, but as usual he'd already anticipated her need and was putting on his winter gear.

"At this rate, you might have the house livable by 2020."

A laugh rumbled from Nick as he bent over to lace up his snow boots, his easy-going nature taking the ribbing all in stride.

He put his shoulder to the door and shoved. It stuck in the jam, and not only because of the snow.

"It tends to stick when the temperature changes."

Laura made a joke about door jams getting another chuckle from Nick, but the joke was on Laura when they walked back through the front door two minutes later.

"So, it's a little deeper than we thought," said Nick. The amount of snow combined with the wind chill factor meant a long walk in below-freezing temperatures, none of which was a smart idea, no matter how awkward the night had turned. "I'm sure the roads will be clear by morning. You can stay the night."

"All right," Laura replied nervously.

"I'm going to take a quick shower," said Nick on his way up the stairs. "The bedroom's this way. It will be easier to stay warm in there, assuming the radiators kick back on at some point." Nick didn't seem at all fazed by the turn of events, and she knew he was simply being a good friend.

"Great!" Laura squeaked.

Nick smiled reassuringly at the high pitch of her voice but didn't say anything as he disappeared down the hallway at the top.

Calm down. It wasn't like they were actually going to sleep together, she reassured herself. At least not in the way her hormones were pleading with her to do. It'll be like sharing a bed with Lon, she tried to convince herself. Except her feelings for Nick went well beyond those of brotherly affection. She'd passed by the no trespassing signs of friendship the moment she'd kissed him at the Memorial.

Who was she trying to kid anyway? She wanted Nick, regardless of how risky his job might be. It was a line she was inching toward again with every hangout, but first, she'd have to get through tonight without totally embarrassing herself.

By the time she'd talked herself into climbing the stairs, she could hear him singing in the shower, which took a little of the edge off. It was so Nick-like. She smiled and stopped to listen for a minute, her forehead against the door.

If only she'd bothered to pay attention to whether the water was running, she might have moved away before it flew open to a still-damp and mostly naked Nick.

"Sweet Mary, mother of God," she murmured at the sight of all his chiseled perfection within touching distance of her. Her eyes trailed over his broad shoulders, to the chest that was a sculptor's dream, down the abdominal muscles carved of stone, and past a happy trail to his narrow hips where fingers barely held onto a towel much too small to conceal every detail.

She swallowed audibly and forced her eyes back up to meet his twinkling ones, a smirk comfortably situated on his lips in light of her open admiration. Laura blushed so hard she knew her face was fire engine red.

"There's an extra toothbrush in the drawer, if that's what you're looking for," he said, watching her burn up in his presence, every part of her entirely hot and bothered, until his gaze moved from amused to…

Was that smoldering invitation? She was at a total loss for words, a rare occasion to be sure. Laura always had a comeback. Instead, she nodded and watched as he strutted past her to a room down the hall, wearing his tiny towel like he was king of the runway.

It was too much to take in. Laura burst out laughing, and Nick's answering wink over his shoulder served to confirm he was everything her quivering, calloused heart could ever want.

Nick

By the time Laura had finished brushing her teeth, Nick had already put on a t-shirt and flannel pajama pants. He thought she looked a little disappointed, which made him smile. Finding her outside the bathroom had been a surprise but not an unwelcome one with the way she'd looked at him. Her desire had sparked his own and been a serious boost to his morale. Attraction was half the battle and, since they were already friends, why not the love of each other's lives?

Laura rubbed her hands together for warmth and complained, "It's like Antarctica in here."

"Have you actually been there?" he asked, digging through one of his dresser drawers. Knowing her record, it wasn't beyond the realm of possibility, but even the North Pole felt a little extreme in terms of running away.

"Nope, but this feels like a close second right now."

Nick tossed something in her direction. "Here, this should keep you warm."

She caught the fabric with her face, bringing the shirt up to her nose a second time and smiling. Nick smiled too, turning away so Laura wouldn't catch him. He could win her over one sniff at a time if that's what it took.

Laura looked down at the long-sleeved thermal Henley and finally bobbed her head in agreement. "Thanks, anything is better than sleeping in jeans and an itchy sweater."

Nick slipped outside into the hallway to give her privacy, knocking a couple of minutes later to make sure the coast was clear.

"Come in." Laura was in the bed with the covers pulled up to her chin, and aside from her teeth chattering, he had to admit with more than a little primal satisfaction that he enjoyed seeing her there. Unfortunately for him, he wouldn't be joining her.

He grabbed the sleeping bag he'd pulled from his camping gear in the closet and started to unroll it on the floor.

"What are you doing?" Laura asked between the click of her teeth.

Nick quirked an eyebrow, no doubt looking as confused as he felt. "Um, going to sleep on the floor."

"Are you kidding me, it's freezing in here."

"So, I can hear. The radiator will probably kick back in at some point tonight."

"Nick Kelly, get in this bed right now," she practically yelled, her teeth continuing to chatter through it all.

"I was trying to be a gentleman. Besides, the bed isn't big, and I'll take up most of it." So much so, he'd be hard pressed not to touch her. His butterflies flapped their wings excitedly, but he shut them down before they could get airborne.

"Please, please, please sleep with me," she whined. "I mean next to me…you know what I mean. I need body heat and I need it now," she demanded, pink-stained cheeks withstanding.

You aren't the only one, sweetheart, thought Nick, though he was fairly sure she didn't mean the same kind of heat he had in mind.

Laura was becoming more flustered by the second and he found it completely adorable. No man in his right mind would turn down the invitation she'd extended, and Nick was not above temptation. May God have mercy on his soul, he thought as he hit the light switch on the wall and slid in next to her. Pulling the covers over his head and resisting the urge to haul her to his side, he closed his eyes and told himself to go to sleep. Maybe if he didn't imagine what it would be like to run his hand up her bare leg, and under the shirt she'd borrowed from him, he might actually get some sleep.

"What are you doing?" asked Laura, sounding a little panicked.

"Going to sleep," he said gruffly.

"No, I mean, with the whole covers over your face. And it's pitch black in here. Don't you think it's really dark in here?"

She definitely sounded panicked, but he couldn't figure out why, she was the one who'd asked him to sleep next to her.

"Yep, it's called nighttime. Go to sleep, Tink." Did the woman think he was a saint? The longer he stayed awake, the more he wanted her. The least she could do was dole out a little mercy and let him drift off into oblivion, instead of keeping him awake with thoughts of everything he wanted to do with her in the dark. Hell, what he wanted to do with her at any given time if he was being honest.

Laura shifted next to him, and he could tell she'd rolled over to face him. He pulled the covers down and turned to look at her.

"I'm afraid of the dark," she said in the smallest voice he'd ever heard come out of her. She sounded ashamed and damn if the knowledge didn't crack his heart wide open.

"Okay. Let me see if I can solve our problem," he said gently.

"You mean, my problem," she said in that small voice again, and his heart started to bleed for the independent woman who'd spent the last ten years of her life pretending she didn't need anyone. He longed to pull her in and comfort her, to tell Laura it was all right to need other people, but he wasn't sure how he would deal with her pushing him away again.

So instead, he said the words she needed to hear, which hurt a little more than he thought they would. "Nah Tink, we're friends, which makes your problem my problem too."

Nick got out of the bed, the mattress creaking with the shift of his weight, and made his way over to the dresser to grab his cell phone. On a whim he snagged the Magic Eight Ball he'd had since he was ten. It didn't actually work anymore, the single fortune left inside of it being "It is decidedly so," but he liked the consistent delivery of hope it offered.

Once he had settled back onto his tiny portion of the bed, facing Laura, he pulled the sheet over his head and tucked the covers around the outside of his body, making a half tent. "If you do this, it'll help keep the heat in and your face warm." Then he placed his phone in the narrow space between the center of their bodies.

Chapter 23

Laura

Laura pulled the covers over her head, tucking them around her to finish the cocoon Nick had started and then stowed her hands beneath the pillow. Face to face with a scruffy, sexy-as-all-get-out Nick, her hands itched to run over the stubble lining his chin and jaw. She refrained, barely.

The backlight on Nick's phone lit up again and she let out a breath she hadn't realized she'd been holding. "Thanks. I know being afraid at my age is silly."

"Lots of people are afraid of the dark," he said, trying to make her feel better.

She let out a snort of disbelief. "I bet most of them aren't almost thirty."

"Maybe. Have you always been afraid to sleep without a light?"

"No, but after Drew died, I started having night terrors. If I kept a nightlight on, I didn't have them. Now, I'm afraid to find out what happens if I don't."

"Got it. Nightlight for life," he said without any judgment, as if it were a regular occurrence.

"I'm tired of being afraid, though, and not only of the dark," she confessed.

Nick moved his hand to rest next to hers, of his own volition or because he needed to stretch his arm, she wasn't sure. Either way, his pinky touched hers beneath the pillow, bringing with it a sense of comfort.

"Stop accepting one side of the story then," he said in a matter-of-fact tone she would've bristled under if it had been anyone other than him. But it was hard to be mad at someone who always had your best interest at heart.

"And how exactly do I do that?" she asked, only to clarify.

"Life is complicated. You can't have light without darkness. You can't experience true joy without knowing sorrow. Or courage without the presence of fear. One exists because of the other. If we accept half of what life offers us, then we're missing the whole picture."

"Resiliency can only be developed with adversity," said Laura, thinking about her recent conversation with the grief counselor Father Hugo had recommended. It wasn't a matter of *if* grief found her in the future, but *when* it found her, how she chose to work through it. Would she lean into the people and resources who could support her, or would she let grief be the only part of her story she told in the end?

In her soul, she wanted everything life had to offer, which meant being willing to open herself up to possible hurt and loss.

As if he could read her thoughts, Nick said, "I don't think my way of dealing with grief is any better than yours, Tink. After 9/11 there were times that I questioned if God even existed. Honestly, on the really hard days, I still do. But about the time I'm ready to give up, my hope is renewed. Time doesn't heal everything, but in my experience, it does make the sharp edges softer, creating space for..." Nick hesitated as if he'd say something else before finishing with, "something more."

"And maybe the possibility of someone new when I'm ready?" she asked keenly aware of how close their bodies were in the small bed.

Nick picked up the Magic Eight Ball he'd placed between them with the phone and shook it. "It is decidedly so. See, it says so right here," he said showing her the blurry words floating on the surface of the tiny screen.

Laura smiled broadly. Nick lifted the covers enough to put the old-school fortune teller on the floor and then tucked them tightly beneath him once more, the back light from his phone glowing eerily between them. It shouldn't have been romantic, but it was. In fact, sleeping next to Nick entirely clothed was easily the most intimate experience she'd ever had. His breathing steadied and her eyes fluttered shut of their own volition, the quiet cadence of his inhale-exhale lulling her to sleep.

Nick

Nick woke to the light of morning streaming through his blinds and a weight on his chest. Sometime during the night, Laura had tossed the covers and thrown herself entirely on top of him. Not that he was complaining. The radiators had hissed to life once more in the middle of the night, but as far as he was concerned, the only kind of heat he needed was what Laura was providing.

Her nose had found its way into the place between his chest and chin, as though she were searching for the spot where his pulse kept time with his heart. The rest of her attempted to encompass his torso and one of her bare legs hooked over both his to hold him hostage. He had died in his sleep, and this was heaven. Frankly, it could be hell and his body would still be as delighted to be under her. Sadly, he wouldn't get to revel in it as long as he would've preferred.

Laura started to stir and as she shifted, Nick let his hand drop away from her hip and slowly to his side, laying as still as possible before she could notice how entangled they'd become. She yawned sleepily and stretched, eventually sitting up, baring the skin of her legs increasingly with her movements. Nick swore quietly and tried to get the lower half of his body under control, which only tortured him further.

Her hair waved in a dozen different directions, calling to him to mess it up even more while he kissed her long and hard. The rest of his body eagerly agreed with the thought, and he forced himself to think about a painful bath in ice water instead.

Laura rubbed the sleep from her eyes and said, "Morning." Her voice was a husky caress stroking the entire length of his body until he felt taut as a bowstring.

"Morning, sunshine," he automatically replied, the sound coming out more like gravel than usual.

"I had the strangest dream last night."

"You don't say?" he asked, keeping his eyes on the ceiling. It was safer than looking at her. One more glance of her in his shirt and he'd never make it out of bed without embarrassing both of them.

"I was climbing this huge tree and when I finally made it to the top, the branches pulled me into this cozy bower."

He almost coughed, but managed to get out a casual, "Huh, imagine that." He'd like to show her how cozy his bower could be. Sitting up, Nick placed his feet on the floor and sang a classic Vanilla Ice song in his head, trying to dispel thoughts of Laura plastered to his body, only to have Sarah McLachlan's *Ice Cream* take over. The music wasn't helping. Hunched over, elbows digging into his flannel-clad knees, he dragged long fingers through his hair, once, twice, three times.

Nope, he was going to burn from the inside out it seemed. At least he'd die a happy man.

Laura didn't appear to notice his distress as she stumbled sleepily from one side of the room to the other, gathering up her clothes. It was cute to watch how much of a morning person she wasn't.

"I'm going to get dressed," she announced, eyes squinting in no particular direction. She'd used the moisturizing eye drops he kept around for the occasional use to store her contact lenses in a plastic cup the night before. "Any chance you have coffee hidden around here, Mister matcha latte?" Laura asked as she passed by him.

She didn't wait for the answer or look in his direction, and Nick sagged with relief as the bedroom door clicked shut behind her. Quickly changing into a pair of raggedy khaki cargo pants he'd had since college and a clean graphic t-shirt advertising his favorite whiskey across the back, he padded downstairs, second guessing his choice to go barefoot amidst the construction. At least the radiators were working again, or frostbite would've been an actuality.

The kitchen was barely functional, but as he pulled the single serve coffee machine forward to load it with a filter and grounds, Nick was glad he'd taken Dean's advice to wait until summer before demolishing it. Next, he filled the electric kettle with water and pulled down a plastic container filled with packets of instant oatmeal from its home on the second shelf of a cabinet without a front.

Laura walked in, looking as fresh as a daisy in springtime, regardless of the white world staring back at him through single-paned windows suggesting winter wouldn't hibernate for a while yet. Nick smiled, no doubt looking a little goofy, at the beautiful woman standing inside his kitchen the morning after they'd slept together. Well, sleeping together of a sort, anyway.

Circumstances may not be what they appeared to be, but he could dream about the possibility of one day if their conversation from last night meant anything. A morning when he didn't only hand his friend a cup of coffee but greeted her with a thorough kiss and a whispered good morning as if all were right with his world, solely because she was in it.

Nick followed her to the two-person, diner-style table pushed against the far wall in front of the large bay window, overlooking a shared backyard. He had snagged the wobbly piece of junk and matching vinyl chairs from a tear-out job near the station a couple of years ago. Laura watched him over the rim of her coffee cup while he scrapped out the last bite of oatmeal in his bowl.

"I still can't get over the fact that you eat oatmeal."

"Why? What did you think I ate for breakfast?"

"Honestly, I took you for more of a cereal guy. You know, the sweet kind little kids like to eat, with a prize somewhere at the bottom."

Nick merely raised his brows at her accusations and went to wash his dish. Finished, he ran a hand up and down the length of his torso, saying as blandly as possible, "You don't get to look like a sculptor's dream without eating healthy."

Laura blanched at the realization her thoughts had been far from only in her head last night.

"I wish you could see your face, right now," he said, rubbing it in a little bit more.

No sooner had the words left his mouth than she marched over to the sink, setting her cup within, but instead of walking away in a huff like he expected, she stepped into his space. Standing on the tips of her toes with one hand at rest on his chest and the other curled around the back of his neck, her pose reminded him of their doomed kiss. Nick's mouth went dry as he waited to see what she'd do next, and Laura obliged, playing with the hair at his nape. His eyes almost rolled back in his head, it felt so good, and when she tugged his head down toward her mouth, he went obediently, fully at her mercy.

"Any time you want me to compare you with a work of art, feel free to go shirtless," she whispered boldly, turning the tables on him.

Nick barely kept from swallowing his tongue while Laura chortled ruthlessly. Before she could get away, though, he snagged her around the waist, bringing his mouth to the shell of her ear, enjoying the shiver he felt wash over her as he whispered, "Just say when, Tink."

When she blinked like an owl waking up from a nap, he slowly released her, maintaining physical contact between them until her feet were flat on the floor once more. Nick held his breath and wondered if he'd gone too far with their game of cat and mouse. It was a foolish risk to take if his heart was the only one involved.

Laura simply sauntered back over to the table, hips swaying

with her movements. She came to an abrupt stop when she finally spotted yesterday's newspaper on top of a pile of recyclables, where Nick had left it, a black-and-white photo splashed across the front page.

Looking flabbergasted, she read the title of the article, "With Love, from New York."

Nick had also been shocked to see the couple passionately kissing against a backdrop of the 9/11 Memorial when he reached for the paper on his stoop twenty-four hours ago. Though he wasn't familiar with the reporter who'd written the piece, the photo of him and Laura front and center had caused him to do more than a double take.

"Who is this Hatta Mann person, and who gave them permission to print this photo?"

Nick raised his hands in innocence. "It wasn't me, and it's not like the paper can retract it now without it becoming an even bigger deal. Besides, no one but us would recognize the couple anyway."

"Did you know about this yesterday?" Laura asked. Nick could tell she was gaining steam, irritation creeping into the color of her cheeks and tone. He should try to talk her down off the ledge before she got any more riled up, but this conversation had been a long time coming. Besides, he liked it when Laura got all fired up about…well, anything.

"Maybe. Nice leg pop by the way," he said with an audacious smirk, adding fuel to her kindling. He refused to apologize for it either. Though taken without their knowledge, the photo was proof of her attraction despite an instinct to flee as soon as her heart became involved in a situation.

"My leg did not pop," Laura argued, snatching up the paper to rake her eyes over the picture, checking again as if her eyesight had failed her the first time.

"Oh, but it did," Nick replied calmly in the face of her denial.

Laura's mouth opened to refute it once more, except she couldn't with the evidence printed starkly in front of her. Nick didn't blame the reporter for wanting to capture the moment. It was iconic, with his hands wrapped around her waist and pulling her flush with his body, her left foot popped up behind her like she was posing for an old school movie. He could almost believe the photograph belonged to a time where people celebrated in the streets, and destiny wasn't something a person waited idly on, but had the courage to make happen.

"The article is about finding love in the city. There's a collage of couples from Central Park, in front of hot dog stands, at Yankee Stadium, on subway cars and anywhere else you can think of," he said, looking over her shoulder to where she'd laid out the paper. "Ours is definitely the one that stands out though."

"How could it not, when it's blown up on the front page of the *New York Herald* for everyone to see?" she asked, eyes big with exasperation. "Never mind that we aren't an actual couple or that we were making out in front of the Memorial," Laura groused, her cheeks stained a lovely shade of pink.

Nick turned to look at her, so close to those lips he wanted to kiss until Laura's toes curled and this inane conversation became nothing more than a fleeting blip on their way to something more closely resembling destiny. "What better place to grab life by the lapels and embrace it? I know my dad and Donnie would never begrudge anyone's happiness," he said quietly as their breaths mingled in the small space between them. It would barely require any movement at all to take her soft lips with his, taste the coffee still lacing her tongue, and thoroughly ravish her mouth.

Kiss her, kiss her, kiss her, chanted his flock of butterflies as if he needed any encouragement. *Sorry guys, it's a no-fly zone today.*

Forcing himself to retreat, he tried to be the voice of reason. "The roads look cleared. I'll call you a taxi."

"Okay," she said, her voice slightly shaky from the interaction.

Good, thought Nick. *At least I'm not the only affected by our close encounter.*

After he'd arranged for a pickup, he walked her to the door, giving them both a fair amount of physical space as she put on her coat and shoes. He didn't want to do anything she might regret, and pushing Laura before she was ready had already ended poorly once.

No sense in repeating the same mistake. Their conversation last night pointed to Laura moving forward with her grief, and he didn't want to hinder her progress. If she wanted to be with him in the future, she'd let him know. And then there was the colossal challenge his career presented.

Laura still might not want to be with a first responder, and though he liked to play off the risk his job entailed, it wouldn't be fair to either of them. He could be honest enough to admit he needed to create boundaries where his family was concerned, but the job was non-negotiable. Livelihood aside, he loved being a firefighter. It was a calling as much as a career, even if it had taken the deaths of his father and brother to help him find his true north.

Nick followed her down the steps and opened the door of the taxi. "So, a group of us are going to karaoke on Saturday night. Dean and C.J. will be there. Any interest in coming?"

"Sure, why not. But under no circumstances will I be performing."

"No pressure. But under no circumstances can I promise C.J. won't try to rope you into it after she's had a couple of drinks."

Laura smiled briefly and slid into the backseat. "Thanks for the warning."

"I'll call you tomorrow with the details." He closed the door, relief and regret fighting within him as he watched her drive away.

Chapter 24

Laura

Laura texted Uncle Joe to let her know she was home. She'd asked him to take Micky home for the night when she got stuck at Nick's, and since he was closing Walker's early due to the snow, it was a win-win situation for all of them. He would never admit it, but she knew he liked having Micky around to keep him company.

It was difficult to picture Uncle Joe retiring, but if that day ever came, she was going to get him his own dog. An older, medium-sized rescue would be the perfect fit. Laura rounded the corner of the building and trudged up the slush-laden stairs, pulling a house key from her pocket as she went. She slipped the key into the deadbolt, pursing her lips in confusion when the door popped open without any effort.

Uncle Joe must have forgotten to lock it back with the spare key she kept beneath a flowerpot on the landing, she reasoned. It wasn't exactly the most stealthy of hiding places, but it came in handy when the walking service sent someone by for Micky on the evenings she worked late. Stepping inside, she meandered down the hall to clean up the mess she'd left on her bed, half of which was from Kate's closet.

Her sister never threw away a piece of clothing, upcycling the older pieces over time, or in this instance supplementing Laura's minimalistic wardrobe. She walked in and stepped back out, thinking she'd entered her sister's room by accident—except the ceiling confirmed she had the right room. It was still painted a midday cerulean instead of an orange creamsicle and raspberry sunrise. She turned on her heel, striding for the other bedroom.

Pushing open the door, she surveyed the neat and tidy space, getting a whiff of Kate's signature freesia. The scent permeated the room—so much so, it was as if her sister had recently been there. Laura sat down at the dressing table in the corner of the room and lifted the glass bottle of perfume to her nose. Kate had probably left it behind in lieu of something more travel friendly. She put the bottle back and jogged for the kitchen, grabbing the phone from the receiver just as Uncle Joe started to leave a message.

"Hey, what's up?" She could hear glasses clinking and the muffled sound of a crowd in the background.

"Hi doll, any chance you can come in early? Half of Brooklyn played hooky from work today and came into Walker's instead."

"Of course," replied Laura, warily eyeing the kitchen sink, or rather the lack of dishes inside the porcelain basin. "I know this is random, but did you happen to come in and clean up around the apartment when you picked Micky up?"

"Micky was waiting for me by the door. I didn't make it past the entryway."

"Huh, that's strange," she started to say, but Uncle Joe interrupted with, "Gotta go. See you soon."

Laura returned to her bedroom and quickly changed into a pair of leggings, tunic, and long cardigan. Inside her closet hung the clothes she didn't remember hanging up, similar to the dishes on the drying rack beside the sink. A feeling of unease churned in her gut.

If last night and this morning weren't message enough, cleaning without any recollection must mean she was a total goner for Nick Kelly. It was only a matter of time before she fessed up lip to lip with him, which was the best incentive she could think of for doing the homework her counselor assigned at their last session. Laura decided it was time to make a visit to a certain engine house.

Nick

Nick dropped the oversized yellow sponge he'd been using to wash the Squad's truck into a bucket of suds when he spied his favorite blonde walking his way with purpose in her stride. She wore a pencil skirt with a tailored blazer, and her glasses perched upon her nose as if to say she meant business. Her stern librarian look was one of his favorites. In one hand she held a large paper bag and in the other Micky's leash, not that he needed one, thanks to Laura's consistent training.

Nick walked out to the street to greet her before anyone else in the Squad could. When he'd called to give her the details for karaoke, he'd also given her his shift schedule for the week in case she needed to get ahold of him to go over anything. Booking the pub for the night meant Joe had looped Laura into the planning and played directly into Nick's fervent wish to spend more time with her. He was a glutton for punishment. Of course, using the pub also made sense since the Squad occasionally used the venue for parties and the like.

"Hey, Tink. Everything all right?" Nick asked, squatting down to Mickey's level, who immediately rolled over for belly rubs. "Hi, pal," he said obliging the canine.

Laura looked at him a little sheepishly from beneath her lashes. "Mm-hm, why wouldn't it be?"

"You're here." Laura had never come by the station before, but then again, he'd never invited her either. Nick was doing a poor job of making her feel welcome but incorporating relationships into his career, aside from the family and Dean, had never been easy for him. Laura was the first girl he'd ever shared anything with in regard to work, and it had totally backfired.

Then again, he reminded himself, he had shoved the most dangerous parts of it in her face and never thought to show her a broader picture. Nick acknowledged that he'd been afraid to give her all of himself—specifically, the part that loved his career. Laura hadn't been the only one afraid to take risks. He needed to take some ownership for how things had gone down between them, and now was the perfect time to redeem the situation with a lesson in Firefighting 101.

She shifted nervously, the bag in her hand crinkling with the movement. "Can't a friend stop by to see a friend at work? I come bearing gifts," she said lifting the paper bag with Squad 2 scribbled in pencil across the front of it. "Ruth says hello, by the way."

Micky sat sentry next to Laura, head swinging back and forth between the two of them, his emotional barometer ticking away with every word. His intelligent eyes landed on Nick as if to say, *Don't just stand there, buddy. Can't you see, this is your chance to get the girl?*

Nick smiled and reached for the bag instead of reaching for her. Not hugging Laura went against the natural order of his whole being, but after their last visit he didn't trust himself not to take advantage of the proximity. Until she gave him tangible proof that she wanted to be more than friends he would keep his hands to himself. Physical distance made his attraction to her easier to bear, if only by a smidge.

"I'm glad you're here. Ready for the official tour?"

"You have time?"

"For you, always. But it helps that today is on the slow side. Depending on the day, a shift can be full of big incidents, while others are all about the little stuff."

"Like what?" she asked, walking beside him into the truck's bay.

"Like checking equipment, making sure everything is in good working order. We take a lot of precautions and safety is at the top of the list for every first responder and those we help," he answered, trying to gage her reaction before he continued, "I usually spend some of each shift making schedules, writing reports, sleeping, and working out to stay fit for the physical aspects of the job."

Laura smirked in the way he usually reserved for her. "I'd say mission accomplished."

His butterflies started flapping with excitement over the flirtatious comment.

He couldn't help the full grin that split his face, or the way her responding one made him want to pick her up and swing her around for the sheer fun of it. "Want to check out the equipment?" he asked instead.

"I thought I already had," she answered with another flirty lift of her brows. "Besides," she mock whispered, "we appear to have a little bit of an audience."

Nick took in the crew watching them and glared fiercely in their direction until they began to disperse.

"Nice to see you around, Laura. Thanks for lunch," said

Sawicki as he snatched the deli bag out of Nick's hand and called for Micky to follow him. "C'mon Eminem, we've got snacks now."

"There'd better still be one of those left for me when I'm done, Sawicki," Nick yelled after him.

"Sure thing, boss." He gave Nick a formal salute and winked at Laura.

Nick shot him the bird, making his crew member guffaw loudly on his way out of the bay.

"Between the accent and *Good Will Hunting* reference, I'm going to venture a guess that Sawicki is from Boston."

"Yep, he loves that movie like it's the national anthem for every kid he grew up with."

"So, does the entire Squad call Micky 'Eminem'?"

"Nah, mostly the guys I'm closest to," he replied. "I might have gushed over him once or twice during a good gossip sesh," he said conspiratorially.

Laura laughed and the strings of his heart sang her praises in response. "Okay, maybe I also gushed about the girl he belongs to," he said quietly enough she could've missed it, but the smile beaming back at him declared she'd heard every word. He cleared his throat. "Anything in particular you want to know?"

"Have you ever saved a cat in a tree?"

"Only once," he chuckled. "Like I said earlier, sometimes things are quiet. There are the typical calls you'd expect for any neighborhood, medical emergencies for the elderly and infirmed, minor car accidents and smaller scale fires."

"But sometimes it's all hands-on deck if the emergency is big enough."

He nodded in the affirmative. "Squads are trained to function as a ladder or engine company, but we also oversee special rescue situations and equipment."

"Ooh, like the jaws of life?" Her excitement was unexpected and absolutely adorable. Nick felt like an idiot for not giving her the whole picture sooner, or maybe this visit was perfect timing. He couldn't decide which. Either way, his butterflies were waltzing around his chest as if it were their personal dance floor.

Placing his hand on her lower back, he kept his touch firm enough to guide her toward the truck, yet light enough for her to step away if she wanted to. "You know how a can opener works. Well, the jaws of life aren't much different except the equipment uses hydraulics and pistons to open the tin can, or car, in this instance," Nick started to explain.

Laura glanced over her shoulder, curiosity and excitement adding to her glow as she leaned further into his hand instead of away.

So much for keeping his distance, physically or otherwise, thought Nick.

Two days after Laura's impromptu visit, Nick parked the bike outside of Walker's, paying homage to the steady fixture she was as usual. This time though, he acknowledged how much had changed in his own life over the last six months. Life was full of moments, those that were significant at the outset, and others a glimpse of potential things to come.

When he'd entered the pub on that fateful day last September, he'd had no idea the woman he met in front of the deli was Joe's niece, or that he'd fall so hard for her. When he'd finally bought the house of his dreams, Laura had still been at the forefront of his thoughts and his hope for a family of his own. Tonight, everything would change once more when Dean proposed to Chaucey. His friends would be moving forward with their own plans, and while he couldn't be happier for them, the idea of doing the same with Laura wouldn't leave him.

By the time she'd left the station, Nick was more sure than ever he and Laura were meant for something more. The Squad had made him proud, giving Laura a warm welcome, taking turns roasting him and lauding his leadership in equal measure. They answered all of her questions thoughtfully as though they understood the gravity of her presence and how the outcome might affect him. Now all he had to do was wait until she gave him a signal.

A large searchlight shining the bat signal into the night sky came to mind and he smiled over the absurdity. He'd settle for more flirting and another hug like the one she'd initiated when they'd parted ways. The bell above the door tinkled upon entry, announcing his arrival to anyone within. Nick headed for the kitchen, where Laura had told him to meet her, passing Amir on his way in.

"Don't leave on my account," said Nick jokingly.

Amir lifted a large plastic container. "Nah man, I'm running an errand on Laura's behalf."

"Oh good, you're here," said Laura, gesturing with a wooden spoon for him to join her at the stove. "Here, try this. Careful, it's hot and a little spicy."

"You certainly are," he said, being deliberately obtuse as he moved in to taste whatever it was. He told himself blatant flirting was up for grabs since she'd initiated the trend already.

"What do you think?"

"Mm, amazing." Why it was the dream of every man to have a beautiful woman feed him, Nick didn't know, but he was pretty certain it had something to do with Adam, Eve, and a tempting apple. Whatever the reason, he was down for it. Now, if he could find an excuse to take her curves into his hands and kiss her senseless, his life would be complete.

One out of two isn't bad, he consoled himself.

"What is it?" he asked around another mouthful.

"Basically, Penang Curry on steroids." She lifted another spoon with a red sauce and chicken to his mouth. "Butter Chicken, but a little heavier on the turmeric. My naan still needs work, so Amir's mom is helping me out. Did you know his parents are from Kashmir?"

Laura pulled a large platter filled with sliced carrots, yellow peppers, cucumbers, radishes, and jicama from one of the oversized refrigerators. She sprinkled kalamata olives and cherry tomatoes over the top and then placed a ramekin with hummus in the center of the colorful veggie wheel. "I guess Mr. Zaman immigrated here as a kid, but his wife came over to attend university in the late seventies. They met through a mutual friend and were married six months later. Sometimes the world seems as small as it is big."

Nick bobbed his head in agreement, lyrics from Led Zeppelin tumbling through his mind courtesy of the geographical reference, and wondered if she had noticed the similarities in their own story. Well, except for the married part. "How are things going at the bodega? Any more harassment?" he asked while taking the platter from her.

"Not recently. Amir and his dad still don't agree on how to handle it, but I guess his mother came with him to the last community meeting, so he's hopeful that his dad might change his tune eventually," she said, removing another tray filled with alternating desserts of chocolate soufflé, fruit tarts, and tiramisù.

Nick followed her through the kitchen door to the smaller dining room at the back of the pub where a makeshift stage had been set up, and a crew from Squad 2 were setting up the equipment for the night's entertainment, namely themselves.

Chapter 25

Laura

Nick and the rest of the Squad had gone all out for their karaoke bash. When he'd mentioned it a week ago, she'd pictured a small club downtown or across the bridge for the venue, not the pub. Though this wasn't the first time they'd transformed the back room for their personal entertainment, according to Uncle Joe, it was the first time anyone had raved about the food. Laura took it all in stride, but the accolades were still nice to hear and a confirmation that her new track in life had merit.

By the time Laura had changed into more suitable party wear, most everyone else had arrived, including C.J.'s parents, who'd flown in for a visit at the last minute.

"C'mon," said Chaucey, taking Laura by the arm immediately. "I'll introduce you to my parents later, but right now, I need a stiff drink."

"I'd say what a fun surprise, but you don't seem very happy to see the parental units."

"More time to prepare would have been ideal. I really do love them, but my idea of fun is not spending a Saturday night with Mum."

"I'll drink to that. I'd ask why all mother and daughter relationships are so fraught with tension, but Kate and my mom get along famously," Laura said with an eyeroll. "I feel like it's impossible to please her, while my sister makes her happy by existing."

"I know what you mean. My brother is in Her Majesty's Naval Service and can do no wrong, whilst I'm the prodigal daughter living in America. Not to mention a poor, starving artist," she sympathized. "Never mind, I'm neither poor nor starving. And I like it here, the most imperative reason being an ocean between me and Mum."

Two drinks in, Chaucey pulled Laura up on stage for a duet, exactly the way Nick had predicted. They sang to Taylor Swift's "You Belong with Me," every woman in the room joining in for the chorus and making the experience one she would always remember. Giving her wing woman a hug, she left Chaucey to visit with Dean's parents, who'd come in halfway through their performance.

Nick caught her hand with his as she walked by on her way to check in with Ronan and Saint at the bar. A very sober Leo sang his heart out on stage, while Vinny watched him with equal parts sappiness and mirth. At the same time, Laura and Nick leaned in to hear one another.

"Trust me, you don't want to miss this next set," he said cryptically before heading to the stage with Dean and three other guys from Squad 2.

Laura took the spot where he'd been standing along the wall as Dean started the music. Each of the men had worn matching slacks, a button-down shirt, oxfords, and a gray fedora. The rat pack may as well have walked in. With that in mind, she relaxed back and waited for a song from Frank Sinatra or Dean Martin to materialize, excited to see Nick croon his way through karaoke. When a familiar song from her teen years started up instead, her mouth almost dropped open.

She knew Nick was enthusiastic about music but watching him sing and do a choreographed dance routine to a mashup of boy band songs from the 1990s was seriously hot. The only thing hotter might have been watching them dance in their gear, stripping away one piece at a time until all they had left was a strategically placed helmet. Or was that called an all-male revue?

C'est la vie, Laura told herself. She was really only interested in a personal show from Nick anyway.

When they finished their routine to a standing ovation, she clapped along, whistling her appreciation with the rest of the audience. Nick sauntered her way, grinning ear to ear, pleased with their performance. He was in his element: confident, sexy, and absolutely alluring to Laura.

She handed him the rest of her drink as he leaned against the wall next to her and took his other hand in hers. It felt like the most natural thing in the world, and her bees buzzed and dipped, drowsy with content.

Okay, so that might be the liquor, she acknowledged, but as far as she was concerned, her merry-go-round had stopped spinning out of control again. For the first time in ten years, she knew what she wanted, or rather whom, in this case.

Nick kissed the top of her head as if he understood exactly where they stood without a single word. He caught her eye and looked back at the stage. "You don't want to miss this."

Dean asked Chaucey to join him on the small stage, while the others dispersed, and Laura assumed they had a duet of their own planned. That is, until he thanked their families for being present for such a special occasion. The entire room watched as he got down on one knee, taking her hand in his, and proposed with his heart on his sleeve for all to see. Gone was the tough guy she usually saw, replaced with the sweetheart her friend had once described.

"Yes, a thousand times yes!" said Chaucey before he could even finish his spiel.

"Did she quote—"

"Jane Bennett from *Pride and Prejudice?*" Nick asked as the room erupted in clapping and congratulations. "Yep, it's the movie they saw on their first date. You'd never guess, but Dean's a total romantic and C.J. has a soft spot for the clueless Bingley."

Which actually made sense to Laura.

Dean and Chaucey's happiness was contagious as everyone took a turn to wish them well. The couple holed up in a corner of the room while their mothers talked about wedding plans and their fathers toasted to family with another pint. Gradually, everyone else started to disperse for other late-night haunts or home.

Someone had started up the pub's usual soundtrack in the background. Uncle Joe finished wiping tables and stacking glasses, giving her a wink as Nick pulled her in for a slow dance. Laura put her arms around his neck, glad she'd worn heels to make up for the difference in height. He moved them in a steady rhythm as they swayed back and forth, his hands wrapped around her waist as he sang the words of the chorus to her.

"Grant my last request…"

By the time the song ended Laura had only one thing on her mind. "Want to get out of here?" she asked, nerves and excitement fighting for space within her stomach as she waited on his answer.

"Absolutely. Your place?" Nick asked at the same time she suggested, "My place?"

They laughed and practically ran through the front dining room of the pub. Ronan raised an eyebrow and Saint blew her a kiss. "You go, girl! Get you a piece of that!"

Laura might have died from embarrassment, but Nick gave her no time to ruminate as hauled her through the door and back into his arms. He slammed his lips on hers, taking both her breath and heart in one fell swoop. She eagerly kissed him back, the rest of the world disappearing around them under the warm glow of a streetlamp.

She couldn't get enough of Nick as they stumbled up the stairs and through the entry into the living room. Somewhere in the middle of making out, he'd picked her up and Laura had wrapped her legs around his waist, every sensitive part of her begging for more contact. She hummed as he trailed kisses down the side of her neck, starting at the tender spot behind her ear. Bliss, that is what this was, unbridled bliss. She tilted her head to give him better access and started to undo the buttons of his shirt, desperate to touch him as he played with the thin strip exposed between her blouse and her slacks.

She tried to peel off his shirt, but the sleeves were stuck on his perfect biceps. "Help a girl out," she pleaded. Nick chuckled and obliged, taking back her lips and flipping them over on the couch so she stretched out beneath him, supporting his own weight on his elbows, and giving her free reign to run her hands over his skin. Legs entangled with one another, she couldn't tell where one of them began and the other ended, and still all she could think about was getting closer.

She was getting ready to take control of the situation herself, when Nick drew back, breathing hard. "I know I'm going to regret this, but I think we should slow down a little."

"Oh." A retreat was not what she'd had on the radar.

He pushed up onto one elbow and cupped her face, his thumb

tracing over her jaw before lowering his forehead to hers. "Believe me when I say wanting you is not the problem, but I also don't want us to do anything you might regret in the future."

"And if I can assure you that isn't an issue?"

He chuckled in the face of her question.

"Tink, you could try the patience of a saint. I'm trying to be a good guy here. It's killing me, but if this thing between us is as real as it feels right now, then we don't need to rush. We have time for this."

"The man who is always telling me tomorrow isn't guaranteed suddenly thinks we have all the time in the world," she pouted.

"I'm not saying no indefinitely, I'm saying no for now. And I have no intention of letting your lips get lonely," he said, kissing them softly once more before sitting up and pulling her with him.

"Fine. If I'm being honest, I find your gallantry kind of sexy."

"Worthy of Colonel Brandon or Captain Wentworth?" he asked, puffing out his magnificent chest.

"Unquestionably, but you should put your shirt back on if you expect me to act like a lady," she replied, disgruntled over the turn of events.

He laughed and tugged her forward for another kiss, torturing them both a little while longer before putting his shirt back on and starting a movie to distract them.

Since Nick had the following day off, they made plans to meet at the farmer's market and head to Greenwood for a picnic lunch afterwards. Nick played with her hand, neither of them being the least bit distracted from their physical connection by the action film blowing up on the screen in front of them.

"I wrote Drew a letter," Laura said in between scenes, a confession of sorts, or a secret only a best friend could understand.

"Oh yeah?" he asked without any hint of judgment.

"Mm-hm. It's not exactly a goodbye letter, but it felt like it was time to get certain things off my chest." His eyes dipped down to the swells pressing against her shirt at the mention.

Laura let out a snort. "Eyes up here, good sir."

"Sorry, just profusely regretting my earlier gallantry. But I do know the perfect place to mail your letter."

Laura dropped the chain with her wedding ring into the envelope and read the letter she'd written to Drew once more to reassure herself the words within it were everything she needed to say. Her counselor had suggested the idea to help her find closure, but also reassured her that the process looked different for everyone, encouraging her to remember moving forward didn't mean forgetting or moving on. She was merely making space for new possibilities and saying goodbye to the former ones.

Dear Drew,

I wonder if we'd had the chance to become an old, married couple, if such a simple salutation would've morphed over the years. Since you're gone, I guess I'll never know if it would have become something more intimate, an endearment born from a life steeped in daily routines, traditions, and time itself.

Would we have become the best versions of ourselves together? Would our children look most like you or me? A perfect pairing of the two, or more likely, an awkward rendering of our gene pools. Yeah, I snorted over that last thought. Were we too young and idealistic to know better, or would it be us against the world, the way we'd planned? These are the questions I wrestle with but will never find answers to, because you're not here.

YOU ARE NOT HERE.

You're not here and I'm angry with you for it! God didn't force you onto that road in the early hours of the morning. It was your choice alone. But it was one you made out of love for me, so I forgive you. And I forgive myself for getting lost along the way.

You will always be a part of me, but I don't want the life we would've had any longer. I'm finally ready for whatever else providence has in store for me, and I actually recognize the person in the mirror again. She's a little older, hopefully wiser, and braver than I ever gave her credit for. The best part, though, is knowing you would love her as much as you loved the girl who came before. So, from this day forward I'm going to live a new dream, filled with infinite possibilities. Today, I'm taking the fork in the road.

Always,

Laura

Green-Wood Cemetery looked much the same as it had the first time she'd come with Nick, aside from the change in foliage. Gone were the orange, gold, and red of fall, replaced with the colors of spring. Green leaves waited to unfurl, while pink and white flowers bloomed from every cherry and magnolia tree. Spring had finally sprung in Brooklyn, the renewal of life evident in every sprout of grass, trellised vine, and soft-downed duckling in the pond.

Laura breathed in the blossom-scented air, the turnover of nature reminding her how to live with a heart wide open for whatever came her way. She had lived for too long in a casket of her own making, keeping others out for fear of losing them, or worse, finding out who she was when they were gone. Walking the same path they'd taken in the fall, she and Nick came to the obelisk she'd been curious about the first time.

It wasn't a monument to the dead, but rather a gift for the living. Engraved with the words, *Here Lie the Secrets of the Visitors of Green-Wood Cemetery,* the open slot below invited the living to divulge their secrets. Nick had explained that there was a watertight container inside to catch whatever burden a person wanted to release into its depths. He wasn't sure what happened to the letters when the space filled up, or whether anyone ever read them, but Laura didn't care. If someone else wanted to bear the burden of her words, they were welcome to try.

There wasn't a soul alive who could judge another person's

grief, the way they moved through it or, in her own case, tried to avoid it. Her grief had been a raging inferno at times and the cold abyss of an ocean trench at others—grief born from a single event, yet part of a thousand moments over the last ten years. But, like a clock counting the seconds, grief had kept its own time, sometimes fading away, only to show up like an unwelcome guest when she least expected. And then there was the guilt of actually living. Such a close companion to grief, it was sometimes hard to tell the difference between them, but it had torn her apart all the same.

Laura pulled the letter she'd written to Drew from her back pocket and dropped the white, folded piece of notebook paper into the slot. Her past would always be with her, but now she could embrace her present for the sake of her future.

Nick held out his hand to her. "Ready to go?"

Laura smiled gently. "I think so," she said and placed her hand in his.

Nick kissed the top of her head as they walked toward the Gothic Gate where they'd entered the Cemetery.

"Do you want to know what the letter said?"

"Only if you want to tell me."

"Not today. But someday."

"Someday sounds good to me."

"It does, doesn't it?" Laura squeezed his hand, enjoying the feel of her fingers entwined with his. They were warm and solid, like Nick. Her life might not look the way she'd planned it all those years ago, but she wasn't the same person she'd been then either. It only made sense for the outcome to change as much as she had.

Chapter 26

Laura

"Sorry, miss. This is as close as I can get. Looks like an emergency," said the cab driver as they pulled over a block from the pub, where a crowd of bystanders had gathered to watch the first responders at work.

None of the chaos in front of Laura made sense. She had left the pub midday to run errands for Chaucey's upcoming bridal shower with a quick stop at the church to speak with Father Hugo. If she planned to stay in Brooklyn indefinitely, then she wanted Walker's Pub to be more involved with the community.

Micky barked incessantly in time with the flashing lights of the ambulance where Uncle Joe sat on the back bumper with an oxygen mask over his pale face. It was more alarming than seeing the pub engulfed in flames, smoke billowing into the cloud-laden sky with its steely tendrils. It looked like her worst nightmare had come to life, especially when she spotted Squad 2's truck parked adjacent to the old brick building.

Micky saw her first and sprinted madly in her direction.

"It's okay, buddy," she said, kneeling down to his level. "I'm here now."

"Uncle Joe, what happened?" she asked when they reached the ambulance.

He removed the mask. "I don't know. One minute I was peeling potatoes, and the next, Micky's barking and running frantically back and forth between the cold storage and the kitchen."

She looked at him in understanding. "You left something cooking for too long."

"Not a darn thing. But that's when I finally smelled the smoke coming from the upstairs." It was his turn to look at her.

"Thanks to Kate's list of dos and don'ts, I'm afraid to even light a candle and I haven't been home enough to cook," she said bashfully. She'd been spending all of her free time with Nick, stoking their relational fire. And with that thought, her entire stomach dropped.

"No, no, no. Where is Nick, Uncle Joe?"

"I haven't seen him, doll. What's wrong?"

"Squad 2's truck is over there, and Nick is on duty right now."

"Calm down. I saw Dean earlier. I'm sure Nick's around here somewhere, doing the job he's been well-trained to do," he said in a matter-of-fact tone, refusing to give her anxiety any room to grow. He was well aware of the hurdles she'd jumped in order to have

Nick in her life.

"You're right," she said, letting out an uneasy breath. She'd made her peace with Nick's career and was taking baby steps in the right direction. The more she understood the precautions firefighters took and the training they went through, the less Laura worried about the job. Of course, visiting the Squad for a more personal tour from Captain Kelly last week hadn't hurt, and neither had the make-out session in his office. His desk was surprisingly sturdy for its size.

The paramedic taking Uncle Joe's vitals said, "Everything looks good, and your oxygen levels are normal. We can still get you checked out at the hospital if you want, but I don't see any reason for concern.

Thank goodness for little mercies. At least she didn't need to worry about Uncle Joe.

It was another hour before the firefighters had the blaze under control. Fortunately, it hadn't spread to any of the other buildings in the vicinity. The pub's impervious brick walls had contained the fire. Unfortunately, for Kate, it meant not having an apartment to return to, though her last voicemail had hinted at extending her time in London anyway. Of course, it also meant Laura was homeless. Again. At least she could stay in Uncle Joe's guestroom for the time being. Tomorrow, she would figure it out tomorrow, *after* a thorough snuggle session with Nick to make herself feel better.

Laura looked around for him, certain he must be in the cluster of coats and helmets standing out front as they wrapped up hoses and carried a ladder back to a truck. The air smelled of charcoal and burnt toast, the last light of day disappearing as she pulled her own coat tightly around her. March had given way to warmer temperatures, but with the oncoming dusk, they were quickly beginning to drop.

Ruth was the first friend to arrive, followed by Amir and Father Hugo, each bringing something different with them. Bread from the deli, Arabic coffee from the bodega, and blankets from the church's donation closet filled her with gratitude. Everything she owned was gone, but every person around them meant more to her than clothing and trinkets ever could.

Letting Ruth fuss over her like a mother hen, she waited patiently for Uncle Joe to finish his conversation with the priest and Amir. It wasn't until the trucks started to load up and Nick still hadn't come to find her that panic began to set in again. Waving frantically, she caught Dean's attention across the street and ran to meet him.

Face streaked with sweat and dirt, Dean looked healthy and whole otherwise. Laura relaxed, taking it as a good sign where Nick was concerned. "Hey," he said, sounding exhausted. "I'm sorry we couldn't do more, but hopefully the insurance will cover the damage."

"I'm sure it will. Uncle Joe doesn't seem overly concerned."

"I can't say for sure, but with no obvious ignitor, this could be a case of bad wiring. Knob and tube is notorious for causing problems in the older buildings these days."

"Any probability of arson?" Laura asked, worried. Kate tended to do things from the ground up on a project, including the electrical. She couldn't shake the feeling that the wiring wasn't the primary cause of the fire.

Dean shook his head from side to side. "An arsonist tends to get bolder over time. The last two incidents were in the warehouse district a couple of months ago, but you'll receive a thorough report after the investigation. I'm glad no one was still inside when we arrived."

"Speaking of, I haven't seen Nick anywhere." Fear reared its anxious head again, as Laura started to envision the worst. Anything could have happened during the time between the Squad's arrival and hers.

"Oh, I thought you knew. Nick is at the hospital," said Dean looking surprised.

"What? Which one?" Laura asked frantically.

"Brooklyn General, but—"

The rest of what he told her floated away in the night breeze as she started sprinting past the gathered crowd.

Nick

Nick was already at the hospital with Leo, supporting him for his next round of chemo, when the news about Jules going into labor reached them through one of the nurses on the oncology ward. Leave it to his mother to make sure every Kelly heard the rallying cry for one of their own. He could only imagine the sheer number of phone calls she'd had to make and to whom when she couldn't reach either of them by cell phone.

"These things usually take a while," the nurse reassured them, giving Nick another once over, which he ignored. Tall and buxom with exotic features to match her accent, the nurse was exactly the kind of woman he would have asked out before meeting Laura. Now, the only woman he looked twice at was a certain petite blonde with a big attitude and pert nose.

"Thanks," he said curtly, jumping back into a conversation with his brother on the pros and cons of the new apparatus safety the department was implementing for the Squad.

An hour later, Luna had tracked them down to a waiting room near the maternity ward to let them know Jules would be heading into surgery for an emergency C-section. Nick felt sick to his stomach. It was the same reaction he had whenever his family faced, yet again, another life-threatening situation.

"She'll be fine, and so will the baby," Luna announced staunchly, but Nick heard the small crack in her voice.

Swallowing back the bile threatening to make an appearance, he stood up to wrap his arms around her. If his mother, their rock of strength and stability was worried, they all should be.

Vinny appeared a moment later and sat down next to Leo.

"Let's get you home and into bed, handsome," she said, putting a beanie over his mostly bald pate.

Leo looked at Nick. "We should stay close. Just in case."

Vinny watched Leo, worrying her bottom lip with her teeth, torn between her loyalty to the family and doing what she knew his body needed.

Peering over their mother's head, Nick said, "I promise I'll call as soon as I hear anything. Go home. You look like death warmed over."

"Nothing like family to keep you in your place. Remind me not to have you read my eulogy."

Nick laughed, albeit lamely, but it was enough to break the vise of fear holding his heart in a tight grip.

Vinny swatted in Leo's direction without any real target and scowled. "Knock it off."

"Not funny, Leonardo Patrick Kelly," said Luna scathingly.

"Come on, Ma, it was a little funny. Besides, I'm not dying today or any time soon. I already told Vinny she's stuck with me until I'm squidgy around the edges."

Vinny's gaze was full of love and promise as she took hold of Leo's hand.

"That's right, baby. You and me on a park bench, my wrinkled hand in yours."

Nick watched them leave and promptly sat down again to keep a silent vigil. He propped his elbows onto his knees and dropped his head into his hands. When his mother joined him, pulling a rosary from her coat pocket, he flinched.

"Pray with me," she commanded, taping the side of his leg with the silver cross on the end of her beads.

"I don't know, Ma. Sometimes, you can't change what's going to happen." He wasn't in the mood to debate the benefits of faith with her. There were days he barely held onto his belief in a higher power, let alone God, and today was turning out to be one of them.

His mother huffed in annoyance.

"God isn't the tragic events of our life, Nicky. He's the response to them."

"And when the response isn't what we hope it'll be?" Nick asked, doubtful.

"We pray for the peace to accept what we cannot change. Your father used to say, 'We weather life to become a smooth piece of glass for someone else to treasure.'"

"After everything this family has been through, is that what you think?"

"No. I know to *live* is to be baptized by fire."

"Let me guess, a phoenix rising from the ashes," said Nick with more flippancy than he should have for his current audience.

"Don't be a donkey's ass. We aren't reborn from the flames; we're revealed in them."

"Scars and all?" he asked, thinking he might be too scarred for anyone to appreciate after today.

"What do you think makes this family so pretty?" said Luna, patting her hair.

Nick laughed under his breath and bowed his head. "Hail Mary, full of Grace, the Lord is with thee," he said, blending his voice with hers before sending up a prayer of safekeeping for his sister and the baby.

<h1 style="text-align: center">Chapter 27</h1>

Laura

Gasping for air, Laura bent over, trying to catch her breath in front of the hospital's entrance. The cabbie hadn't understood a word of English, dropping her somewhere near Brooklyn Bridge. She'd had to run the last fifteen blocks. It was also conceivable she'd spent more time doing kissing marathons than actual running recently, a situation she would need to rectify for any future emergencies.

The thought should've terrified her, but if being with Nick meant accepting every potential disaster her overactive imagination could conjure, he was worth it. Because Nick Kelly was a man worthy of falling in love with, even with the risk to her own heart.

Brooklyn had become her home, because he was her home, and if there ever came a day when he wasn't, she'd be devastated, but she'd survive. Not because she was strong or brave, but because he was worth every moment of a life together, no matter how long it lasted. She would simply have to trust in providence for the twists and turns in the road ahead.

Aside from her labored breathing, the hospital lobby was warm and hushed. Sweat plastered Laura's hair against her head and slid down her back in rivulets beneath her coat. She sniffed her arm pit discreetly.

Note to self, don't skip the second swipe of deodorant next time. Not that she owned any after today's catastrophe, she mused.

"Hi, I'm looking for Nick Kelly," said Laura, reaching down to move her ankle boot away from a newly formed blister.

"I'm sorry, who did you say you were here for?" asked the receptionist absently as she entered information into a computer.

"The last name is Kelly," Laura repeated firmly, feeling frustrated with the delay. She raked her hands through her matted hair as she waited.

"Ah, yes, fourteenth floor. Room 1401. Are you family?"

"Um," Laura hesitated briefly before saying, "Yes, I am. I'm family." Laura smiled brightly to cover the truth. She'd confess to Father Hugo later, but was it really a lie when it was true in her heart? If anything, this whole escapade had shown her exactly how much she wanted to be Nick's family. She only hoped it wasn't too late to tell him. Besides, she reasoned to cover her horror over the alternative, someone needed to marry the man and help him fill his disaster of a house with children. She intended to volunteer at the earliest opportunity.

The elevator moved at a snail's pace, as if the entire universe were conspiring against her getting to Nick. "Ha, ha, God. Very funny. And now I'm talking to myself in an elevator."

To make matters worse, the elevator had stopped at the cafeteria to let an elderly woman shuffle in with a walker.

"It's okay, dear, I talk to the voices in my head too," she reassured Laura, her white hair a glowing halo under the lights, the gas she passed loud and sulfuric.

"Oh, don't mind Fred; he had the lentil soup for lunch today," she excused.

"Lentils will get you every time," Laura replied seriously while her eyes watered and she tried not to breathe.

When they finally reached the older woman's destination, she shuffled out the same way she'd shuffled in, leaving Laura with an oxygen-deprived headache and a sage piece of advice: "A girl should always have a backup plan for when the dog's not around."

Laura shook her head up and down in agreement as the doors closed. She punched the floor number a few more times for good measure. Watching the wall of buttons light up the last three floors, her shoulders relaxed when the doors finally opened onto the fourteenth floor.

Under normal circumstances she might have stopped to admire the hallway painted robin's egg blue with a garden motif along the bottom half, but the spiking adrenaline making her quads cramp urged her on. She waived the wristband the receptionist had slapped on her at the nearest nurse and lunged toward Room 1401, throwing the door wide in her haste.

Nick

His brand-new nephew tucked securely into the crook of his arm, swaddled, and sleeping soundly, Nick turned to see who had entered his sister's hospital room with so much flourish. There stood the woman he adored, rosy-cheeked, hair sticking out on end, and her tan trench coat wrestled into submission by any means necessary.

Laura had stopped dead in her tracks, and he couldn't quite distinguish the look on her face. Part relief, part denial, she appeared to be debating something internally in those hypnotic green eyes of hers. To stay or go seemed to be the question at hand.

"Hey, Tink," he said soft and low, not wanting to wake the baby in his arms. "I'm glad you're here." In his worry for Jules, he'd forgotten to call her, but she was here now, which was all that mattered.

"Uh, hi," she replied uncertainly and scratched the top of her head. "I'm sorry. I shouldn't be here. This is all a big misunderstanding."

His family filled every possible square inch of space in the tiny room already, but still insisted on crowding him and Laura out until they were stuck in the alcove between the door and bathroom. Because, unlike normal families, they needed to make a complete spectacle of themselves. Nick took a long breath through his nose and tried not to elbow anyone, accidentally or otherwise.

"Of course you should," said all of his sisters simultaneously.

"Uncle Nick, tell her she belongs here," said his nieces, jumping in.

"You're in trouble now," sang Leo from the corner, who'd insisted on coming back after a nap. Finn giggled obnoxiously, and even Dae laughed over his predicament.

Then came a swat to the back of his head from his mother. "Ouch, what'd you do that for?" he asked, rubbing the spot she'd so callously accosted.

"Because Laura shouldn't need to question whether or not she's welcome. I raised you better than that," she said, her faux Italian accent on full display.

"I know, Ma," said Nick, taking another breath to center himself. He yanked the flimsy cloth curtain across the tiny entry, effectively cutting off the circus behind him.

"Hey," he said. "Let's start this conversation over again, shall we?"

Laura nodded, still speechless, eyes glued to the bundle he carried.

"This is my nephew, Owen," he said, grinning ear to ear, his uncle pride on full display.

"I thought you were on shift today," she whispered, confusion written all over her beautiful face.

"I was supposed to be, but swapped with Marsden, who needs the time off next week for a school activity her kid has."

"Okay."

She didn't sound angry, but he could hear something off in her voice. "I knew you had plans and it seemed like the perfect opportunity to give Vinny a break. We were here for Leo's chemo appointment when Jules went into labor," Nick explained.

"It's okay, really."

Her easy acceptance made him feel worse. "I'm sorry, Tink. I was worried about Jules and found myself caught up in little man here," apologized Nick, smiling down at his nephew again, the idea of having a family with Laura in the forefront of his thoughts. He was completely smitten with the newest Kelly, but more so with the woman standing in front of him.

"By the way, how did you know I was here?"

Laura started to laugh. Nick chuckled along, though he was a little uncertain as to what they were laughing over, until Laura's laughter turned into gut-wrenching sobs. His sisters occasionally got their wires crossed, but this was more tormenting than a passing moment.

Nick quickly handed off the baby to his mother behind the curtain, every set of female eyes glaring at him for the tears he'd unwittingly caused.

Taking Laura immediately into his arms, he held her until the sobs began to subside. "Shh," he soothed. "Everything's going to be okay. We'll work through whatever the problem is together."

Laura shuddered against his chest, and he held her tighter in response.

"Walker's Pub is gone."

"What do you mean it's gone?"

"I mean it no longer exists. Poof," she said, adding a snap of her fingers to emphasize the point.

The whispers behind the curtain abruptly stopped.

"Tink, start from the beginning," he commanded.

Laura took a shuddering breath and let it out slowly. "I came home from my errands to find Uncle Joe and Micky in the back of an ambulance—don't worry, both are fine."

Nick rubbed small circles up and down her spine, waiting patiently for the rest.

"Squad 2 and another engine company were on site, but the pub went up in flames like the pile of tinder it was inside."

His first thought was about how he could've lost her. Nothing frightened him more. Making plans for the future was useless if he never had the chance to put them into action. He'd been holding back, afraid of scaring Laura off again, but it was time to lay his cards on the table. As soon as they left the hospital, he'd put his heart on the line, and tell her exactly how he felt.

"The façade is still standing, but nothing else is left," said Laura, interrupting his thoughts.

"So, Dean told you I was here," he deduced, since the Squad

had been on site.

Laura started to laugh again. "Something like that. When I realized you weren't there, I panicked, and assumed you'd gotten hurt before I arrived," she said, flushing with embarrassment. "Dean said you were at the hospital, but I didn't stick around to find out why."

"Why not?"

"All I could think about was getting to you," she said as the last of her tears slipped down her cheeks.

His thumbs swept gently over them, wiping away the tracks on her cheeks.

"I am completely, hopelessly, head over heels in love with you, and I was so afraid I would never get a chance to tell you," she confessed, the tears starting in earnest again.

Nick pulled her close again, tucking her against his galloping heart. Laura loved him. His colony of butterflies soared, their wings thrumming until every molecule in his body zapped with electricity.

"Leave it to Dean to be my fairy godmother. I'm going to owe him a lifetime supply of beer after this," he mumbled into her hair.

Laura leaned back slightly in his embrace and lifted her eyes, hope shining brightly within them.

Nick cupped her face in his hands and let her see all of the feelings he'd kept pent up for months. "Tink, I will love you until the stars have all gone out, and the world is nothing but a cold, empty shell. And even then, my soul will find your light in the dark," he said, and kissed her tenderly, a taste of what was to come when he could finally get her alone.

The curtain behind Nick suddenly whooshed back, hooks screeching on the metal rail above. Fluorescent light flooded the small space, causing them both to blink at the hash intrusion.

Nick had *almost* forgotten his family was listening to every word in the room behind them. Leave it to a Kelly to butt in at the most inopportune time. He should be showing Laura how much he loved her. Instead, he was going to have to deal with what he knew was par for the course, where his family was concerned.

Laura hadn't been wrong about him needing to set boundaries with his family. The happiness of his lips was seriously in jeopardy with this latest interference. Of course, she simply raised an eyebrow and snickered over his predicament. Nick finally deigned to glance over his shoulder at the circus behind him, his annoyance over the interruption on display for all to see.

His mother ignored it. "Here," said Luna, grabbing Nick's hand to place something tiny in his palm. "I think it's time I gave you this."

He looked down at the gold claddagh ring his mother had worn all of her adult life, an opal set in the center of the heart, an infinite symbol of his parents' love, loyalty, and friendship. He closed his hand around the band and kissed her soft cheek.

"Thanks, Ma," he replied, feeling overwhelmed by the unexpected gift.

She gave his arm a pat in return. "Love should never be wasted, and neither should time," said Luna, the moisture in her eyes giving away the depth of her feelings. Nick pulled the curtain back into place, ignoring the rest of the Kelly clan behind him, the screech of the hooks all the more jarring under the circumstances.

Laura followed the trajectory of Nick's hand, eyes round, darting back and forth between his face and the precious ring he held.

He could either make light of the situation, and the last couple of minutes, or he could ask her to do what she'd been doing since the first time he saw her at Walker's Pub: tug the strings of his heart for the rest of his life. As his mother had said, waiting would be a waste of time in a world constantly in motion. There were no guarantees tomorrow would come, but he was certain every fork in their journeys had led them to right now.

"I'd imagined doing this somewhere more romantic," said Nick, taking in their meager surroundings. "Or at least putting together a convincing speech beforehand."

"Oh, get on with it," heckled Gina from behind the curtain.

"And my family would be nowhere in the vicinity," replied Nick, loudly.

"You know you love us," interrupted Aria and Jules together.

"Jesus, Mary, and Joseph!" Luna swore. "All of you, pipe down. Your brother is trying to propose," she yelled, waking the baby in her arms. "Now look what you've done," she said over his cries.

Laura laughed with abandon, tugging the strings of his heart, her light a beacon in a lifetime filled with grief and joy in equal measure. It was all the encouragement Nick needed as he dropped to one knee. Wherever she was going in this world, he wanted to be the one by her side for every part of the journey.

Chapter 28

Laura

Laura maneuvered her pregnant body clumsily onto the chaise lounge Nick had placed under a sun umbrella and was getting ready to open her latest read when he handed her a cold, banana-peanut butter smoothie.

"I should probably refrain from having another one," she grumbled, trying without success to tug her bikini bottoms over her growing rump. While she welcomed the generous cup size and heaping portions of peanut buttery goodness, she was a little worried that her rear end intended to keep pace with her baby bump.

He took a sip when she tipped the cup toward him. "I love all your curves. They're more than a handful, like the woman they belong to," said Nick, his lip inching up at the corner as he settled into the sand next to her chair, the waves rolling in mere feet away.

Never willing to turn down a good excuse to travel, Laura had announced it was the perfect time to take a babymoon. Uncle Joe offered to keep Micky for a long weekend since reconstruction of the pub was still underway, and Nick finally made it to the West Coast. Funny how so many things in life were all about timing, she thought.

Laura laughed as she watched him bury his toes in the soft sand. "You know if you sit in the sand, you're going to have it everywhere, right?"

"Yep, but I like the way it feels when I dig my feet in. Besides, I don't remember you complaining about sand on our honeymoon."

They had wasted no time getting married, opting for an intimate church wedding instead of the extravagant affair her mother would have preferred. Of course, her father had simply been content to be present to give her away this time around. Father Hugo had performed the understated ceremony and Squad 2 had somehow commandeered a command vehicle for the getaway to the airport, complete with lights and sirens.

"In fact, the way I remember it, you offered to help me clean off in the shower," he said with a seductive smile.

Sardinia had been everything she'd dreamed it would be for a honeymoon—white sand beaches, delectable food, and time together without any family obligations or distractions. "Oh, so that's your game. Well, Mr. Kelly, we wouldn't want to leave any sand in those hard-to-reach places," she replied with a saucy wink.

Nick grinned and reached up to place a hand on her belly, waiting for the little girl within to move. "I'm pretty sure that's how we wound up in this situation to begin with."

Ailis Sebina Kelly was due to make her appearance in time for spring. Laura closed her eyes, enjoying the weight of his hand on her ever-expanding skin, and thought of all the memories they'd made so far and hoped to make in the future.

Love had the power to change everything, including her life. Laura's heart brimmed over with gratefulness for the new home she'd found in Brooklyn and, if Nick had anything to say about it, their house would be almost as full. He never spared an opportunity trying to convince her to have a large family.

Laura laughed every time he brought it up, which was part of why Nick did it so often. "Your momma is a saint. I think one to start will suffice, but I'm open to negotiating in the future."

Nick smirked back at her. Chasing his wife until she succumbed to his charms was his all-time favorite challenge. As far as he was concerned, he had every negotiation won, and Laura couldn't fault his thinking since his record was nearly spotless.

Laura moved her hand to rest on top of Nick's, watching the man she adored and her proverbial fork in the road. Life was unpredictable, and there were no guarantees of the future, but she knew one thing without a doubt: a life with Nick was worth any risk.

Her husband placed an earbud into her ear and pressed play, singing along close enough for the baby to hear. The birds played in the distance, skimming their wings daringly over the water to cool themselves from the heat of the sun's rays. It was a perfect moment in a world filled with imperfection. There was no changing the past, but they could embrace life to its fullest, shaping the present and their future.

As the song came to a crescendo, Nick leaned in to kiss her swollen belly and rose abruptly from his spot, picking her up as he went.

"You wouldn't dare!" she squealed, as he walked them into the waves.

"Come on, Tink, let's put sand in all those hard-to-reach places. I promise to give you a bath later," he said with a smirk and waggle of his brows.

She laughed and leaned in to kiss him, lingering. "You come up with the best plans."

"I'm pretty sure providence gets to take the credit for this one," Nick replied, this time placing a kiss on the gold band encircling her left ring finger.

Nick was right; they had always been on their way to each other. All she had to do was walk through the door of his favorite pub.

Micky sat outside, basking in the late-spring sunshine, and

greeting those who walked by with a bark or a paw shake. Children giggled with delight, ruffling his fur while adults urged them on or inside. Laura watched as Uncle Joe refilled his bowl and watered the hanging flower baskets at the same time, leaving him to his canine antics. He'd find his way back into the pub when he was ready to eat.

Laura let her eyes travel around the newly finished space, jampacked with family, friends, and regulars, along with fresh faces for the grand re-opening of Walker's Public House. She'd chosen to replace the bar with an exact replica, but everything else was an updated take on the traditional pub interior. Wainscotting in cyan lined the walls of the first floor, the exposed brick above it whitewashed, and a raised ceiling through the former apartment created a bright and airy space as people came and went on the staircase. Polished concrete floors in light gray lay in contrast to the overhead wood beams stained a walnut to match the bar and tables, each bench and seat cushion wrapped in the Walker tartan of red, blue, mustard, and green.

Looking around for Nick, she spotted a crew from the Squad seated with him at a long table opposite the bar. He bounced with Ailis in the front pack, which only made her want to negotiate another addition sooner rather than later. The man without a baby in his arms was hot, but with one, he was a five-alarm fire. Feeling her appraisal, he looked in her direction and winked. She raised a brow in challenge, which he returned with a wide smile and sauntered over at the invitation in her eyes.

"We should go home and negotiate making another one of these," he said, reading her mind.

She ran her fingers over the umber hair covering the top of her daughter's head. With each passing month she increasingly resembled Nick's baby photos, except for her cute little nose. That feature alone belonged to her momma.

"I can't leave for at least an hour, but I wouldn't complain if there was hot bath waiting at home and an already sleeping baby."

"Consider it done," he said, leaning in to kiss her. Laura melted under the warmth of his lips, the heady feeling of anticipation coursing through her body at the contact.

"Hurry home, Tink," he said with a smirk.

Laura smirked back, caught up in a haze of desire. She watched him disappear through the door, tucking their daughter close to his body in that protective way of his and whistling for Micky to follow.

Saint and Ronan worked at the bar, the new cocktail menu as much in demand as the usual pint request. Amir had taken on two sous chefs in the kitchen to accommodate the increase in daily customers and a weekend brunch menu. Business was booming, thanks to the reconstruction the pub had undergone and Laura expected even more once the rooftop venue was complete later in the summer. Kate, who had returned for the wedding and then again for the birth of her niece, got credit for the brilliant idea to host private parties and events. But a garden that bloomed three out of four seasons had been Nick's idea, something about bees and butterflies coexisting peacefully.

Laura wiped the bar clean and pulled out dessert menus for a table of four, instantly spotting the newcomer as he came in. He looked exactly the way she remembered, even with his hair cut short. The tie around his neck was an exact match for the icy color of his eyes and his tailored suit, which couldn't disguise the cruel twist of his mouth no matter what it cost, a perfect fit.

"Laura, it's good to see you," he greeted, all smarmy charm.

"I wish I could say the same, Preston."

"If that's the way you want to play it."

"Kate's not here, so why don't you go back to whatever slimy hole you crawled out of and leave her alone."

"You know I can't do that, Laura. Kate and I belong together," he said, plainly annoyed with her attitude as he adjusted the expensive cufflinks at his wrists.

"Whatever; you sound like a creep. Get out before I call the cops," she said with no room for argument.

He laughed harshly, revealing the monster lurking beneath his polished surface. Laura turned on her heel to walk away. Engaging was what he wanted, and she had more important things to do, like warning Kate off. If Preston poked around enough in Brooklyn, it wouldn't take him long to track her to London, especially if he found her boutique.

His hand shot out and grabbed her upper arm in a bruising

grip. "I see not much has changed where you're concerned. You always were a bit of a brat."

Laura met his glare reluctantly, refusing to yelp despite the pain; she wouldn't give him the satisfaction.

Leaning in close to her ear so no one else would overhear, he said, "I like what you've done with the place. So much nicer than before."

A sense of foreboding slid over Laura, setting her teeth on edge as she clenched her jaw.

Preston pulled a folded piece of paper from the inside pocket of his suit coat and laid it on top of the bar. "Thanks for the help, little sister."

Laura cringed at the familial title and waited for the door to close before reaching for the newspaper he'd left. Front and center was the picture of her and Nick kissing at the 9/11 Memorial next to the original column with a follow-up interview they'd done to promote the reopening of the pub. Laura gasped and froze in place, chills snaking down her spine. There, in a tiny block print at the end of the story, were the words she feared.

"It would seem business is blooming in Brooklyn this spring, especially for these two sisters." The wedding announcement photo her mother had insisted on flashed like a Las Vegas neon sign beneath, and though it was slightly grainy, there was no mistaking Kate for anyone else.

"Swing by Walker's Pub for their grand re-opening on Friday, and while you're in the neighborhood, check out my favorite skin care line at Lavender Honey & Co."

Apparently, Hatta Mann was a better reporter than her fictional predecessor, except the villain in Kate's story was real. Laura had no doubt Preston Toliver would use every resource at his fingertips to make her sister pay for leaving him.

The End

Author's Note

In my effort to honor those who gave their lives without causing further harm, I chose not to mention any of the actual heroes of September 11, 2001. The FDNY's Squad 2 exists only in my imagination, and any coincidence in character names or actions are exactly that. Please visit the 9/11 Memorial & Museum in person or online at www.911memorial.org for more information.

I took the liberty of adding a dog run to Prospect Park before 2020. And though Micky had the luxury of walking through Green-Wood Cemetery as a "emotional support animal" for the sake of the story and raising awareness, please refrain from taking those who don't qualify as a service animal. Also, the blizzard in New York on Valentine's Day 2012 is fictional. Sometimes, snow makes for a more plausible scene.

For those who appreciate accuracy, *The New York Herald* once did exist, eventually becoming the *New York Herald Tribune* from 1926–1966. *Here Lie the Secrets of the Visitors of Green-Wood Cemetery* is an art installation by Sophie Calle from 2017. I chose to include it in the timeline, because it contains a slotted base through which visitors may slip their written secrets into a watertight casket, and it was a fun way to connect Laura, Drew, and Nick with one another. Please visit www.green-wood.com and www.prospectpark.org for more information on these natural treasures in Brooklyn.

While our nation and the world forever changed on 9/11, I still believe our courage to be greater than our fear and love a stronger voice than hate or prejudice will ever be.

Acknowledgments

Heavenly Father, thank You for all of my forks in the road. They have been my greatest challenges, but also my worthiest adventures. I can hardly wait to see what You have planned next.

Mark, we are twenty-one years into this crazy experiment, and you are still my favorite. Thank you for being my best friend, a steady rock in the face of my doubts, and my biggest fan. Moving abroad was definitely a fork in the road, but I know wherever it leads you'll be beside me. Keep talking nerdy to me, baby.

H, G, & A, you keep my feet planted firmly on the ground while I plot out entire lives inside my head. I know moving across the world hasn't been easy, but in the end, I hope it makes your story a little bigger and the future a little less predictable. I love you to the stars and back.

To the rest of my clan, given and chosen, you are the best gift of providence ever. I'm beyond fortunate to call you family. Relationships are complex and rarely perfect, but they bind us together, sewing our frayed and worn-out covers until we feel whole again. Thank you for helping me keep it together when I start to unravel.

Brianna Showalter, thank you for your enduring friendship and advice. You fill my life with beauty, color, and incredible book covers. Your talent is truly awe inspiring. I have missed solving all of the world's problems with you this past year, but know that when next we meet, we will pick up right where we left off as only the best kind of friends do.

Arlyn Lawrence, editor extraordinaire. Your kindness, encouragement, and knowledge are priceless. As always, thank you for your patience and diligence. Without Inspira Literary Solutions, my stories would drown in commas, darlings, and dangling participles. Thank you for the lifeboat!

And finally, my readers. Thank you for reading *Walker's Pub*. I hope you enjoyed Nick and Laura's story, and that you embrace your own forks in the road. They can be small or beyond your wildest imagination, easy paths to tread or difficult mountains to conquer. You never know where they might lead, but I like to think it's somewhere providential.

Feel free to email me cuppakindnessyet@gmail.com if you'd like to receive updates on new releases.

Appendix

Author's Playlist

I Had A Dream by Priscilla Ahn
Man on a Mission by Oh the Larceny
Happy by *NF*
She Sets the City on Fire by Gavin DeGraw
Heaven by Niall Horan
Made for This by Carrollton
So Will I by Phillip Phillips
Just Friends by Why Don't We
What's A Man Gotta Do by Jonas Brothers
Lovesick by Jenna Raine
My Weakness by Kris Allen
Beautiful Things by Benson Boone
Oh My Love by The Score
West Coast by One Republic

Nick & Laura's Mixtape

Beautiful Day by U2
Put Your Records On by Corinne Bailey Rae
I Try by Macy Gray
Lose Yourself by Eminem
Pennies from Heaven by Frank Sinatra
We Are the Champions by Queen
Waterfalls by TLC

Single Ladies by Beyoncé
Waiting on the World to Change by John Mayer
Route 66 by Natalie Cole
Empire State of Mind by JAY-Z and Alicia Keys
Dancing Queen by ABBA
Little Wonders by Rob Thomas
Short Skirt / Long Jacket by Cake
Gravity by Sara Bareilles
Do They Know It's Christmas by Band Aid
There She Goes by The La's
I Want You Back by NSYNC
Stayin' Alive by Bee Gees
Ice, Ice, Baby by Vanilla Ice
Ice Cream by Sarah McLachlan
Kashmir by Led Zeppelin
You Belong with Me by Taylor Swift
Last Request by Paolo Nutini
And the Birds Sing by Tyrone Wells

About the Author

Jaclyn Robinson calls Washington State home but was born in New Jersey and has lived in multiple places in between. She currently resides in Seoul, South Korea with her husband, three children, and a cairn terrier named Mungo. Though she holds a B.S. in Exercise and Sport Science from Colorado State University, she's been plotting stories in her head for as long as can remember. Her reading habits are a bit compulsive and while she has a penchant for romance, she'll read whatever is at hand. This tendency can sometimes make for interesting, if not downright, awkward conversation on her part. She drinks copious amounts of tea and adores sea salt caramels with her scotch. Neat and smooth, please. Ms. Robinson believes one can never have enough books in any form and, if given the choice, would spend eternity in an incredibly old and famous library.

Also by the author, *The Christmas Tea Shoppe*, available on Amazon.

Abigail Hart is a hometown girl. Okay, maybe not in the traditional sense. But she does love her aunt, who owns The Christmas Tea Shoppe on Main Street, which is why Abby moves back home to help out when Aunt Sara gets sick. Now, if only she could stuff her emotional baggage into a suitcase the way she did her clothing. Homily may be small, but its gossip mill is thriving and so are some of its more eccentric residents. How bad could it be?

Matthew Dixon has life figured out. He's living in the only place he ever wanted to call home and working as an ER attending physician at the local hospital. That is, until Abigail Hart makes an appearance in his waiting room. Suddenly, life has so much more to offer. All he has to do is convince her life would be better together.

How hard could it be?

Looking for a little Christmas spirit all year round? Get cozy with a soft blanket and a cup of grace in *The Christmas Tea Shoppe*, offering a sweet romance and a little magic no matter the season.

Scan here to purchase your copy
of *The Christmas Tea Shoppe*

9 781952 943447